AN UNJUST JUDGE

AN UNJUST JUDGE

A Burren Mystery

Cora Harrison

This first world edition published 2016
in Great Britain and 2017 in the USA by
SEVERN HOUSE PUBLISHERS LTD of
19 Cedar Road, Sutton, Surrey, England, SM2 5DA.
Trade paperback edition first published
in Great Britain and the USA 2017 by
SEVERN HOUSE PUBLISHERS LTD

British Library Cataloguing in Publication Data
A CIP catalogue record for this title is available from the British Library.

ISBN-13: 978-0-7278-8672-9 (cased)
ISBN-13: 978-1-84751-775-3 (trade paper)
ISBN-13: 978-1-78010-843-8 (e-book)

All Severn House titles are printed on acid-free paper.

Severn House Publishers support the Forest Stewardship Council™ [FSC™],
the leading international forest certification organisation.
All our titles that are printed on FSC certified paper carry the FSC logo.

Typeset by Palimpsest Book Production Ltd.,
Falkirk, Stirlingshire, Scotland.
Printed and bound in Great Britain by
TJ International, Padstow, Cornwall.

One

Triað 96

There are three ruins of a kingdom:
1. A lying chieftain
2. A lustful priest
3. An unjust judge

When Mara, Brehon of the Burren, attended judgement day in the neighbouring kingdom of Corcomroe on October 11th in the year of 1524, she had not the slightest inkling that the man in the Brehon's chair in front of the people of north-west Corcomroe had less than another day of life left to him. She had, in fact, arrived at the proceedings held beside the ancient burial mound on the Atlantic clifftop of Knockfinn, without feeling much interest in them. She was not there as a judge or investigating magistrate, as she would have been in the kingdom of the Burren, but rather as the wife of King Turlough Donn O'Brien, lord of the three kingdoms of Thomond, Corcomroe and Burren. The appointment of this new Brehon, judge and investigative magistrate had been made by Turlough; her attendance was purely a matter of form and courtesy.

The elderly Brehon of Corcomroe, Fergus MacClancy, had become incapable through old age and poor memory of conducting the business of the area, so the king had placed him in a pleasant home by the sea and had appointed a replacement. Today would be the inaugural judgement day for Gaibrial O'Doran from the kingdom of Ossory. He was a young man in his mid-twenties, a member of the numerous legal clan of the O'Dorans.

Looking down upon the dead body of the newly appointed Brehon the following day, Mara recalled the feeling of dislike which had come to her as she listened to his high-pitched

voice with its unfamiliar accent passing harsh judgements on
the five cases that came to him. She had told herself that she
must not be too censorious, that this was the young man's
first day among the people of the kingdom and that the
harshness might only be a lack of confidence, that he was
trying, perhaps too hard, to stamp his authority on these
people. Nevertheless, she remembered that she had been
apprehensive. Her eyes had gone to another surprised and
sceptical face, that of Boetius MacClancy, a man learned in
English law as well as in Irish law and a nephew of the elderly
Fergus MacClancy. His period of banishment from the
kingdom was over; he had expected to be the inheritor of
his uncle's position and law school and had returned from
England several weeks ago when he had heard news of that
descent into senility. But he had been disappointed; Turlough
had never forgiven Boetius for his part in some unsavoury
events ten years ago and he had refused to entertain the possibility of installing a man like that in a position of trust. Now
Boetius looked grimly satisfied. It was easy to sense that mood
of the crowd. The new judge was not going to be popular.

Of course, she acknowledged to herself, while outwardly
paying polite attention to the severe voice interrogating Donal
O'Connor, a young musician accused of infringing a copyright,
of course it may be that I am just annoyed that Turlough didn't
consult me over this appointment. She had suggested that
together they interview some of the young lawyers that clus-
tered around his court in Thomond, but the king had heard
of Gaibrial O'Doran from Ossory, the kingdom of one of
Turlough's enemies, and he had rapidly seized the opportunity
to deprive King Brian Fitzpatrick of one of his men. The
appointment was made before she had even met him and she
was furious with Turlough. After all, the Brehon who was to
work in the neighbouring kingdom to hers should surely be
someone who met with her approval. Still, perhaps he would
settle down after his first performance in front of the king and
his wife, famous as the only female Brehon in Ireland. Perhaps
he was just trying to impress with a show of decisiveness and
authority.

She turned her attention to the cross-examination. There

were two young bards, both sharing the clan name of O'Connor, Breacain O'Connor and Donal O'Connor, the one accusing the other of copying a song written years ago and both glaring angrily at each other. The Brehon directed his young assistant to call for witnesses.

'I remember Breacain singing that song at the Michaelmas Fair at Noughaval,' called out a voice from the crowd. 'It must have been a good four years ago,' he said in a slightly hoarse voice and then cleared his throat noisily. 'I remember it well because it was a frosty day and I noticed the words of the song that he sang because there was something about the deer making tracks on the frosty grass and about an icy wind.'

'That's nonsense,' whispered Mara's scholar, Cian, in her ear. 'I remember all that business about deer making tracks in frosty grass in one of Suibhne's poems and the other bits about the icy wind, too. And Suibhne must have written it about three or four hundred years ago. The pair of them copied it. One is as bad as the other. Should I tell the new Brehon? You'd think that he would know the poems of Suibhne by heart, wouldn't you? We learned them when we were little.'

'Shh,' said Mara. Cian had a point, and Brehon law did encourage bystanders to put in comments on judgement day, but as he was one of her scholars it would look as though the king's wife was questioning the judgement of the king's appointed man. In any case the sentence must be trivial for such a trivial offence, she thought, and then caught her breath in astonishment as the harsh voice raised itself above the muttered comments of the bystanders.

'I declare that you, Donal O'Connor, are guilty of theft. You will pay a fine of—'

The voice that interrupted him was stronger than his own, a fine, well-trained voice that rose effortlessly above the harsh, high-pitched words.

'Surely,' said the voice in a polite, mellow tone, 'the law decrees that the penalty is for the copy to be returned to the original owner of the work.' Boetius MacClancy, nephew of the former Brehon of the area, was on his feet. He spoke in Latin, but every head turned towards him with interest.

Many of the people of north-west Corcomroe had expected
Boetius to inherit the position of Brehon from his uncle
Fergus MacClancy and now all eyes were on him. He enjoyed
the attention for a few seconds and then switched to Gaelic,
the soft Irish words of his youth now spoken, after his ten
years in exile, with a strong English accent. Boetius, according
to Turlough's sources, had done his best to ingratiate himself
with the powerful Cardinal Wolsey and Bishop Stephen
Gardiner while in London. This did not seem to have worked
so well, however, and at the news of his uncle's senility he
had returned to Ireland. Ready to make trouble, thought
Mara.

'The first case of copyright that Irish law recognized,
occurred almost one thousand years ago,' he said, ignoring
Brehon O'Doran and speaking to the people as though he
were the Brehon. 'It was the case of St Colmcille who had,
without permission, copied a book written by St Finian.
Diarmuid, the High King of Ireland, passed judgement and
these were his very words,' said Boetius solemnly. '"To every
cow its calf and to every book its copy." This occurred in
the year 563, so our poets tell us. So this means that the song
which was copied by Donal from one written originally by
Breacain merely needs to be returned to its owner. Possibly,'
he concluded with a condescending smile, 'the new Brehon
is not aware of all the laws of our country yet.'

'The fine based on the offence and the honour price of
the owner of the song is two *séts*, or six cows or six ounces
of silver,' said the new Brehon, doggedly keeping his eyes
averted from Boetius. 'Next case,' he called out, ignoring the
gasp from the people gathered on the hillside of Knockfinn.
Donal was a young bard who probably barely made a hand-
to-mouth living singing at fairs and selling a few copies of
his songs. It would be as impossible for him to find six ounces
of silver as to produce six cows. Even Breacain, himself, looked
thunderstruck by the verdict in his favour.

'Next case,' repeated MacClancy angrily and his assistant
hastily called out for Ciarán and Emer and Emer's mother to
come into the court.

'He should have settled that business of the two bards

before it ever came to court.' Mara could not resist murmuring this in the king's ear, though she felt a little ashamed when she saw how uncomfortable Turlough looked. The trouble with her husband was that he tended to take talkers at their own valuation. Despite his high office, he was a humble man and respected scholarly learning to a degree where it over-shadowed the judgement that he would use in evaluating a soldier. Still the deed was done, Gaibrial O'Doran had been appointed Brehon and she should keep her thoughts to herself and learn to work with such a near neighbour, just as she and Fergus had collaborated over the last thirty years. Nevertheless, as the next sorry tale, with many interruptions from a hard-faced, middle-aged woman who held Emer firmly by the elbow, unfolded of too much to drink and furtive lovemaking, or rape as Emer's mother claimed, in the bushes beyond the alehouse, Mara had to bite her lips to avoid whispering the same comment in her husband's ear. Why, on earth, she thought with irritation, hadn't the Brehon talked to the two young people in private beforehand, got Emer's mother to see that there were faults on both sides and that compensation would be made in the form of an offer of marriage. In fact, Ciaráin was emphatically now declaring that he had offered marriage and Emer was looking at him with a half-smile on her lips. Her mother, however, was insistent that compensation had to be paid for her daughter's loss of honour.

'The fine for rape is six *séts*, eighteen cows, or eighteen ounces of silver,' announced Gaibrial O'Doran, cutting short Ciaráin's stumbling apologies and explanations. For a moment it appeared as though the boy could hardly believe his ears and then as a gasp went up from the assembled clans, he went very white. He was the youngest son of a large family, Mara seemed to remember. There was no way that his family could afford a fine like that. She clenched her hands in an effort to contain her anger, but Boetius was on his feet again. This time he spoke in Gaelic and it was obvious that he was speaking to the crowd, that he was stirring up the feeling that he would have been a better choice as their new Brehon.

'Surely this was not a case of *forcor* but of *sleth*,' he said suavely and his tone was the tone of a teacher rather than that of a bystander. 'There is no evidence, I presume, that the young man used any force to induce his young woman to go into the bushes with him. I gather that Emer went unaccompanied by a father or a brother, or even her mother, to the alehouse and while there, she, also, drank ale. And it appears to me that she is not adverse to marriage with the young man. While not condoning Ciaráin's behaviour, I would ask the learned judge to consider whether anything is gained by this large fine if the two young people do get married, anything, in fact, except the fee paid to the judge.'

And with that he sat down, smiling gently to himself. Mara felt herself grow hot. This was a great insult to her profession. Many Brehons, she knew, took a levy from each fine passed, but there was something distasteful about the process. Her own father had negotiated with the king, at the time of his appointment as Brehon of the Burren, that he would receive land and a yearly stipend for his services and she had continued that arrangement. So far as the people were concerned, the judge had to be, and had to be seen to be, impartial and incorruptible. Obviously, Gaibrial O'Doran, since he did not deny the charge, had opted for a levy of a tenth of each fine.

The case of arson, where Seán set fire to a stack of old hay belonging to his neighbour, Brendan, was judged with similar harshness. The hay in question was very old, poor stuff according to Seán, mainly rushes, mouldy and unpalatable and standing abandoned for a year at the junction of the two farms. Seán had set fire to some gorse and the flames had spread. Despite the offer of compensation with a stack of new hay, the fine, once again, was a savage one and Boetius was on his feet again, protesting about the difference between *comraite* which showed deliberate intent, and *anfor* where the damage was caused by simple carelessness. Nevertheless, once again the maximum fine was imposed, as it was in the next case where, in a fight in an alehouse, Ronan knocked out a front tooth of the alehouse owner, a man named Barra.

This kingdom will soon become ungovernable, thought Mara. That last fine was absurd. True it was a front tooth, but the law took into account the damage which such disfigurement would cause. In the case of Barra, the man was already missing several teeth and previous fights had resulted in a lump taken out of one ear and a scar across his cheek. It seemed to her that the new Brehon had gone around the small territory of north-west Corcomroe, inviting people to bring cases for his first judgement day and probably hinting at rich rewards. He had been installed in the Brehon's house at Knockfinn over a week ago. She had ridden across to welcome him and had listened to his plans to set up the law school again. He had already one scholar, a boy of about fifteen named Niall MacEgan and told her that he was going to make enquiries in the villages and farms and of the priests to find some intelligent boys whose fathers could afford the law school fees.

Now, it seemed to her that he had done more than look for pupils. He had scoured the countryside seeking grievances and had, doubtless, promised rich rewards. She looked at the gloomy faces of four ordinary young men declared guilty and facing fines that would be an impossibility for them or for their immediate families: Donal the infringer of copyright, Seán the arsonist, Ciaráin the rapist and Ronan the assailant, all of them ordinary young men who might have drunk too much, or been careless and now their lives would be haunted by guilt and debt. Was there anything she could do at this late stage, she asked herself, but could not see any possibility; the man had been appointed to his position by the king, not just her husband, but her overlord, and only the king could remove him from his position or reverse his decisions. Mara gave one quick glance at Turlough's gloomy face and then braced herself to hear the last case.

Peadar O'Connor was known to her. As a boy he had worked for Setanta the fisherman, the father of her scholar, Art, and at that stage her son, Cormac, had been fostered by Setanta and his wife Cliona. Peadar, she remembered, was a thin, nervous boy. Setanta had told her that the boy's father was unkind to him and favoured his eldest son and neglected the youngest. Now he stood passively in front of the new Brehon, his eyes wide with apprehension.

'I call on Clooney O'Connor as a witness,' said the Brehon's assistant, the boy Niall. His voice shook slightly and Mara felt sorry for him. He, if not his master, sensed the hostility of the crowd. There had been a lot of discontented murmuring from the crowd at the harsh sentences passed in the previous four cases and only the presence of the king had subdued the unrest. They waited in silence for the questioning of the witness, but there was a feeling of tension in the air.

'Peadar O'Connor was the only living son of your uncle, Cillian, when he died last month, is that correct, Clooney?' asked the Brehon.

'That is correct.' Clooney, first cousin to Peadar answered with the air of a man who has something shocking to relate.

'And your uncle was in bad health for months before he died.'

'That he was,' said Clooney, nodding his head emphatically.

'And needed assistance for daily living?'

'He could walk well enough when he wanted to,' put in Peadar. His voice was hoarse, with anger, or with apprehension. Mara thought that it was the latter. The young man's eyes were dilated and his large hands twisted in and out of each other in a convulsive fashion.

'Silence,' said Brehon O'Doran sternly and then turned back to Peadar's cousin, Clooney.

'And your uncle's son, Peadar, did he care for his father as the laws of the people dictate?'

'Never did a thing for him,' said Clooney emphatically.

'Perhaps he did not know of his father's plight; is that correct?'

'No, it is not. He knew right well. I sent messenger after messenger. Any boat that went to sea carried a message from me to Peadar. "Come home", I said to him. "There's plenty for you to do here on the farm, you don't need to scour the seas for a living. There's cows to be milked, bullocks to be slaughtered, hens' eggs to be gathered, oats to be harvested." But he never came back. That is,' continued Clooney, 'until two days after his father died when he turned up and laid claim to his father's land and uncovered his father's hearth.'

'Perhaps he had not received your earlier messages?' suggested the Brehon. He had an ironic smile on his face and Clooney sniggered.

'Oh, that he did! I questioned all the fishermen. Yes, my messages were delivered to him. And the man who brought the news of his father's death was the same man who delivered some of the messages telling him that the poor old man needed his son back home to work the farm.'

'Is this true?' asked the Brehon looking at Peadar. 'I can call additional witnesses, if you wish.'

'It's true enough.'

'So why did you not return to take care of your father?'

'I didn't chose to.'

Peadar, thought Mara, was going the wrong way about this. There was obviously tension between him and his cousin Clooney, but a wiser and perhaps an older man would not have risked antagonizing his judge at a trial.

'You didn't choose to!' Gaibrial O'Doran repeated the words in tones of incredulity. 'But we cannot always choose what pleases us most. There is the law of God, the law of man, our own laws that governs our conduct towards our family, our neighbours and our king,' he finished with a polite bow towards Turlough.

'I owed nothing to my father.' Peadar's loud, discordant voice caused the Brehon to swivel back in his direction. He straightened himself and rearranged his legal gown on his narrow shoulders.

'You owed nothing to your father,' he repeated so softly that even people in front few rows at Knockfinn strained their ears and looked at their neighbours for enlightenment.

'No, I didn't. He never did a thing for me. His only interest was in my brother, Stiofan. He got the praise and the presents. I got nothing but hard words and harder blows.' Peadar's voice was loud enough to reach the back of the crowd and Mara saw several heads nod. She was not the only one who had witnessed the young boy's battered face and noted how he flinched at a raised voice. It was not, she thought, surprising that Peadar, as soon as he was old enough to be given a place on a fishing boat, had left home and had never returned, not even when the news of the death of Stiofan in an alehouse brawl had reached him.

'You should be ashamed of yourself,' said his cousin Clooney severely and the Brehon did not reprove him for an unasked intervention.

Mara's eyes found Setanta who was standing in the front row and saw him look with sympathy at Peadar. Setanta was a former inhabitant of north-west Corcomroe, but when he married Cliona, a sheep farmer and nurse to Mara's son, he had moved to the Kingdom of the Burren. He would not be allowed to speak in favour of Peadar, and no one else, so far, had yet found the courage to stand up before this harsh-voiced new Brehon. Setanta turned around and seemed to be speaking urgently to some men standing behind him.

'Silence in court!' Niall tried to roar out the command in imitation of his master's voice, but the first word came out as a high-pitched squeak and the next two as a rusty growl. Several men in the crowd laughed good-naturedly and women smiled.

There was a notable slackening in the tension and one tall, very brown-faced man behind Setanta shouted out, 'You know full well, Clooney, that if the lad had returned, his father would have had nothing to say to him. Peadar would have had a beating for his pains and nothing to eat or to drink and no bed for the night. It's well known that he had to seek the roof of a stranger whenever he came into the kingdom.'

'You wouldn't be wanting the farm for yourself, Clooney, would you?' Another neighbour joined in and there was a burst of laughter.

'Silence in court,' said Niall again in an uncertain voice, after a quick, fear-filled look at the fury on his master's face.

'Justice in court!' shouted another of the men standing beside Setanta. Fishermen, all of them, thought Mara. More outspoken and more independent than the farmers. There was something about facing rough Atlantic seas, winter as well as summer, to build a man's courage and independence of mind.

But all the comments were ignored by the new Brehon. He did not, as Mara always did, ask if anyone had anything else to say, but continued his merciless accusations against Peadar, reciting long sections from the law book *Berrad Airechta,* citing him as a *macc úar* (a cold son), one who has failed in his duty to provide filial service and obedience to his father.

Mara began to grow apprehensive. The man had the law texts by heart but so had she and she knew what was coming next. Surely he would not do this, no matter how eager he was to stamp his authority on the kingdom. The crowd shifted uneasily, but the relentless voice went on fluently reciting the law texts. From time to time the Brehon was interrupted by Clooney eagerly relating the complaints made by Peadar's father, but Peadar himself said nothing. He had even begun to look flustered and a little ashamed.

'And so,' ended Gaibrial O'Doran, 'I condemn you, Peadar O'Connor, as a *macc úar* and I sentence you to the full penalty of the law.' He waited for a moment glancing around at the now silent crowd. Mara felt cold with apprehension. Surely the man was not going so far. Brehon law always took into account mitigating circumstances, and surely there had been evidence that the father of Peadar had failed in his duty to his child. But she feared the worst, looking at the cold, merciless face.

'You left home when you were seventeen years old. Was that with your father's consent, or without it?'

'Oh, he didn't mind a bit. He was all for my brother Stíofan. Stíofan was two years older than me. He was the favourite, always had been and always would be. I just went off and got myself a berth on a Spanish ship.' Peadar O'Connor was probably doing himself no good by this aggressive tone, but Mara could see how the boy was pale under the brown of his skin. His eyes were showing their whites like a frightened horse. It was time to question him more gently, she thought, but the new Brehon pressed on aggressively.

'And you came back to Formoyle last year?'

Peadar shifted uneasily. 'Just for a few days.'

'And you heard the news that your brother had died and that your father was alone?'

Surprising that he did not stay then, thought Mara. The land owned by his father was poor barren land, just a few acres near to the sea, nevertheless, it was probably better than rowing and hauling in nets on a Spanish boat. The land at Formoyle had been in the family for many years. She knew the place well. A cousin of her housekeeper, Brigid, lived near there. Yes, it was surprising that he did not stay. She, like the rest of people on Knockfinn, that high, stony hill overlooking the sea, turned her eyes onto the young man's face and waited for his answer.

'I couldn't stand him,' he blurted out at last.

'You couldn't stand the company of your own father?' Brehon O'Doran waited for a comment on this, but none came. Young Peadar had shut his lips firmly.

'So you didn't care whether he lived or died? Your own father, you left him there in his misery, an old man, a man who had sired you, who had brought you up, you left him, didn't you, you walked off, turned your back on him as though you were a wild dog, left him to die alone in that lonely place.'

How did the new Brehon know all of that, wondered Mara. Her eyes sought the face of the *taoiseach* Finn O'Connor, but he had a look of distaste on his face and, when he saw Mara's eyes on him, he slightly shook his head. He, the message was conveyed to her, had nothing to do with the knowledge of local affairs which tripped so readily off the tongue of Brehon O'Doran. He had, indeed, been busy during the week he had spent in the MacClancy house nearby.

And he seemed to have amassed plenty of information. Now he consulted his notes, deliberately, thought Mara, building up the tension. The unfortunate Peadar had begun to sweat heavily and from time to time, he mopped his brow with the back of his hand.

'Did you say these words, overheard by a witness: "I hope that the next time I come back here that you will be six feet underground." Are those your words?'

'No,' said Peadar sullenly, but the word lacked a ring of conviction.

'Two witnesses overheard you say that.'

Ask to see them, ask to cross-question them. The words screamed in Mara's head and she tried to project them across to Peadar, but it was no good. After a minute he nodded slowly.

'Answer me!'

'Yes,' said Peadar reluctantly, 'but it wasn't like that. It—'

'You admit it. That's good. Now we come to sentencing.'

Everyone looked startled. Wasn't Peadar going to be allowed to say anything, to explain his words, but the new Brehon raised his voice to almost a shout.

'Peadar MacSeán MacDonal MacTeige O'Connor, I sentence you, according to our ancient laws which lay down that a man should care for his father. You, Peadar MacSeán MacDonal MacTeige O'Connor have failed in that duty. And now, I, Brehon of Corcomroe, sentence you to banishment from the kingdom.'

There was a murmur from the crowd, but Peadar stood as though like the biblical Peter, he was made from rock.

'You are now an outlaw,' said Gaibrial O'Doran solemnly. 'You are a man beyond the law, a man whose contract is invalid and who cannot be harboured by anyone in the kingdom, no man or woman can give you shelter or food or drink. You are a man who is now without protection in the kingdom and who can be slain by anyone who finds you within the boundaries of the kingdom after twenty-four hours have elapsed. This banishment will, according to the law, last for a period of ten years.'

And then he turned his back on the people, replaced his law documents within his satchel. Only when that was done to his satisfaction did he look again at the aghast crowd.

'Go, you are all dismissed,' he said abruptly.

And then, stern-faced, he bowed briefly in the king's direction and, without a backward glance, he strode across the hillside to where his horse stood cropping the grass. The four young men, Ciaráin, Donal, Seán and Ronan, stared after him as though frozen to the spot, but Peadar, now condemned as an outlaw, started violently and then began to run like a deer down the hill towards the sea.

Mara's eyes met Setanta and Setanta immediately followed him. After a moment's hesitation some other men did also and she held her breath until she saw them catch up with Peadar. Then she gave a sigh of relief and then realized that her own sigh was echoed by the crowd. That high cliff above the foaming hollow of Hag's Kitchen was a place that had seen many deaths. No one wanted to see another young life extinguished for ever among the sharp rocks of this inlet of the ocean.

Two

Brecha Nemeð
(Judgements of Professional People)

There are seven props which serve judgement:
1. *The law relating to the rights of sons;*
2. *The law relating to monks or monastic clients;*
3. *the law relating to lordship;*
4. *The law of marriage;*
5. *The law of kingship;*
6. *Boundary law;*
7. *Laws relating to a treaty between territories.*

'But, Turlough, every single one of those judgements was incorrect. You must do something.'

'I was thinking about that.' Turlough's face beamed at her with simple pleasure. 'It just came to me this morning. I went for a ride while you were having your bath and it suddenly dawned on me. I get all my best ideas when I am out on a horse. So I sent a boy down to the priest with a message and he came back with the answer straight away. I know what to do now.'

'What?' Mara stared at his pleased face with exasperation. She had spent most of the night before awake and worrying about what was to be done about the unjust judge. Setanta had called into Ballinalacken Castle some time before sunset while she and Turlough were at supper and had sent a message by his son, Art, her scholar, to say that Peadar was safe and was having supper with Setanta and Cliona. That was a temporary solution, but a good one for the moment as Setanta lived in the Kingdom of the Burren, quite near to Mara's law school. However, there was no reason why the young man should be permanently excluded from his farm and his place of birth. And then there were the cases of the four other young men.

There was little chance of Ciaráin marrying Emer if that heavy fine was exacted from him. It would cause a permanent rift between them. And the families of Ronan and the innkeeper, Barra, would be enemies for ever because of the crippling debt that the fine would place on them – and all for a drunken fight where there appeared, from Ronan's stumbling words, to be faults on both sides. And Seán had meant no harm – it had been a simple piece of bad luck that the wind had veered towards the haystack. As for the copyright issue, well that was a piece of nonsense. Donal had used some words from a song that had stuck in his head for a year and which originally belonged to Suibhne, now dead for about four hundred years. These poets borrowed lines from each other without realizing it.

'Stop frowning. I tell you that I have a good idea,' said Turlough proudly.

'Tell me about it.' Mara resigned herself to listening. Turlough's way of solving problems usually involved either a warlike attack or else having a quiet word with someone. Neither solution could she see working in this case.

'Well, I thought of pardoning everyone in honour of St Leger.' Turlough beamed at her.

'Who on earth is St Leger?'

'His feast day is today. The second day of October is the feast of St Leger. That's what the priest says, anyway.'

'I never heard of him.'

'Nor me, neither,' said Turlough, 'but I once had a horse called St Leger and he was a great horse. Had a bit of an Arab in him – that sort of head, small ears, you know. Anyway, you needn't look so impatient because it's a great idea. I'll announce that everyone convicted yesterday will be pardoned in honour of St Leger and any claims for compensation will be looked after by one of my Brehons in Thomond and paid by me. Then you need not have anything to do with it.'

'It's an idea,' said Mara slowly. She didn't like it much. It was a bad precedent, but on the other hand, the king was known to be generous and impulsive and most people would evaluate this offer as an effort to save the face of the newly appointed Brehon and would not expect it to become a habit that wrong-doers were freed of responsibility for their actions.

'Well, there you are then, that's that,' said Turlough heartily. 'The trouble with you is that you think too much and you worry too much. Look at me. I slept like a log last night and this morning went out for a ride without the slightest idea in my head. Just was riding along enjoying the morning, thinking about nothing much when the notion suddenly popped into my mind. As soon as I got back I sent a lad down to the priest. I knew there would be some feast day or other. There always is, but I was pleased to find that it was St Leger. He was a great old horse. I was sorry when I lost him.'

'But Turlough, this might work for this occasion, but it can't keep happening. The Brehon of north-west Corcomroe is going to have at least six judgement days in the year and more if it is necessary. You can't keep finding obscure saints and pardoning everyone just because it is someone's feast day. And how are you to explain it to the Brehon, the new one, I mean, Brehon O'Doran, not dear old Fergus?'

'He has heard about it all, you know; Fergus, I mean. I dropped in to see him when I was riding along the cliff. The couple that are looking after him said that silly boy, the song-writer, Donal, wasn't it? Well, he's written a song about it all and he popped into Fergus last night and sang it to him. Poor old Fergus. Gobnait and Pat, they were trying to keep him busy making sloe wine, but he kept coming back to the wretched judgement day. He was a bit muddled but he had got hold of the fact that Peadar had been made an outlaw and he was repeating over and over again, I never declared anyone to be an outlaw, never in my whole life. I kept saying, Never mind, Fergus, don't you worry. I'll settle everything. But he didn't listen to me, just wailed like a child. I tell you, Mara, I had tears in my eyes listening to him. If anything like that ever happens to me, just push me over the cliff.'

'Turlough,' said Mara earnestly. 'Never mind about Fergus for the moment. We need to settle this matter now. You've come up with a good temporary solution and it's generous of you to offer to pay the fair fines, but now you need to think of a permanent solution.'

Turlough's face fell. 'You don't think that the new Brehon, Brehon O'Doran, will have learned his lesson?' he enquired.

Mara thought about the performance yesterday. Brehon O'Doran had not once shown any sign of self-doubt, of any hesitation, any compassion or any effort to seek for a solution that would keep the peace among the people of the kingdom.

'No, I don't,' she said firmly. There was no point in giving any false hope to Turlough, although she was sorry to see the cheerful look fade from his face. 'At least you will have bought some time with this decision. But,' she finished warningly, 'Turlough, something will have to be done. This is not a man to take a hint. This man believes in himself and his knowledge of the law.'

'But he did seem to know a lot, didn't he?' Turlough looked hopeful. 'There were a lot of these things from *Berrad Airechta, Bretha Crolige* and all those fellows. I thought you'd be very impressed by him. Never stopped for a word, did he?'

'That was true,' said Mara. 'And I'm afraid that worried me even more. He never stopped for a word, and he never hesitated and wondered whether he was right, and above all he never listened. It was supposed to be a trial, a time where the accused and accuser say what they have to say in front of the people of the kingdom, but his response was always to get that wretched child, his scholar, to shout for silence. A man, or a woman, who will not listen, will never learn, Turlough. I am deeply worried about this.'

'Well, let's deal with one thing at a time,' said Turlough. 'I'll just pop down to the Brehon's house and have a quiet word in his ear. Have a chat with him. Tell him that we don't do things like that here. After all, the poor fellow comes from Ossory and that's just near Kildare's lands. And you know what the Earl of Kildare is like: would hang a man for looking sideways at him. O'Donnell was telling me that he heard talk that the Great Earl, as he calls himself, threatened to cut off the right leg of men who did not kneel to him as he passed. "Bend the knee or lose the knee" that's what he shouts at them. It stands to reason that this fellow, the new Brehon, might have picked up some odd ideas about how to treat people.'

'Do that, then,' said Mara. She suppressed a sigh, unwilling to dishearten him, but she did not think that Brehon O'Doran would take too much notice of a quiet word from Turlough. After all, the appointment was made and it would be difficult now to dismiss a man because of one performance. There would have to be many complaints over a long period. In the meantime, of course, it was the people of north-west Corcomroe who would suffer. 'I'm going back to the law school now, Turlough, and I'll see you this evening at supper. You can tell me then how you got on.'

During the ten-mile ride between Ballinalacken Castle and the law school at Cahermacnaghten on the Burren, Mara resolutely kept her mind off the subject of the new Brehon O'Doran. There was nothing that she could do, she told herself. The affair was for Turlough to manage. He had been king now for twenty-five years, a most successful reign and a most popular king who ruled in his own distinctive style. She would not interfere any more in this matter, she promised herself and turned her mind to her own law school.

The new school year began traditionally on Michaelmas Day, the 29th day of September, but this year that had fallen on a Saturday and so the school had opened on Monday. She needed to recruit more pupils, she thought as she rode in through the gates leading to the cobbled yard of the law school. Her thirteen-year-old son, Cormac, had left the school to undertake military training with a friend of Turlough's in the north of the country and her two oldest scholars, her grandson Domhnall and his friend Slevin had passed their examinations in the summer and were now qualified as junior lawyers. Slevin had gone back to his home kingdom in Mayo to take up a post there and Domhnall had stayed with her as a teacher. This just left her with three pupils: Art, the son of Setanta the fisherman, and the MacMahon twins, Cian and his sister Cael. She had arranged that two eight-year-olds would join the school next week, a boy, named Davin, the son of the Brehon MacEgan from Ormond, and a granddaughter of a local farmer, named Ide. She could, though, do with another thirteen- or fourteen-year-old to support the gentle, self-effacing Art against the twins Cael and Cian who both very strong characters. Art was missing his foster brother, Cormac, intensely and had looked depressed during these last few days as he slumped over his desk in the law school. Her mind went to Niall, the new Brehon's assistant. She had liked the look of his face and he had winced at the brutal judgements as though he knew that they were not made in accordance with law.

And then she saw him. Niall must have been following her. She had heard the clip-clop of horseshoes on the limestone road for the last few minutes. He was riding his pony so recklessly that he came around the piers of the open gate and almost crashed into her. His face was a dead shade of white, the blond hair dishevelled and his pale blue eyes wide with horror.

'Brehon!' he shouted, almost screaming the word.

'Get your pony under control,' she snapped. He must have set off in a hurry because the saddle was twisted and girths either broken or not fastened. The pony neighed loudly and rolled its eyes. The boy fought with him as he reared up and tried to knock his rider off his back. Cumhal, Mara's farm manager, came running from the woodshed where he was stacking the logs ready for winter fires and Domhnall followed by the three scholars erupted from the schoolhouse.

'Careful,' said Mara. Her own horse was restive, but she murmured a word and stroked him. Niall clung desperately to his pony. The reins had been jerked from his hands which were bleeding from a scrape against the rough stone of the entrance and he hung on desperately to the pony's mane.

'Whoa there, whoa,' called Cumhal and for a moment the pony turned his head towards the calm soothing voice and that moment was enough for Domhnall who managed to snatch the reins and hold the dancing pony for long enough to enable Cian to put a heavy arm over the creature's neck.

'Whoa there, whoa,' repeated Cumhal and, producing an early apple from his pocket, held it out. The pony paused. He did not accept the apple, but the smell was enough to calm him for long enough so that Domhnall could hold him next to the bit and bring him under control.

'Down you get, young man,' said Cumhal, handing the apple to Domhnall and keeping a steady grasp of the boy's arm as he slid unsteadily from the saddle, holding him until he was steady on his feet. And then Niall looked at Mara with dilated eyes.

'He's in a lobster pot,' he said unsteadily and then he began to laugh in a slightly hysterical fashion. 'A bird nibbled his hand, thought he was a lobster.'

And then, quite suddenly, he vomited onto the cobbles. Cian took a hasty step backwards and Art's hand went to his mouth. Cael, quick-witted and sensible, grabbed the boy's arm, while Mara hastily dismounted, handing over her horse to a wide-eyed stable boy.

'Bring him over here, Cael,' she said. 'Sit down, Niall, sit on the mounting block. Put your head down. Art, get a drink from Brigid. Don't worry, Niall, take your time. You can tell us all about it as soon as you feel better.'

'Get some turf mould over that,' muttered Cumhal to the stable boy and in a minute the pungent smell of peat dust overcame the sharp acidity of the vomit. The boy's colour began to improve as he sipped the drink held solicitously by Art. Mara took one look around at the crowd that gathered: two or three of the farm workers had ceased their wood chopping and peat stacking, the lads in the orchard abandoned their baskets and the girls in the kitchen had all accompanied Brigid out to look at the stranger.

'You're looking better now, Niall,' she said cheerfully. 'Let's get you indoors. Art, you help him into the schoolroom. You go, too, Cael and Cian. Cumhal, perhaps one of your men could look after this pony until Niall is feeling better.' And then, in a low voice, she said to Domhnall, 'That boy is the pupil of the new Brehon in Corcomroe.'

Domhnall nodded. He was always very discreet. Now he said nothing, asked nothing about lobster pots, did not speculate about why Niall had come hurtling through the gate of the law school in the Burren. He waited knowing that all would soon be made clear and held the door open for Mara as she passed into the schoolhouse.

'Feeling better, Niall?' she asked. The cup had been drained and the air smelled of chamomile, Brigid's remedy for all upsets. He nodded, but his face was still very white and his eyes still large with horror.

'He was tied into a lobster pot,' he said, the words spurting from him. 'A very large one.'

'Who?'

He looked puzzled. 'My master, Brehon O'Doran.'

Mara waited. Surely a prank like tying a man within a lobster pot was not enough to cause the boy to look like that. Niall, however, said no more, just put his two elbows on the desk in front of him and rested his face within his hands. Mara could see that he was trembling.

'A crime of murder has to be reported immediately to a Brehon; but the Brehon is the one who is dead,' he said suddenly and there was a tremor in his voice. He took his hands from his face and once again shook with uncontrollable laughter. He was on the verge of hysteria.

'Stop that,' said Mara sternly. 'You're not a child. Tell me sensibly. Is Brehon O'Doran dead?'

The boy nodded. His lips trembled but he had managed to stifle the hysterical laughter. 'I didn't do it. I had nothing to do with it. I wouldn't have done that. Why should I? This was a great chance for me. My father said that. He said I would learn so much more than in a large school. He said that Gaibrial O'Doran was a clever man and . . .' The boy's voice shook again, but he swallowed hard. 'My father said that he had a long life ahead of him as Brehon and that he could teach me, but he didn't have a long life, did he?'

'Where did you find him?' asked Domhnall quietly. He put a hand on the boy's shoulder and Niall looked up trustingly at him.

'In Hell,' he said.

'By the ocean?' asked Art and then, to Mara: 'That's what they call the place near the harbour, Doon MacFelim, that place where the water foams up. You've seen it, Brehon, haven't you? No boat dares to go near to it, but you can see it from the cliff above.'

'I remember it,' said Cael. 'It's that massive fissure in the rock. You can see the ocean through it. Do you remember, Cian? We got drenched once when the seawater suddenly spurted up through it. There's that big blowhole a bit further up and—'

'And Bones' Bay below it,' said Art nodding. 'That's the place?'

'Did he fall, did your master fall, Niall?' Cian repeated the question twice before Niall's eyes focussed on him.

'Fall, no, I don't think so. I don't know. He's still there. He's squashed into that lobster pot. The birds were eating him. People eat lobsters and birds eat people.' Once again Niall's voice broke hysterically and he strove to keep back another fit of laughter. The three scholars looked at him with astonishment, and Domhnall's eyes met Mara's. He slightly shook his head and she nodded. Whatsoever was the truth of this matter it needed to be investigated immediately. The man, she thought, might not be dead. He might just have stumbled and become entrapped within the ropes of a lobster pot. He might just be stunned. Hopefully he might be saved. She made up her mind to waste no more time.

'We need to get Nuala,' she said decisively. 'You go, Art. You know this place and you can take her directly to it. Cian, go and see whether Niall's pony is fit for the journey, or better still, ask Cumhal to find something for him.' Nuala O'Davoren was the physician of the kingdom; the daughter and granddaughter of former physicians, she had excelled her forebears by her knowledge and skill. If the man were to be found still alive, then she might be able to save him. If he were dead, then she would be able to tell Mara whether he died of drowning, or a broken neck, or whether something more sinister might have been involved. Several years of study in Italy had given her the skills to open a dead body, to look at the contents of the stomach, to trace a wound or to examine the heart.

And if the man had been murdered, there would be plenty of suspects. As she climbed on her horse, she thought to herself of the extraordinary scenes at the hill of judgement, yesterday, and of the shocked faces of the five young men who had received such heavy and such unjust sentences. Sean the arsonist, Ciaráin the rapist, Ronan the brawler, Donal the infringer of copyright, Peadar the undutiful son; each one of them, or indeed any of the relations who would have to help pay the fine, could be the guilty one. And in particular she thought of the one who had been declared an outlaw, had been banished from his own kingdom and declared to be without the protection of the law, a target for any man who wished to rob, or even to kill him. Perhaps a messenger should have been sent to ascertain whether Peadar was still with Art's father, but she was unwilling to cause gossip before the facts were confirmed. Niall did not seem a very reliable witness. The story of the lobster pot and the nibbling birds was quite strange. Or did he mean fish?

Mara's eyes went to the slumped-over figure of the exhausted scholar of Brehon O'Doran. Niall looked as though he had not slept all night, she thought suddenly. He was white with black circles under his eyes and he was yawning repeatedly. Domhnall was riding very close to him, and she knew that her astute grandson had noticed how the boy swayed in his saddle and was alert to catch the pony's rein if sleep or hysteria overcame him.

Might Niall, also, she wondered, be a possible suspect if this affair of the Brehon and the lobster pot turned out to be a murder case? For a boy of his age, he had shown an undue amount of upset in his account. By the age of fifteen, he would have seen many dead bodies. What had caused such hysteria?

Three

Bretha Forma
(Judgements of Trapping)

*No bird trap may be set without the permission of the landowner.
If a bird is trapped with permission, then two-thirds of the flesh and
one-third of the feathers may be retained. If trapped without permission
a fine must be paid and the bird given to the landowner.*

*However, there is no penalty for trapping very small birds, or birds of
prey such as herons and hawks.*

*If a landowner is absent for some length of time, then birds may be
trapped on his land with immunity from any legal action.*

'Look, Cian,' said Cael as they crossed the boundary line
between the two kingdoms. 'Look at the geese! Do you
remember we used to shoot these when we were young, at
Urlan, do you remember? With our bows and arrows. Feels
like a long time ago, doesn't it? I don't think I would do it
now. It seems a shame.'

'Tasted good, though, didn't they? The cook was delighted
when we brought them in. Cooked six of them that very
night,' said Cian, his eyes following the V-shaped trail of long
necks and wide stretched wings outlined against the pale blue
of the autumn sky. Mara listened with interest. The twins very
seldom talked of the past. This summer she had talked to them
about their father's death at the hands of the king years earlier
when the MacMahon had been hanged for treachery and found
that both knew of the event, had known for a long time, but
neither had wanted to discuss it, nor to bring to mind anything
about their past. This reference was an unusual one, she thought,
and then forgot the twins as Niall suddenly turned his head and
looked at her.

'It was that which brought my master out of doors last night,'
he said unexpectedly. 'The geese were coming in from the sea.'

'He went shooting, did he?' questioned Domhnall, his voice quiet and relaxed.

Niall shook his head. 'Not shooting,' he said scornfully. 'The man was blind as a bat. He went out to bring the law on the shooters. He saw them from his room. He went running down the stairs, and out of the door. I could see him pelting down the hillside, his lawyer's gown flapping out behind him like a black sail. He was shouting at them. He was threatening that they would be brought to the next judgement day.'

'Did you go with him?' asked Mara, adopting Domhnall's neutral tone of voice. Niall still looked ill and still rode slumped into his saddle, but Cumhal had given him a very quiet pony, a nice old animal that he used to teach a new scholar to ride across the stone-laid fields of the Burren. She didn't think that he would fall off now, though she noticed that Domhnall still rode very close to the boy and kept his head turned towards him.

'No, I didn't,' said Niall, and this time his tone was raucous and defiant. 'You can't pin this crime on me. It was nothing to do with me. He didn't order me to come and so I kept out of his way. He had stirred up enough hatred already. I didn't want to be in it. *Hell*, that's a good name for the place. A good place for him to end up in.' He gave a short, abrupt laugh.

'Did you see who they were, the huntsmen?' asked Mara. 'You looked out after them, I suppose.'

'No, I didn't see who they were. I don't know the people here. They were just the usual sort of people you get around here. Very brown, very black hair. All about the same size. All dressed the same. Just wearing a *léine* and sandals. When they heard him shout, they went running down the hill towards the sea. He followed them, shouting at them.'

'How many of them, were there?' asked Mara.

'Five,' said Niall.

Five, she thought. That is a coincidence. 'Are you sure?' she asked.

'Five of them,' repeated Niall.

'And you're sure that you didn't recognize them? Could they be the five young men that you saw at the law court?'

Niall was silent for a moment. 'Could be,' he said then. 'I think that the fellow Peadar was there. I thought I heard Brehon O'Doran shout out something about banishment when he went flying down the hill after them. I was saying to myself, Is that man going to banish everyone who commits the slightest crime out of the kingdom? But I suppose it could have been the fisherman fellow, Peadar – he had already pronounced a sentence of banishment on him.'

'Where were they?' Art was the one who knew this district the best as his father, Setanta, often fished from Doolin Harbour.

'They were down by the hedge, just where the oats had been harvested. I suppose the geese come in off the sea to eat the stuff.' Niall seemed better, more animated and he moved up to ride beside Cael who was discussing with Cian the legal rights of hunters. Domhnall hung back and looked at Mara.

'Would Peadar have dared to go hunting on the Brehon's own land?' he asked and without waiting for an answer, continued, 'And would Setanta have permitted him to go back to Corcomroe. It seems very strange, doesn't it?'

'Well, strictly speaking, Peadar had twenty-four hours before he had to leave the kingdom. Perhaps he thought that he would take one more look at the farm that should have belonged to him.'

'Perhaps he went to the alehouse and met the other four drowning their sorrows,' said Domhnall shrewdly. 'Would they have dared to hunt over the Brehon's lands, though?'

'It might have been something that they had done over the years from time to time. In fact, I'd say that a lot of young men had hunted over the Knockfinn territory during the last few years, and perhaps longer,' said Mara. 'Fergus would not have stopped them and his farm manager had been complaining to me that Fergus did not allow him to drive out any trespassers, or even to get a fair price for the produce. Fergus had turned very obstinate about things like that. The more he felt his wits and his memory slip from him, the more he stood his ground on being the one to make the decisions. And, of course, every layabout and every idle person took advantage of him, nothing too much, but something like bird hunting, well, I doubt that Fergus would claim his share or allow the farm manager to do it. I think that Fergus would only be too pleased to think that the cooking pots were filled.'

'It would be a good place for hunters,' called back Cael. 'The grass is very good on Knockfinn; I was thinking that yesterday and of course geese love grass and they love oats.' She rose up in her stirrups, her hand shielding her eyes from the overhead sun. 'Look, look down there. That's not geese. Look at all of those hawks down there, Cian, they are diving down, there must be some prey down there, perhaps some dead fish.'

'Oh, my God,' said Domhnall. 'And that's the place that they call Hell, down there. Do you remember Setanta telling us some stories of that place? Quick, ride as fast as you can, you two, shout and wave your arms. They might be attacking the body. If he is still alive by any miracle, they'll kill him. That's a golden eagle there hovering just above the cliff edge.'

'And that's a peregrine falcon. Look at his wings. He's going in for the kill.' Cian screamed the words as he clapped his heels and flew ahead of them. 'Come on, Cael, ride like the wind, keep yelling. Oh, if only I had my bow and arrows!'

And then the two of them were off, riding recklessly, shouting at the tops of their voices. First Cael and then Cian leaped the stone wall at the bottom of the hill at Knockfinn. A few seconds later, they were lost from sight.

'Go after them, Domhnall,' said Mara urgently. 'I hope they don't break their necks.' She was not truly worried though. The MacMahon twins were born horse riders. They had been so neglected in their youth that they had formed the habit of doing most dangerous things and emerging unscathed. She drew nearer to Niall. The excitement about the birds of prey had brought a little colour to his cheeks and he sat far more steadily on the pony and looked alertly ahead. Mara thought that the time might have come for a few questions.

'How did you come to be the pupil of Brehon O'Doran, Niall?' she asked, making her voice sound casual. She did not look at him, but as they rode steadily up the next hill, she scanned the distant view waiting for the first sight of the Atlantic and of the Aran Islands ahead of them. She hardly listened to his long-winded explanation but strained her ears to hear the shouts from the twins or from Domhnall. They were loud and angry, but no note of alarm in them, and she relaxed. They were just frightening the birds away. Now she and Niall had surmounted the brow of the hill and the sea stretched out in front of them. The land here around Knockfinn was very green, right down to the cliff edge, but even from the distance she could see how the smooth curve of the hill was broken off at one spot and a white plume of sea rose up. Hell. It had been named, she supposed, by some fisherman whose boat had been swept in to the inlet by the rocks. Setanta had told her scholars some stories of it. The name of Bones' Bay probably evoked several past events. Domhnall was riding back up the hill towards them, so the twins must have the bird situation in control.

'That's a buzzard rising up, now,' said Niall looking up into the sky. 'I used to shoot those back in Ossory. I was the best of all the marksmen there,' he boasted. Somehow his earlier horror had gone and he looked with interest at the birds beating their wings above the foam that rose up from the cliff edge.

Mara glanced at him with interest. 'You're a bowman, then, are you?' And was not surprised when he nodded. He had broad shoulders for his age. It made it slightly surprising that he had not gone out with his master to witness the shots of the five hunters on the evening before.

'Look, there's the body down there in that big lobster pot?' he said pointing towards the cliffs. 'That's what the birds were attacking all right. See them hover above it. They want to get back down and finish their meal.' He gave a slightly hysterical laugh.

'Your eyes are better than mine,' said Mara amiably. She would not cross-question him now. First they had to see whether there really was a body there, and then wait for Nuala's verdict before deciding whether the death was a murder or an accident. Domhnall was returning. He would bring the news.

'Niall, Niall,' called a voice from behind them, a childlike voice, high and wavering. Mara turned in her saddle just as Domhnall joined them. A young girl, her hair streaming out behind her, was running down the hill from the Brehon's house at Knockfinn.

'Christ, I forgot about her,' said Niall.

'Her?' Queried Mara. 'Who is she?'

'She's Ríanne, she's the wife of the Brehon, the wife of Gaibrial O'Doran.'

'What?' The same word burst from Mara and from Domhnall. They looked at each other.

'I didn't know that he was married,' said Domhnall.

'Nor did I,' said Mara. 'And the king never mentioned a wife. Are you sure, Niall?'

'He just got married the day before we left Ossory. She brought him a big dowry, my father told me that. He said that Brehon O'Doran would become a rich man.' Niall gave one look towards the girl and then turned his head back towards the sea and the circling birds.

'Does she know about her husband?' Mara made no attempt to ride back up the hill towards the girl. She needed a few facts before she met this unexpected wife.

'She was the one that sent me out looking for him. She woke me up. She told me that he hadn't come home. She was pestering me. She kept on saying, Where is he? As if I should know!' Niall's tone was sulky but now he watched the girl avidly. 'She's going to get a shock,' he added and, unbelievably, there seemed to be a note of satisfaction in his voice.

'Didn't you tell her?' Domhnall stared at him open-mouthed and Niall flushed.

'I had enough on my mind.' The wind carried away the next few words but the boy's expression was now more indignant than embarrassed. Mara could distinguish a few muttered words, 'Always pestering me.'

'He's dead, all right,' said Domhnall briefly when she looked a question at him.

'I see,' said Mara. There was no point in cross-questioning him. In another few minutes she would see for herself. The MacMahon twins were clearly visible now. Cael still sat on her pony. She had taken the belt from her *léine* and every few seconds she whirled it around her head to keep the birds at bay. Cian had dismounted and was searching the edge of the broken cliff, picking up large chunks of white limestone and piling them up in a heap beside him.

But now she had to deal with this child.

The Brehon's wife, Ríanne, looked about the same age as Niall, or even younger. Thin and small, dressed quite simply, just a pale blue gown over her *léine* with her dark hair hanging loose. The wind from the sea flattened her clothes to her figure and the lacing of the gown showed small breasts, but there was something very immature and childlike about her.

'Don't say anything now, let me break it to her gently.' Mara kept her voice low but made it authoritative.

'She won't care,' said Niall. 'She's always crying and wanting to go back to Ossory. She'll just be pleased.'

Almost as though she heard the words, the girl slowed down and then advanced hesitantly. Domhnall jumped from his horse, tossed its reins to Niall and came forward to assist Mara to dismount. Once she was on the ground, he stood back, placing a restraining hand on Niall's knee. Mara went swiftly uphill, her hands outstretched.

'You poor thing,' she said. 'You've had a worrying time.'

The girl's thin face flushed and she scrubbed at her eyes with a small piece of slightly grubby linen. 'What's wrong?' she asked. 'I've been waiting and waiting for Niall to come back.'

'We think that there's been an accident, Ríanne,' said Mara. She could rely on Domhnall to keep Niall silent. Despite the young scholar's words, this must come as a great shock to a bride of one week's standing. Barely fourteen, she thought, scanning the childlike face before her.

'Is he dead? Did they kill him? Those men with the bows and arrows, did they kill him?' Despite Niall's words, she sounded upset and frightened. Her eyes went to the cliff and then to the circling birds. She shuddered and looked slightly sick. 'I don't want to see him,' she said then.

'No, no,' said Mara soothingly. 'But I'm afraid that I have some bad news for you. Niall thinks that your husband is dead. He came to fetch me and we've sent for the physician.'

The girl's face was very white and at these words, her teeth began to chatter. Mara took the two cold hands between hers and began to rub them.

'Is there anyone in the house with you, Ríanne?'

'No, Niall left me alone.'

'Orlaith comes in everyday to clean the house and cook the dinner,' said Niall, from the background.

'Well, she didn't come today,' said the girl resentfully. 'She knows what happened, I suppose. Everyone knows what happened except me.'

That, indeed, was possible, thought Mara. News would have got around quickly in this small community. And if it was rumoured that five young men, related to most of them, had been responsible for the murder, then there would be an unspoken resolve to keep clear of the body and to avoid suspicion. And this, Mara reminded herself, was not her own kingdom. She was a stranger here.

But what to do with this child while she checked on the body?

And then an elderly figure came walking slowly and hesitantly, up from the cliff edge. Fergus MacClancy, one-time Brehon, had been drawn to the scene by instinct. He came towards them and Mara grimaced. Now she had two problems on her hands. Turlough had reported how tearful Fergus was about the unjust verdicts at what had been his court for over forty years, and now the sight of a dead man in his territory was bound to upset him far more.

But Fergus did not look upset. In fact, he appeared more like the Fergus that she had known from the time that she was a child, better than she had seen him for many years. He nodded gravely to her, gave a puzzled glance at Domhnall and Niall as though he wondered who they were, and then went straight across to Ríanne. 'You poor child,' he said in his quavering old-man voice, 'your husband is dead, but never mind. He was not a good husband to you. We'll send you back to your family and they will find a better one for you. Now, you come back to my new house and you'll sit by the fire and we'll look after you.'

'Go with them, Domhnall,' whispered Mara. 'Just make sure that all is well and then you can come back.' Turlough had reported how the couple that he paid to look after Fergus were kind and reliable. Once little Ríanne was in their care, then she could get on with the business of the morning. Aloud she said, 'Go with them, my dear. I'll come and see you afterwards and we will discuss what should be done. It will be your decision. My grandson, Domhnall, will walk back with you, Fergus.' She waited until they disappeared before turning to Niall.

'We'll walk the horses from here,' she said. He was not, she thought, a particularly good rider, and Domhnall's horse might resent another hand on his bridle. 'You go ahead,' she added. 'I'll follow.'

He was a puzzle, this boy, she thought, eyeing him as he walked ahead of her. She had thought to like him better than she was doing. He had shown himself hysterical and immature and his attitude to the bereaved child-wife had been that of a selfish young boy. How could he have forgotten to go back to the empty house and to tell her the truth about her husband, and to find somewhere to shelter her while he rode the ten miles into the neighbouring kingdom to report the death to the Brehon of the Burren? And, her thoughts continued, was it not odd behaviour of a boy of fifteen not to go to one of the nearby houses to look for help. After all, the man may have looked dead, but he might just have been stunned and lain insensible. At the very least, a guard should have been set up to make sure that the body was safe from the birds of prey who might peck out the eyes of an unconscious man.

No, she decided. The king would have to detail a guard of men to bring Ríanne back to the kingdom of Ossory and it would be the sensible thing to send Niall MacEgan back with her. The MacEgans were the foremost legal family in Gaelic Ireland and they had Brehons who worked for the majority of kings towards the north-east of Ireland, as well as working for some of the great and powerful families near Dublin such as the Kennedys and the Butlers. A place would be found for young Niall in one of the many law schools in these areas. Unless, of course, he needed to be detained to face a court here in the kingdom where his master had died.

Murder or an accident, this matter would have to be sorted out before young Niall left for his journey back east.

'Look out, Brehon,' shouted Cian. A stone curved through the air, falling not too far from the feet of Mara's horse. Overhead a white-tailed eagle banked and then flew back towards the sea, squawking angrily. The birds were avoiding the MacMahon twins and were turning their attack on the newcomers. Mara felt that it was rather beneath her dignity to shout and wave her arms and Niall had bridles in both hands, so they would have to rely on Cian and Cael. A surprisingly huge bird, she thought, trying to repress a feeling of nervousness. Perhaps they made their home in the tall cliffs that fringed this kingdom of north-west Corcomroe. Thankfully, she saw that there was a small lane, edged with the spiky-branched blackthorn, just ahead of her and leading towards the cliff. The horses would be safer there. Wild birds were frightened of anything that appeared to be a trap and the bushes would shield them. She steered her horse into that refuge and heard Niall follow behind. She heard him stop once. The bushes were studded with blue-black sloes, a good year for them, there were more of them lying on the laneway, as though the thrushes and hawfinches were sated with the fruits. Niall was not a country boy, she thought, as she saw him eagerly bite into one and then spit it out vigorously. He was, she guessed, apprehensive about seeing the body again and trying to delay the moment, as he lingered to survey the bushes and then followed her reluctantly.

After a bare two minutes, they were out on the cliff side again, out in the sunlight. It was a beautiful day. The sea shone a bright turquoise, bluer than the sky. Crab Island, just below the cliff, was covered with seabirds and in the distance, the Aran Islands floated in the mist, as insubstantial as the islands of legends. As they emerged, a foaming jet of seawater shot up through the blowhole and sent billowing jets of spray all around the cliff. Cael and Cian ran back towards them. The birds soared higher in the sky, and hovered there, baulked once more of their prey. And then a few seconds later, as the waves retreated, the pillar of spume subsided.

And then they could see what was drawing the birds to the spot. A large wicker pot seemed to be stuffed with wet black cloth, but as the mist cleared Mara could see that something glistened pink under the sunlight. The birds squawked noisily and dropped down. One managed to land despite the shrieks from Cael and Cian, but then the waves rolled back in again to the shore, the jet of water spurted up through the blowhole and once again the basket was shrouded with water. Nevertheless, Mara had seen enough. That was a human face, a human head on top of the shapeless heap stuffed into the basket.

'We'll have to drag it out,' shouted Cian in her ear. 'We were waiting for you to come, Brehon, but we'll have to get it out of there. Nuala will need it away from the spray so that she can examine it.'

He was right, of course. Mara knew that. Although Nuala had always impressed on her and on her scholars that a body should not be moved until she had a chance to view it, it was impossible to view anything in the couple of seconds when it was uncovered. The waves were crashing against the cliff face of the inlet at their side but this remaining section of the cliff was far out and got the full force of the sea. They might have to wait for hours for the arrival of dead tide and even then that hole might still be spurting out its water.

'We're wet already,' screamed Cael. 'We'll do it, Brehon. We'll take it back as far as possible. Niall, you get those stones. Give us cover from the birds, keep firing.'

Mara assessed the situation. The basket was near enough to the blowhole to get soaked every time that the seawater shot up it, but it wasn't so near that there would be any danger to the twins. She was tempted to wait until Nuala arrived with her apprentice, but the body might have been battered all night by the tide, and if there was the slightest chance that the man were still alive, then no moment should be lost.

'Take care!' That was all that she could say and she thought that there was no more that she could add. The twins would have summed up the situation and they were a competent pair, so she helped herself to a couple of stones from the pile and stood beside Niall. Cael was yelling something into Cian's ear and he nodded. Both were alert, ignoring the birds now and waiting as near as they dared to the lobster pot.

'Now!' screamed Cael. The spurt of foam had just wavered when the twins plunged into it. For a moment Mara could not see them and for a moment her heart skipped a beat for fear that they might go too near the edge of the blowhole – about five or six feet across, she reckoned. But then the water slipped back down, the noise of the waves grew less; its place taken by the raucous cries of the hovering birds.

'Quick, Niall,' said Mara, resolutely turning her gaze from the twins. She hurled one stone and then another and another at the white and black shapes that jetted through the air down towards them. There was a shout from Cian but still she fired the stones one after the other, hoping that Niall was doing the same thing, but not daring to pause in the rhythm of stoop, pick and fire; stoop, pick and fire.

'We've got him! Keep firing, Niall!' Cael's voice sounded thin and high above the roar of the sea and the shouts of the birds. The enormous jet spurted up again, but now the twins and their burden were safe from its reach. Mara threw her last stone and moved to their side.

'Weighs a ton. Must have a rock at the bottom of it.' Cian was breathless with the exertion and Cael had slumped onto the grass. She sat up quickly, though and then, with one glance upwards at the hovering birds, she turned her head towards the body in the lobster pot.

'He's dead alright, Brehon. Look at his throat.'

Under the white face and the empty eye sockets there was a gaping hole, a long slit that stretched almost from ear to ear. Cael was right. The man's throat had been cut. No one could have lived for hours with a wound like that. As Mara came nearer she could see that a piece of white linen had been used as a gag, had been tied around the mouth that had been so eloquent and fluent on judgement day. The hands that held the law scrolls were tied behind his back, attached to the ankles and the whole bundle inserted into the lobster pot.

And then as she concentrated on the dead body, to her relief, the birds hovering above all rose high in the sky and then flew noisily out to sea. There was a shout from the hillside and Mara turned back. A man with a stick in his hand had appeared at the top of the hill and was making his way down towards them. It was Setanta, Art's father.

'I met Art on his way to the physician, Brehon,' he explained. 'I told him that I would come across to see if you needed any help.' Once again he raised the short straight stick and pretended to aim at the birds and once again the whole flock went noisily off to descend on Crab Island.

'Learned that trick on board ship when you have a big catch,' he explained. 'The birds will keep away if they think you have an arrow trained on them.' And then he looked down on the dead man and his eyes widened.

'That's the new Brehon of Corcomroe; Art didn't tell me that, just that there might have been an accident.' Without waiting for her comment, he said urgently, 'Better get him out of that quickly, Brehon. There's a chance that he might not be too stiff if he has been under that cold water all night.'

Mara forced herself to reach over and to touch the dead man's fingers. They were pockmarked with pecks, she noticed but no blood appeared. Her mind registered this while she tested the flaccidity of the body. They felt quite loose, but the sun, despite the October date, was quite warm and the man would probably start to stiffen now that the body had been moved out of the icy temperature of the water.

'You're right; we'd better get him out,' she said and watched while Setanta cut with his knife the rope that bound the man and then with the help of Cian and Cael, plucked the body from the wicker pot. He had been trussed like a chicken for the boiling pot, legs and arms closely bound to the trunk. Niall turned aside and Mara heard him gulp heavily, but she had a feeling that he was now only pretending. At any rate, he did not vomit so she ignored him and turned her attention to the pot which had imprisoned the body.

The pot was more of a creel, a large basket woven from willow and bleached a pale tan colour by the sun and the sea. The top half of it had been broken off at some stage and the container itself had probably been discarded as past repair. It had still been solid enough to contain a man.

And then she turned her attention to the body. Setanta was on his knees, knife in hand, cutting the remaining pieces of rope.

'Take his shoulders, Cian,' he said and together they stretched the corpse out on the grass. Mara winced at the noise of two sharp clicks. The body had begun to stiffen at the joints. Setanta, however, did not hesitate, but continued straightening out the limbs, the legs stretched out very straight, the sodden lawyer's cloak pulled straight under the body and the arms placed one on either side of the trunk. Mara forced herself to gaze steadily at the man, trying to ignore the horror of the missing eyes.

'Yes, it's Brehon Gaibrial O'Doran,' she said aloud. She would say no more about the matter for the moment. It was important to observe the law and to take all the steps in due order. Now the corpse had been identified, Nuala would perform the autopsy and then the legal work to ascertain the cause of death would begin. Speculation at this stage could be misleading.

'Cael and Cian, you are both soaking wet,' she said. 'Take your ponies and ride as fast as you can to Fergus's house. See if you can borrow some dry clothing and wait by the fire there. I'll come and collect you when we are ready to go back to the law school.'

For a moment she thought of sending Niall with them, but then changed her mind. She wanted, she decided, to keep him under her eye.

Four

Bretha Cróliqe
(Judgements of Blood-letting)

In the event of an illegal injury, the victim is brought to his home or to the physician's hospital and nursed for nine days. If he dies during this period, the culprit must pay the full penalties for the killing.

It took quite some time before Nuala, accompanied by Art, arrived. They had kept pace with the cart driven by Nuala's apprentice, Ulan, and had come around by the road, rather than cutting across the fields as Mara and her scholars had done. Setanta had rigged up a shelter against the birds for them and for the corpse by cutting some branches of a spindly ash tree, inserting them in the ground and tying their tops together. After he had made sure that the birds were not approaching again, he had departed for a day's fishing. He reluctantly confirmed that Peadar had not spent the night with him, but had gone off when his friend, Donal the bard, had called to the house just after the evening meal.

It was just as well that Setanta had gone because Nuala was not at all pleased with his efforts to lay the corpse out for her. As Art was listening in an embarrassed fashion, Mara tried to save his feelings by claiming that it was she, not his father, who had taken the decision, but Nuala was scathing about the bull-strength that Setanta had used in order to straighten the bent limbs of the dead man. She reluctantly admitted that it was probably useful to have taken the lobster pot from under the spray of the blowhole, but declared that she would have removed the body, still encased in the wicker pot, right back to her hospital in Rathcorney, if it had not been interfered with.

'You see, Mara,' she said severely, 'those cuts on the hands. I suspect they are not caused by birds, but by the wicker.' She surveyed the pot and then went back to studying the long scratches on the man's hands.

'You won't find any blood marks on that,' said Niall scornfully. 'The sea would have washed them off.'

Nuala gave him a long cool look.

'Get into the basket,' she commanded.

'What!'

'Go on,' said Nuala impatiently. 'Ulan is too big. Your master was a small man, no bigger than you. If he could fit in, then so can you.'

'What about Art?'

'I'll do it, if you like,' said Art heroically.

Nuala gave him a glance. 'No, you're too long-legged. Niall is a better match. Go on, get in. Stop making a fuss.'

'But he was trussed up, bound with ropes!'

'We can do that, if you'd prefer,' said Nuala glancing at the pieces of rope lying on the grass.

'No, no,' said Niall hastily. He climbed into the basket and crouched down awkwardly, managing to kneel on its base.

'And hands behind your back,' commanded Nuala. 'Tie his wrists, Ulan.'

'I don't think that is necessary,' said Mara firmly. 'Just pretend to struggle, Niall. The physician wants to see whether the hands would have moved against the broken pieces of cane.'

'That's freshly done,' said Ulan, bending down and examining the side of the basket. 'You can see that the inside of the canes are still white, look just there.'

'That's what I was thinking,' agreed Nuala. She went back to the cart and examined the hands, now neatly tucked against the man's sides. 'Yes, I'd say these marks look more like scratches than pecks from birds. They would be smaller and deeper. Look at the marks on the cheeks. They are bird damage, now, but the marks on the hands are something else.'

Mara grimaced. 'You think that the man was alive when he was tied up and put in there. Deliberately tortured and then his throat cut.'

Nuala ignored that. Mara did not repeat her question. It was never any use to rush Nuala. She wouldn't give an opinion until her work was done and the body had given up its secrets.

She turned her attention to Niall. The boy looked sick again and she took pity on him.

'Well done, Niall,' she said cordially and stretched out a hand to him. 'I think that the physician has a good idea now of how the corpse was packed into the basket.'

Calling Brehon O'Doran a corpse perhaps took away some of the horror that a living man might have been bound, trussed and then his throat cut.

But why stick the basket under the drenching spray of the Atlantic waves? There didn't seem to be any reason for that.

'So we'll take him away now, and the basket, Ulan, store that carefully. I'll need that beside me when I am examining the body. Come and see me before supper this evening, Mara, and then I might be able to give you some information, despite the interference with the body. We'll be off then, if that is your instruction,' she added.

'Yes,' said Mara trying to make her voice sound humble and apologetic.

And then she thought of what she should have remembered before.

'Oh, my God,' she said aloud. 'My instructions! You'll have to wait, Nuala. I'm very sorry. I must get Turlough. I have no right to be here, in reality. I have no jurisdiction over this kingdom. I'm Brehon of the Burren, but not of Corcomroe. In law, I have no standing in this kingdom, no authority to give orders. What was I thinking of? Art, get on your pony and ride up to Ballinalacken Castle. The king is still there. I can see his flag fluttering from the turret. Tell him what has happened and ask him to come here as quickly as possible as I need him. If he can't come himself, then perhaps he could send some sort of written authority.' She watched him go flying up the hill towards the castle perched high above them and to the north. Turlough, she guessed, would laugh and would consider it all a lot of nonsense, but Mara knew that it was important always to keep to the letter of the law as well as the spirit of the law. The people of the Burren accepted everything she did. She had been Brehon there since the year 1494, almost thirty years, she thought ruefully. Her authority was absolute, but she really had no right to question the people of another

kingdom without the king's authority. And yet there were five
young men somewhere in this small kingdom, all of whom
received an excessively severe sentence by an unjust judge. And
that judge now lay there with his throat cut. These five needed
to be found and questioned without any further delay.

She had been rather outside the law in sending for Nuala,
she thought. True, there was now no Brehon in the kingdom
so her arrival might be excused, but there was a physician, a
man who lived by the sea and who was reputedly good at
sawing off mangled legs from injured stone workers. Apart
from his skill with a saw, she had never heard anything good
about that physician, in fact, most of his amputees seem to
have died in the weeks following their operation, from what
she had heard, and he probably would have done little other
than confirm that the man was dead and that his throat was
slit. Her instinct had undoubtedly been correct to send for
Nuala. In any case, there was nothing that she could do now,
except pray that Turlough had not yet returned to Bunratty.
She watched Art ride rapidly up the hill and then turned her
gaze back to the flag. It still fluttered in the wind from the
sea. If Turlough was on the move, that flag would have been
taken down and given to the bearer before the main party
assembled in the courtyard. There was, she comforted herself,
always a lot of fuss before Turlough managed to get underway.
His favourite dogs had to be assembled, the servants at
Ballinalacken had to be thanked and rewarded and various
items from the state rooms suddenly recollected as necessary
for his journey. Mara hoped for the best and went to join
Nuala who was standing at the cliff edge, smiling at the antics
of the small comic puffins that inhabited it.

'Strange how the birds of prey just took themselves off
once Setanta put up that bit of roof over the man.' Mara
scanned the skies, but there was no hovering menace. Eagles,
buzzards and falcons had all removed themselves to attack
their normal prey.

'He'd have been better doing that in the first place and
leaving the cadaver as he found it,' said Nuala testily. 'I've been
trying to think how I will be able to work out whether the
man was dead or alive when he was put into the lobster pot.

I was thinking that it's not positive that those scratches happened before death. The seawater has washed away all evidence of bleeding. He might have been dead and they occurred while the body was being stuffed into the basket.'

'Alive, almost certainly,' suggested Mara and Nuala turned surprised eyes towards her.

'Really! How do you make that out?'

'The rope tying wrists and ankle.'

'Perhaps done just after death to make a neat bundle.'

'But not the gag, surely. That would be pointless unless the man was alive and could shout for help.'

'You may be right,' said Nuala grudgingly. She turned back to the cliffs while Mara gazed out to sea and tried to imagine the last minutes or even hours in the life of the young man who had just been appointed as Brehon of a small kingdom. Somehow the crime did not make sense. What was the point of the lobster basket? What was the point of putting the man under the drenching spray? Why not cut his throat, throw the body over the cliffs and into the sea and hope that the turbulent waters would wash it far away and that Brehon O'Doran would just disappear.

Unless . . . she began to think and then Nuala interrupted her thoughts.

'Isn't that Boetius MacClancy? Coming across the cliff with Domhnall? I heard that he had turned up again. Is it really ten years since that affair?'

'It is,' said Mara grimly. 'And now he's turned up looking for a position and, if I know him, hoping to get not just Fergus's job but also his lands, his goods and his money. But I won't have that. Fergus is not fit to make a will, and I remember that he destroyed the previous will where Boetius was named as his heir. Poor Fergus came to see me, while my hands were still bandaged, do you remember how burned they were? He was so upset about it. He came across to Cahermacnaghten and he showed me the will, told me that Boetius would never have a penny of his and then he rolled it up and stuck it into the fire. I remember the smell of it burning.'

The vellum she remembered had smelled like burning flesh

and it had reminded her of that terrible day with Stephen
Gardiner and Boetius MacClancy. The thought of it still filled
her with horror, nevertheless, she stood very tall and waited
for Boetius to approach.

He didn't come towards her, though. Suddenly he pulled
up his horse. His head swivelled in the direction of Ballinalacken
Castle and she guessed that he could see what she was still
unable to see: Turlough and his men must be coming down
in answer to her summons.

'I must go, Nuala; Niall, you stay here,' she said. Explanations
might take too long. She crossed over to where the horses
stood tied to a lone hawthorn bush growing up through the
loosely piled stones of the wall. In a moment she was on its
back and urging him towards the steeply climbing hill.
Domhnall, she saw, altered his course to join her, but she did
not look back again. She didn't care where Boetius went so
long as she reached Turlough first. He had already refused, and
angrily refused, to give the position of Brehon to Boetius, but
anger with Turlough never lasted long and now he might just
think that since the man he appointed was dead, then the best
solution might, after all, be to appoint a man already on the
spot, and the nephew of the former Brehon to boot.

She met them at Knockfinn Crossroads. Boetius bowed
respectfully, almost touching his forehead to the upright of
ears of the showy grey horse that he rode. She gave him a
curt nod.

'You'll have heard of the death of the Brehon of the kingdom,
Boetius,' she said. 'I am taking over the legal affairs of north-
west Corcomroe for the moment and I will need to question
you, but first I wish to speak privately with the king. Would
you wait here and I will return shortly. Domhnall, perhaps you
would bear him company. I'm sure that Boetius can tell you
some interesting information about the court of Henry of
England, the eighth of that name. And, of course, about
Cardinal Wolsey and his secretary, Stephen Gardiner. You can
see, Boetius,' she continued, 'you can see how well I remember
them all and how clearly I remember the events of ten years
ago and of the chain of evidence that lead me to discover the
truth of what had been plotted.'

His cheeks turned a darker shade of purple. There was a hint of menace in his eyes.

'Ten years is a long time to hold a memory,' he said in a low voice.

'It doesn't seem long to me,' said Mara emphatically. 'Now, please excuse me. I will be back soon, Domhnall.' And with that she rode as fast as she could up the road. Boetius would, hopefully, be taken aback by her decisiveness. In any case, Turlough had already refused his uncle's position to Boetius, so, even with this sudden and unexpected death, he would have been prepared for a long argument as to whether he was the most fit for the position. Nevertheless, she turned from time to time to make sure that Boetius was not following her or trying to take a shortcut through the fields in order to reach Turlough first.

'Have you heard the news, my lord,' she called out as they came near and he nodded. He waved to the men surrounding to wait and then moved forward, accompanied only by Art.

'Hold my horse for me, like a good fellow,' he said to Art and then came forward on foot, taking Mara's bridle from her.

'God, would you believe it,' he said explosively. 'You were right. This fellow was nothing but trouble from start to finish. Not a nice way to kill a man, though. Young Art was telling me all about it as we rode down. Couldn't believe my ears. You'll sort it out for me, Mara, won't you? I have to get back to Thomond today, should have left over an hour ago, but I couldn't find my favourite dagger. You wouldn't believe it. I'd put it in that old jerkin that I keep at Ballinalacken and I just couldn't for the life of me think of where it had gone.'

'The thing is, Turlough, the crime has been committed in Corcomroe and I am Brehon of the Burren. I have no jurisdiction here.'

'Yes, of course, you have,' roared Turlough. 'Who is it that says you haven't? Tell me who said that and I'll have a quiet word in his ear.'

'No one has said it, but this needs to be officially done. Could your steward ride to the blacksmith and to the mill and perhaps first of all to the Fisher Street alehouse? Look, I've written out something.' She delved in the satchel hanging by the horse's side and pulled out the piece of parchment, handed it to Turlough to read and then pulled out a quill and an ink pot, passing these to Art. 'Unscrew the lid, Art, and hold it steady for the king,' she directed and then looked back at Turlough. To her annoyance, he was not reading her carefully phrased lines, but was gazing down the road.

'Was that Boetius?' he enquired, adding, 'Oh, well, I suppose that you can keep an eye on him. He's probably more scared of you than he is of me. Anyway, I'll leave you a few men.' And then, accepting the pen from Art, he scrawled his name at the bottom of the page and handed it over to his steward.

'You should read things before you sign.' Mara felt her face relax into a smile. Turlough had a knack of making everything seem very simple.

'You're better at all those legal terms than I am. Here, Murty, take this thing off down to the alehouse, read it to them and then get someone to tell you where to find the nearest black-smith and mill and after that then you can follow us. Pick out a few men and quarter them at the alehouse and then the Brehon can find them whenever she needs them.' He looked up at Mara and nodded his head. 'My uncle, the Gilladuff, God have mercy on his soul, taught me that trick,' he said, without lowering his voice. 'He reckoned that the men would always be looking for an alehouse if you quartered them anywhere else, but once they were there just beside the beer barrels, well, they just stayed put.'

'I'll remember that,' said Mara gravely and was glad to see the grin on Art's face. He had been looking rather miserable since term started. He was missing his foster brother, her son Cormac. They had been so close since the time that they were both tiny babies and now Art was left without a brother and a best friend.

'You go on now,' she said to her husband. 'I won't delay you any longer.' She leaned down in her saddle and kissed him. She had in the past felt slightly embarrassed about doing that in front of his men, but she knew that it hurt him if she allowed him to go with just a formal farewell. He was a man who never considered his dignity, but was, nevertheless, a natural ruler and one who had brought peace to the three kingdoms of Thomond, Corcomroe and Burren.

'I'll come and tell you how this works out,' she promised, 'and, of course, then you'll be coming across to us for the *Samhain* celebrations.' She added that knowing how much he minded parting from her and how he wished that she could just be a wife to him. She waited while the cohort turned around and waved her farewell and then turned her horse back towards the sea, beckoning to the steward and to the six men to follow.

'I think,' she said in loud clear tones to them as they approached the spot where Domhnall waited, 'I think that we'll ask Boetius MacClancy, the nephew of the former Brehon of Corcomroe to accompany us to the alehouse and then you can take him on to the blacksmith and to the mill. He will be a witness to the king's proclamation. I need to get back to the physician and give directions about the body.'

Fisher Street was a small settlement of fishermen's cottages and an alehouse. It was quite near to Crab Island and to the cliff where the body was found. It was only a few minutes' ride away and was the obvious place to make a proclamation. However, the alehouse itself was of interest to Mara. After the judgement day many people would have gone back there for an evening's drinking and discussion of the controversial verdicts. It may also, she thought, be the place where Boetius was lodging. When he arrived back from London, he would have found that Fergus's previous home was then in the hands of the newly appointed Brehon and Fergus himself was lodged in a small house by the cliffs and was in the care of a married couple. The most likely place for Boetius to go would have been the alehouse at Fisher Street.

In the meantime, she thought, as they rode down the hill towards the portly figure of Boetius, she was going to enjoy the look on his face when he saw her escort. She still felt a shiver of disgust and almost of fear when she saw him and she told herself that she must overcome this. The events of ten years ago must be buried and forgotten. For now he was just a man with a possible connection to the murder case she was about to investigate.

'Come with us, Boetius,' she said when they arrived at the place where he and Domhnall waited. With an effort she kept her voice cool and neutral. 'Let's ride quickly. The physician is waiting for me and I have much to do in order to solve this crime and to find the person who was responsible for this terrible death.'

The innkeeper was alone when they arrived at the alehouse. He listened, gravely nodding, to the words read out by the steward.

'Not a man who was greatly liked,' he said to Mara when the proclamation had been read and the steward was scrolling the vellum.

'You would have heard talk last night,' prompted Mara. The small room was filled with the scent of the ale. There had been great drinking on the previous evening, she reckoned.

He shrugged. 'Wild talk. I don't take too much notice. It's the froth on the beer, my poor wife, God have mercy on her, used to say that.'

'A wise woman,' murmured Mara.

'She was that. Let them talk, she used to say. Let them talk and drink and go out to . . . well, you know, she used to just say this to me, private-like, but she used say, They'll piss the bitterness away and then they'll all be best of friends. That's what she used to say.'

'But last night,' said Mara suppressing a smile as she noticed a shocked look on Art's face, 'but last night the one that they were so bitter against, well, he wasn't here, was he?'

'Just as well,' said the innkeeper. He cast a curious glance at Boetius. There was a measure of speculation in it, noted Mara, but thought she would question him in private later on. In the meantime, she needed to get back to Nuala and to allow the steward, his men and Boetius to move on to the blacksmith and to the mill.

'You had a full house, last night, then,' she said as she moved towards the door. He sprang to open it for her.

'Twenty, I counted at one stage.' He had a pleased look on his face. Judgement days were good for business. 'Including the gentleman who is staying here. At least I saw him a few times at the back of the room, but you know what it's like,' he added lowering his voice, 'I was that busy that I couldn't have eyes in the back of my head. Ah, but I miss my old lady,' he said raising his voice. 'It's she that could tell you everything that was going on.' And with that he bowed respectfully and she heard him asking Boetius what time he would be back for his dinner.

'Wish we had her here, his old lady. We could do with someone who was keeping an eye on who was inside and who went out,' muttered Mara as Domhnall held her horse and helped her to mount.

'Twenty or more people,' said Domhnall thoughtfully. 'And that place would be quite dim by late afternoon. There was quite a wind got up yesterday by midday. He's just got the one small window and that would be shuttered. And only three candles in the whole place. I had a good look around when he said that there were twenty people there. It would be hard to be sure how many people, wouldn't it? They'd be people coming and going. Having a drink and leaving or else staying longer and going outside, as he put it. Plenty of bushes behind the place. No one would know, would they, what was going on?'

'It must have been light, though, for the man to be tied up and gagged, wouldn't you think?' Art moved his pony up to ride on Mara's left side.

'It's a different matter, though isn't it, if you were on top of the cliff, just near the sea? You'd get the last few rays of sun from the north-west up there. Inside a small alehouse, with that low roof and a shuttered window crowded with people, it would be dark long before. And those candles would have flickered. And the door would have been opening and closing. Even if the landlord counted twenty people at one stage, there is nothing to say that it would have been the same twenty fifteen minutes later.'

Five

Cáin Qdomndáin
(The Law of Adomndán)

Duinetháide (secret killing) is a crime as serious as causing another's death by magic spells.

Nuala had not wasted her time while they were absent. Ulan, her apprentice, was writing industriously as Nuala moved around the body of the dead man, calling out her observations from time to time. She gave an irritated nod when Mara told her that officially she was now in charge of the case and that she appointed Nuala as physician with powers to examine the body. Nuala went ahead with her curt observations while Mara waited patiently.

'You can take him back now, Ulan,' she said eventually. 'Get him onto the marble slab ready for the autopsy if you arrive before me.'

'One thing for you to be going on with, Mara,' she said when Ulan had gone ahead, driving the cart. 'I am fairly sure that the man was alive when he was tied up and put into the lobster pot.'

'Yes, I thought so,' said Mara.

'I'm talking about scientific proof, not guesses.' Nuala swung herself onto her horse with an ease that Mara envied. What it would be to be twenty years younger, she thought as Nuala went on: 'I've examined the scratches and abrasions on the hands and they are very consistent with being done before death. And, although it's not conclusive, there is heavy bruising to the upper arms which possibly occurred when the man was held while his wrists were tied. Not utterly conclusive,' said Nuala in her lecturing voice, 'but in my experience, bruising that occurs after death, is usually at the lowest part of the body. In this case, there are bruises around the knees and the calves and these are probably post-mortem. The ones on the upper arms are probably pre-mortem.'

'Thank you,' said Mara humbly.

Nuala's grin flashed out. 'Don't try to soft-soap me, Mara. You always get your own way in the end and you always manage to get everyone to work for you. I hope you find the man who did this, though. It was a very ugly way to kill anyone.'

'What did you make of that? I mean the possibility that the man was alive when he was placed inside the lobster basket,' asked Domhnall as Nuala rode off.

'I'm not surprised. I always thought the gag was meaningless if the man was already dead. Now I think that we should go back to the innkeeper and question him again. I didn't want to say much in front of Boetius, but I would like to try him with a few names, including that of Boetius himself.' Mara stared around the hillside and then back up at the Brehon's house at Knockfinn. What had happened on the previous evening? According to Niall's story a group of men, seen only from the back, had been shooting on the Brehon's lands. Gaibrial O'Doran had jumped up and hurried out, to read the law to them, his apprentice had said.

'Where's Niall?' she asked. She had not noticed his absence before.

Domhnall looked all around. 'The pony is still here, tied up over there,' he said with a frown.

'Wretched child. As though I haven't enough to do.' Mara stared towards the cliffs with a worried frown. The waves still crashed against the rocks of the inlet and a long pillar of spume still rose into the air looking quite like one of those fountains in the books that her father had brought back from Italy.

And then she saw him. His head appeared first and then his shoulders rose above the jagged edge of the cliff.

'Niall,' she called authoritatively and he hurried across to her. He was looking better, she thought. There was a tinge of colour in his cheeks and his eyes were brighter.

'There's a pathway leading down there,' he said breathlessly, 'not to the beach, but it leads into a sort of cave. You can

see light coming through it. The walls are all full of little
pools and there are pieces of seaweed lying around on
the rocks. The sea must come quite far in at high tide. The
seaweed is fresh and it's wet, soaking wet. That means that
someone could have murdered him and escaped that way,
perhaps in a boat.'

'Perhaps,' said Mara. She did not think it likely, but it was
good to see Niall being active rather than standing around
with a sick look on his face. 'Now tell me about yesterday
evening, Niall, the time when your master saw the men
hunting birds and went out after them.'

'There were five of them,' repeated Niall.

'Did you see their faces?'

'They had hoods over them.' Niall had a puzzled look on
his face.

'Cloaks?'

'No, just jerkins, but hoods, I think, something covering
their heads, I think.'

Mara gave him a moment. The boy seemed to be thinking
hard. Eventually he spoke.

'Do you know, I think, they were like the mummers'
hoods. Do you have mummers, here? We had them in Ossory.
Ríanne and I went to see them once, at Bealtaine, before she
was married, I mean.'

'So you knew Ríanne before she was married.'

Mara made her voice sound casual, but the boy bit his lip.
'I should have said that the household went. She's the daughter
of O'Kennedy.'

And one of the MacEgans was Brehon to the Kennedy
family and there was a law school somewhere on their lands,
thought Mara. There was a good chance that Niall and Ríanne
had grown up together and knew each other very well. But
why try to keep it a secret? What had Niall to hide? Still,
the important thing at the moment was the question of those
men who went hunting across the Brehon's land, deliberately
in full sight of the Brehon's house, it seemed, just on
the evening after the unpopular and unjust sentences at the
morning's judgement day. Was it a way of drawing him out
of doors?

'Mummers' hoods,' she said aloud. 'Yes, I've seen them. Some young men in the Burren were wearing them at the *Samhain* celebrations just over a year ago.' She did not say that she had immediately ordered them to remove the disguise. These boys, she had thought at the time, would be drinking fairly heavily as was the custom and what with the drink and the excitement of the bonfire and the talk of the souls of the dead and wild stories about the emergence of the old gods from the caves, Mara had instantly decided that wearing those hoods over face and head would have emboldened the young men to break the law in various ways and had confiscated them, politely inviting the wearers to collect them from the law school on the following day. Fergus, she had heard afterwards, had allowed them to be worn in his kingdom and there had been lots of complaints afterwards. It was very likely that many of those mummers' hoods had remained in this locality, tucked into the bottom of chests, or stuffed to the back of the shelves. Those that Mara had collected, she suddenly remembered, were still at the back of her cupboard in the schoolhouse. Still, that would have nothing to do with the present case.

'But you thought, Niall, that one of them might be Peadar, the man who was accused of neglecting his father; that's correct, isn't it? You did think that you might have recognized him, didn't you?'

Niall looked uncomfortable and unsure, so she added, 'What made you think that one of them was Peadar? Were you at the door?'

'No, at the window,' he said. 'I might have been mistaken. You could ask Ríanne. She was there, too.'

'Let's go back and look at the lands from the window,' said Mara. 'Where were the hunters when you saw them?'

'Just about where we are standing now, I'd say.' Niall looked back up at the Brehon's house and then down towards the sea. He looked uncertainly from Mara's face to Domhnall's and then fell back to walk beside Art as they all climbed up the steep slope, leaving their horses tied to the lone tree.

The Brehon's house was perched on a height, overlooking the sea. A lovely place to live and to work in, Mara often thought, though her recent visits had been clouded with sadness as she realized how much Fergus's memory was deteriorating. He retained his power of judgement and his knowledge of the law but he was, he had to be made to understand, unfit for the task of ruling the portion of Corcomroe that had been assigned to him. Wrongdoers and their families soon got to know that Fergus forgot a judgement almost as soon as he had uttered it and this led to trouble between neighbours and clans. Eventually, Turlough, though full of compassion for the old man, had acted decisively, finding a new home for Fergus, a couple to look after him, and a man to replace him all in the space of a few days.

And now that man was dead.

Little had been changed within the house. Of course, Gaibrial O'Doran had only lived there for just a few days. Nevertheless, he had a wife with him and Mara would have expected that Ríanne would have brought some of her own wall hangings, some articles of furniture, some new candlesticks to replace the tarnished pewter of the ones left behind by Fergus. The same unsteady table made from oak occupied the centre of the paved floor, the wall facing the window was still covered with the almost completely faded stitched picture of a lady on a bench outside a window. It had been old over forty years ago when she was a girl, Mara reflected. Fergus had bought it from a Spanish ship in Galway. Distressingly, in his last years of occupation of this room he had insisted on telling her that story again and again, with the very same words, the very same gestures, even a laugh at the very same place in his tale and now she averted her eyes from the wall hanging.

'And this was the window, was it, Niall. The shutters were open.'

'That's right,' said Niall. 'My master was getting me to write down the judgements. We had just come to the last one, the case of "the cold son". I had just written the first line when my master looked up.'

'He was sitting here, looking this way, looking towards the window?'

Niall nodded again.

'What made him look up?' queried Domhnall. He seated himself at the place Niall had indicated and looked towards the window, narrowing his eyes and leaning forward. Mara could see the point of his question. The window frame was filled with very small panes of glass, enclosed within large thick strips of lead. The glass, itself, was of a poor quality, not coloured, but heavily blemished with bubble marks.

'I think it must have been the cackle of the geese,' said Niall after a minute. 'I wasn't paying too much attention. I was concentrating on my pen. Brehon O'Doran was a hard man to please. A blot would start him shouting and swearing.'

He did not, Mara noticed, utter the usual prayer for the dead man's soul when mentioning his name.

'So he looked towards the window, attracted by the sounds of the geese,' she said. 'What did he do next?'

'And then he jumped up, he swore, he shouted out, *As ucht Dé*! If anyone is hunting over my land I'll have him up before me on the next judgement day. And then he just ran out of the room and I heard him slam the door in the passageway.'

'And you?'

'I went to close the window. It was blowing smoke into the room.' Niall sounded defensive. 'I just took one look out to see what had put him into such a passion and I saw five men with bows and arrows and the geese were flying overhead. Then I went back to my work. He calls out the words so quickly that I can't keep up with him, so I was glad to have a few minutes to myself.'

'And where was Ríanne at this time?' asked Mara.

He shrugged, but there was an uneasy furtive look in his eye. 'Don't know,' he said.

'But you said that she was there,' blurted out Art. 'I distinctly remember you saying that Ríanne was there too. You said, You can ask Ríanne; she was there, too. You said that, didn't you?'

It was unusual for Art to intervene when the Brehon was questioning a suspect. Scholars were supposed to keep silent, to listen and to learn. There was an angry look on the boy's face. Perhaps he had sensed that Mara might accept Niall into the law school as a substitute for Cormac; maybe Art was, perhaps, sending a message that this boy would be no substitute for his best friend and his foster brother. Mara decided not to reprove him, even by a look. She kept her eyes fixed on Niall and slightly raised her eyebrows.

'I suppose she was looking out of the upstairs window, that's what I thought, anyway,' he said eventually. 'She came down complaining as usual. She was saying, What is he doing, Niall? I want my supper. I thought you'd be finished ages ago. Orlaith had it ready ages ago. She wants to go home.'

'And did Ríanne go out after her husband?'

Niall shrugged again. It seemed to be a habitual gesture with him. 'How do I know? I just went back to my notes. I could get on better without him shouting in my ear. I've a good memory, better than his, anyway.'

Mara studied him. 'You seem unhappy with your master, Niall. But your father thought this was a good prospect for you, didn't he? Were you at your father's law school before you came here with Brehon O'Doran?'

The boy's sullen expression deepened. 'No, my uncle's. My father wanted him to take in my younger brother at Michaelmas, but he said that he never had more than ten scholars and he never would. And the next thing was that I found myself shunted off into the wilds, just to make a place for that nuisance Tadgh that my father thinks is so clever.'

'And what will happen now?'

'I'm going back,' said Niall with an air of satisfaction. 'I'm going back to Ossory. The king, your husband said so. He sent me a message and to Ríanne. He said that he would send an escort in a week's time and then we could both go back. Young Tadgh can wait another year or go somewhere else. I'll be back with my friends.'

'And is Ríanne pleased?' Mara thought that she must see the girl herself but it was worth getting Niall's opinion now that he seemed to be in such a talkative mood.

'Should be. She's been crying her eyes out ever since she got married. She used not be like that. She was always coming down to the law school and all the boys thought that she was great fun. Sometimes she'd sit in on the lessons. She's not stupid. You'd be surprised how much of the law that she knows. She'd even play at hurling with the other lads.'

'So you grew up together. You would be friends,' said Mara. There was, she thought, no hint of a romantic interest, but friendships could be strong at that age.

'Well, sort of,' he said with a shrug. The look of uneasiness was back on his face.

'And was Ríanne present at the judgement day? You thought, did you not, that she might have recognized Peadar?'

'Yes, she was.'

But nowhere in sight. And how very strange would it be for a man with a newly-wedded wife not to bring her up to introduce her to the king and to Mara who was not only the wife of the king, but also his future colleague, the Brehon of the nearby kingdom, working and living only a few miles away.

'Did the king know that Brehon O'Doran was married?' she asked.

'I don't know,' said Niall unhelpfully. His lips were tight, and his eyes darted apprehensive glances at her.

'But you said that he sent a message.' It would be most unlike Turlough, the most gallant of men, not to immediately think of a distraught young bride. Mara would have expected that at the first news of the murder that he would come straight over, would immediately have thought of what to do about her. It seemed strange just to include her in a casual message to Niall. 'Did he mention her by name?' she finished.

'I told the man about her. I asked him if Ríanne would come, too. And he said that she could.'

'I see.' It was as she thought. Turlough knew nothing about the girl. His messenger probably thought that she was some hanger-on, a washerwoman, a cook or even a bedfellow of the Brehon's.

'And what's going to happen to your Brehon's wife until next week?' She asked the question, not because she thought that he would have any useful suggestion, but just to gauge his reaction.

'Well, I suppose we'll just both wait here.' Niall sounded

uninterested. Domhnall's eyes met Mara's with a glint of amusement in them.

Mara nodded gravely. 'We'll see,' she said. 'And how old is Ríanne, do you think?'

Niall thought for a moment. 'She'd be about my age, about fourteen, I'd say. Yes, she is. She was making a big fuss about getting married. She was going on about how she had been promised by her father that she wouldn't get married until she was sixteen. But I suppose it was a good match.'

I can't leave her there for a week. And that couple have enough to do to look after Fergus. I'll take the girl back to the law school and put her in Brigid's care, thought Mara and then a better idea came to her. Cahermacnaghten was a good ten-mile ride from Knockfinn. Why not move her scholars and herself into the kingdom of Corcomroe while she was dealing with this murder. Cael could look after Ríanne, share a room and Niall could share with Art and Cian. The Brehon's house was a bachelor establishment, but it had three bed-chambers as far as she could remember, as well as a room by the kitchen for the woman who had cooked and cleaned for him. They would all manage well there. She would make sure that her presence was widely advertised and people who had evidence, suspicions or even items of gossip could find her quickly and easily if she took up residence in the Brehon's house at Knockfinn. She looked across at her grandson. Domhnall was not a Brehon, but he was now a qualified lawyer, an *aigne*. And, more importantly, he was careful, discriminating and of sound judgement. She could trust him to deal with small matters, the daily queries about boundaries and the requests for deeds to be drawn up relating to the buying and selling of land. Domhnall could manage all of this easily. He had worked side by side with her for ten years and knew all of her methods. If he needed any help, then Fachtnan, her previous assistant, though occupied with the new school that had been set up, would certainly be available for advice. And what was even more important, the people of the Burren trusted Domhnall. He was seen as the natural inheritor of the law school, following in the footsteps of his grandmother and his great-grandfather. Only last week, she remembered, Fintan, the blacksmith, had sent a message to Cahermacnaghten asking whether *the young Brehon* could call in to give him some advice about taking on a new apprentice.

'Domhnall,' she said aloud. 'I'm going to trust the affairs of the Kingdom of the Burren to you. I think myself, Art, Cian and Cael will take up residence here in the Brehon's house at Knockfinn. I'm sending you back to Caherma-cnaghten. And would you get Brigid to pack up clothes for us all and to come herself and –' she glanced around at the dusty room and the dirty flagstones on the floor – 'tell her to bring a few girls with her to do the scrubbing and bring enough food to keep us going for a few days. We can find out where to purchase more supplies if I have to stay longer. Will you be happy about that, Domhnall? Do you think that you can manage?'

'I'll do my best,' was all that he said, but she could see how his eyes shone and how pleased he looked, with a small smile curving his lips. 'And you won't be too far away if I need help or advice,' he added.

'That's settled, then,' said Mara briskly. 'You set out straight away so that Brigid and the cart can travel in daylight. Art, you and I and Niall, of course, will go and collect Cael and Cian and Ríanne.'

'But what about the alehouse, the meeting that you were going to have there. Won't you need me to help to set it up?' Domhnall's expression showed that he was torn between excitement at the prospect of his new dignity and his conscience which told him that he might be needed in Corcomroe.

'I've been thinking about that,' said Mara, 'and I don't think that I'll rush into organizing it for today. Tomorrow is Sunday. I'll get the priest at Killilagh Church to make an announce-ment about the death of Gaibrial O'Doran and asking that all who know anything about the hunters on the cliffs, or who have any information for me, should attend the alehouse after Mass has finished.'

'That should be popular,' said Domhnall with a grin. 'And what about the physician?'

'You call over to Nuala and if there is anything important for me to know, then just send a letter with Brigid,' decreed

Mara. Nuala, she knew would have a lot of medical details about the dead body, but really, for the moment, all that concerned her was whether the man was alive or dead when he was tied up and placed in the broken lobster pot. And she was fairly sure that she knew the answer to that question.

Six

Cáin Lánamna
(The Law of Marriage)

A wife in a marriage of joint property is entitled to make contracts regarding household and farm, including the renting of land, purchase of provisions and buying of young animals.

Mara delayed for some time after Mass was finished. The priest was talking with Ciaran and Emer and she stayed in the background until they left, going down the road towards the alehouse. Then she stepped forward and greeted him. The priest, she was relieved to find, was eager to discuss the situation, to express his horror at the deed and to enquire about the funeral. Mara listened to him patiently, told him that the king would be sending the body back to Ossory and then enquired tentatively about the feelings of his parishioners about the new Brehon. The man had a keen, intelligent face and she thought his opinion would be worth hearing. She waited, however, until the rest of the congregation had straggled out through the gate and were walking in twos and threes and in small groups down the road towards the sea, or back up the cliff. There was, she noticed with satisfaction, a good crowd streaming across the grass towards the alehouse.

'I couldn't speak for others, and to be honest with you, I carefully avoided making any enquiries, but I thought last week that he was building up trouble for himself,' said the priest.

'In what way?' asked Mara.

'Encouraging complaints, opening up old wounds, rousing up feelings of greed and revenge,' said the priest succinctly and Mara nodded an agreement. She said nothing, however. The priest would be satisfied with her nod and nothing then could ever be quoted against her. From her earliest days as Brehon she resolved to guard her tongue always, to listen and to weigh her words. It had made for a lonely, though satisfying life, until she had married Turlough, but she had kept to that resolution made almost thirty years ago.

'Were you there at Judgement Day?' she asked. She knew he had been; she had seen him there, standing quietly in the background, but her query opened an opportunity to him. He could answer with a simple affirmative or he could volunteer some information. The choice would be his, but she knew, by his quick look around to make sure that no one was within listening range that he would share his opinions and knowledge with her.

'I must say that I was surprised, surprised and upset,' he said. 'The old Brehon, God bless him, he was a gentle soul. People respected him and his judgements were always carried out. No one ever complained of him in all of my time here – if a wrongdoer began to say something, he was quickly silenced by his clan. But this time, well, those judgements were very harsh, Brehon, very harsh indeed. Especially poor Peadar.' He paused for a moment and then said tentatively, 'I would not have thought that there was any harm in those boys.'

'You would know them,' said Mara.

'Yes, of course. Baptized them all, knew them seed, breed and generation,' he said briefly. 'Peadar is a good lad. As for Ciaran and Emer, well they'll settle down to married life when they grow up a bit, always did quarrel, that pair. And Seán is a good lad. Not like him to be careless, but sure, the wind here, on the cliffs, well . . . You never know the hour or the minute when that starts blowing. Well, I'm delaying you, Brehon, and I mustn't go on gossiping. God bless the king for lending you to us in our troubles.' And with that he went off hastily, leaving Mara to ponder his words. He had not mentioned Ronan's attack on the innkeeper, nor Donal's copying of his friend's song; perhaps regarding these offences as too trivial to bother about, she thought, as she followed the MacMahon twins and Art and Niall, down the hill to the alehouse. Ríanne had not come to Mass. The woman who looked after Fergus had met her just before she spoke to the priest and said that the girl complained of a headache and had taken the old man for a walk.

'She's a great girl with him. Not many of that age would have the patience to keep explaining and repeating things. The Brehon, God bless him, has got very fond of her.' The woman's words were in Mara's mind. She eyed Niall's back as he walked stiffly by himself. He had painted a very different picture of Ríanne as spoiled and demanding. Why, she wondered, had he done that and why had he left her alone in that house all night and never once mentioned her presence? Mara resolved that once her meeting at the alehouse was over that she would go on down to the little house on the cliff, pay a visit to Fergus, and have a chat with Ríanne. In any case, as wife to the dead man she should be kept informed about what was happening in the investigation into his death.

The alehouse was full. Everyone wanted to know the latest news about the strange death in their midst. Mara was feeling rather sorry that she did not have Domhnall when the door opened and Domhnall came in. He was carrying his satchel in one hand and in the other a large canvas bag of the type that Cumhal, the farm manager, used for carrying apples from the orchard. He stood at the door for a moment, assessing the size of the crowd, and then came straight across to Mara.

'Don't worry,' he said in a low voice, 'Fachtnan came up to the law school this morning. He had a message from Nuala for you and when he heard about you staying in Corcomroe, he said that he would look after everything for today as the school is shut. Nothing ever happens on a Sunday, anyway, that's what he said. Here's the message from Nuala and here in this bag is the broken lobster pot, the one that the body had been stuffed into.' He cast a quick look around the crowded room and slipped the bag unobtrusively under the table in front of Mara. 'It was quite an important message and I thought that you would want to know as soon as possible. Nuala thinks it is possible that the knife was wielded by a left-handed person. She said to tell you that she could not be sure, but that she thought it was a possibility.'

'I see,' said Mara slowly.

'Does it help?' he asked.

'It should do, I suppose, or at least it would do if she were sure about the matter,' said Mara. Niall, she had noticed

immediately, was left-handed. A handicap, she had always
thought it to be for any scholar.

She wondered whether this accounted for some of his surli-
ness. There was usually an effort to force such a child to write
with their right hand. In fact, she had, herself, tried that with
a scholar in her early days of teaching, but had given up when
she saw that she was making the child anxious and furtive and
from then on concentrated on helping left-handed children to
achieve a neat script, even seeking help from Fergus as she,
herself, was strongly right-handed.

However, many well-respected teachers persisted in enforcing
a scholar to use the right hand. She could understand their
frustration. There was, she knew, a prejudice against left-handed
people. One of the ancient Gaelic words for 'clumsy' was the
same as the word meaning a left-handed person. All through
the tales of antiquity, through the Bible verses, the importance
of the right hand was always underlined. "Him hath God
exalted with his right hand to be a Prince and a Saviour, for
to give repentance to Israel, and forgiveness of sins". When,
in 1494, Turlough's uncle had confirmed her appointment as
Brehon of the Burren, and Fergus, dear Fergus, had whispered
in her ear, 'Raise your right hand', she had thought of these
lines from the Bible. They had, she thought, great relevance
to the law to which she had sworn allegiance. 'Repentance
and forgiveness of sins'; these had been the functions of a
Brehon. The accumulated thousands and thousands of words
which her scholars memorized on a daily basis provided fixed
penalties for each case and had allowed the sinner to repent
and the injured to forgive.

If Niall had killed his master then she would have to handle
the matter with great sensitivity. Still, she thought, there may
well be other left-handed people among the suspects. She
turned back to Domhnall who waited patiently while she
digested the news that he had brought from Nuala.

'Shall we get them into groups?' he asked. He did not question her and she thought that was typical of him. 'I've brought
spare pens and pieces of vellum with me,' he said in a business-
like way. 'Would it be best to investigate the story about the
hunters first?'

Mara suppressed a smile. Her grandson had read her mind, or else just reasoned the matter out correctly.

'I'll just talk to everyone first,' she said and immediately he stepped forward and waited. With a few quiet words and a couple of glances at Cian, Art and Cael, Domhnall managed to get most of the crowd sitting on benches or stools in three neat lines while the alehouse keeper inserted a tap into a new barrel of beer. Niall stood with his back against the wall, his mouth set in a straight line and his blue eyes were hard and full of hostility. Mara looked at him. She would have expected him to offer to help, but he made no move towards Domhnall or any of the scholars. Still, she would have time enough to talk with him afterwards. Now was the moment to deal with this unexpectedly large crowd who had turned up to hear what she had to say and to share their knowledge of the events of the previous day, she hoped. She scanned Domhnall's note on Nuala's findings. Yes, as she had guessed, the man was alive when placed into the pot. Death, according to Nuala, Domhnall had written in his precise neat hand, probably occurred about two hours after supper. Mara beckoned to Niall.

'How long after supper was it when your master saw those hunters and went out after them?'

Niall thought for a moment. 'Not long,' he said. 'Straight after, really. He was pacing around waiting for Orlaith to take away the dishes and ordering Ríanne to help her.'

'I see,' said Mara. 'Thank you, Niall. Could you show me your knife, please.'

He put his hand into his pouch and then withdrew it and shook his head. 'I haven't got it. It's broken. I left it behind.'

By now Domhnall and the scholars had everyone sitting down and all heads were turned towards her. Mara abandoned the questioning of Niall. That could wait. As she moved forward the low-voiced conversations ceased and all heads turned towards her.

'A death in a community is always a very difficult thing to deal with,' she said, speaking clearly so that those in the back could hear, but keeping her voice low and unthreatening. There had been enough shouting at that judgement day. 'The king has authorized me, as you will all have heard, to take charge of this matter so I would urge everyone to confide in me and to keep nothing back. Let me be the judge of whether a matter is of importance or not. It is, I know that you recognize that it is of great importance that this crime is solved, that retribution is paid and that the community can trust each other again.' She paused for a long moment and then said gravely, 'One murder can result in another murder unless the matter is solved quickly. It is dangerous to keep information hidden. This opens the way to blackmail and to more deaths. Now,' she said changing the tone of her voice and speaking more briskly, 'I have two immediate concerns. One is to ascertain the identities of the five men who went hunting the wild geese in front of the Brehon O'Doran's house and the other is to know whether any of you recognise this.' And with that she bent down and plucked the enormous lobster pot from the canvas bag at her feet.

It worked very well. She had thought that it would. Immediately the tension vanished, the tight-lipped expressions on the faces of these people who were not, unlike the people of the Burren, used to a female Brehon, and not used to her methods and her authority. All tensions seemed to melt away. A buzz of talk arose. People turned to talk to neighbours, to call questions across to others in the row behind them, or leaned across neighbours to speak to someone further along the bench. After a while heads were nodded and the conversations ceased. All eyes were turned in one direction. Peadar rose to his feet.

'It appears, Brehon, that it belonged to my father. I'd be last person to know that; he wouldn't ever have wasted lobster on me,' he added bitterly.

'Who recognized it?' Mara turned her head towards the crowd. The lobster pot had been broken for a long time, she reckoned by the look of it, and there did not appear to be any recent attempt to mend it. All of the canes were silvered with age. This was an unexpected development. She had asked the question purely with a notion of breaking the ice rather than find any useful pointers to the murderer, but now Peadar's admission had changed matters. Several hands were raised and after a few minutes more went hesitantly up. Mara picked out a brown-faced, white-haired man. He would be the nearest fisherman in age to Peadar's father. She smiled reassuringly at him.

'I don't know much about catching fish,' she said, trying to sound modest and friendly. 'I would have thought that one lobster pot looked very much like the other. What makes you think that this one belonged to Peadar's father?'

'This man was a neighbour of Peadar's father, Brehon,' put in Art in a low voice and she nodded her thanks to him. She was glad that he spoke and that he addressed her as Brehon. There had been a tendency to call her 'Noble Lady' which she deprecated. She was here as an investigating judge, not as the wife of the king. As she had hoped, the man took up the name.

'That's right, Brehon,' he said. 'Many a time I've seen the old man with that. I used to say to him, "It's too big!" but he was a greedy man, God have mercy on him. He wanted to catch six lobsters at the time and sell them at the market, but I never knew him to get more than one and after a while he just left it lying around. He was getting too old to bother, too old to be wading through seawater.'

'And where would it have been left? Have you seen it recently?' asked Mara.

There was a moment's uncomfortable silence and then the man said, 'It would be in the old man's yard, I suppose.'

'I'm sure that I've seen him carry in some sods of turf for the fire in that very basket,' said his wife. 'He was coming out of his barn with a load and I called out to him not to slip because the yard was a mess after the cattle had walked through it. He'd keep it for turf now. It's just the right size.'

That was true, thought Mara. Turf as a fuel for the fire was very light, but quite bulky. An ordinary log basket would not be at all as useful as that tall lobster pot, made light by dozens of years' exposure to seawater and sunshine. What was interesting was the uneasy atmosphere. Something had occurred to the majority of her audience there. Heads were turned, glances exchanged, almost silent whispers were spoken into a neighbour's ear. Most of these people here before her had some knowledge of what had occurred on the night that followed the judgement day and the verdicts of the unjust judge, Brehon Gaibrial O'Doran.

'That's very helpful,' she said aloud. She would ask no further questions about the oversized lobster pot, but she would, perhaps, have a word in private with that helpful man later on. He had the look of one who knew more than he had told. She noticed him exchanging meaningful glances with his wife.

'And now to another matter,' she said aloud. 'There were five men who went out hunting on the lands and cliffs at Knockfinn in the evening. It is very possible that these men have no knowledge of what occurred later on at that place, but on the other hand they may have some information which might prove valuable to me in my investigations into the death of Brehon Gaibrial O'Doran. So if these five men would identify themselves, then this would be very helpful.'

It was a high-risk strategy and it did not pay off. Glances were exchanged but no one volunteered any information. And yet, perhaps it had been valuable. Mara was alive to the atmosphere and she sensed that it was hostile. Not perhaps to her personally; as the wife of their popular king she would have their respect, but these five savagely unfair judgements had made Gaibrial O'Doran deeply unpopular with the people of this small area in north-west Corcomroe. There was probably a lot of local sympathy with his murderer, or murderers, and no one appeared willing to help to convict.

'Of course,' said Mara artlessly and in her most chatty manner, 'it may be that this crime has nothing to do with anyone in the area. The man was less than a week here. He came from Ossory on the other side of the country and it may be that an enemy followed him.' Her mind was on Niall and on Ríanne, but she was glad to see that no eyes looked at the boy. She would not want him to be victimized. Everyone nodded wisely and the faces that she could see clearly in the front row seemed to look relieved.

'And now,' she continued, 'I don't want to delay you too long on this fine Sunday morning, but perhaps you would just give your names to my scholars and to my assistant and any information that you think might be useful. Just one last thing, I shall be staying in the Brehon's house at Knockfinn until this matter is cleared up so that if anyone wishes to see me, then they should just . . .'

And then she stopped. Peadar was on his feet, making urgent signals to others in various parts of the room. Reluctantly Donal, who was seated beside him, stood up also and then, after a few moments, Ciaran was pushed to his feet by Emer. Ronan and Seán whispering to each other, joined them. Peadar was the one that spoke, though, and the others just nodded in agreement.

'There's been a lot of talk about this murder and how it might be one or all of us five who might have done it. That's the story anyway; that's what some people have been whispering,' he said, his voice overloud for the small room. 'Well, I'd just like to say, Brehon, that all of us five spent Friday evening in this very alehouse and any man who says different is a liar.' There was a tremor in his voice, and he glared around the room in a nervous fashion.

'And I'm witness to that,' said Emer emphatically. Mara waited, but no other voice was raised. Glances were exchanged, but that was all.

'That's the truth, isn't it, Barra?' Peadar turned to the alehouse keeper.

'If you say so.' Barra's response was that of a man who liked to keep his customers happy. Peadar's shoulders slumped. He looked around the room appealingly, but no eye met his and no voice was raised in his support. After a minute he sat down again with a deflated expression.

'Good,' said Mara firmly. 'Now, if we can just divide you up so that we keep no one waiting for too long.' Her eyes met Domhnall's and she was not surprised when she found that the short line waiting for her attention included Barra as well as Peadar and Ciaran. Her grandson worked fast. Within minutes Art, Cian and Cael each had a table, a candle, a piece of vellum, a couple of pens and a carefully selected number of people to interview. Emer, separated from Ciaran, was tactfully placed at the head of the line to be dealt with by himself and Mara was amused to see a simper on the girl's face as the handsome young man said something to her.

Then she turned her attention to questioning the alehouse keeper.

'It must be difficult for you, Barra,' she said quietly, 'to know everything that is going on here on an evening when you have lots of clients.' She cast a look around the room. Though small, it was partitioned into various cubicles and the bar where the beer barrels were stored was quite high. Barra, despite his bulk, was not tall. It would be difficult for him to see people seated on low benches and stools.

'Well, that's the way of it, Brehon,' he said. His hoarse whisper sounded relieved. 'You can see for yourself, there's not much light here at the best of times. And then when someone opens the door to go around the back, well, the candles all flare and smoke.'

'I can imagine,' said Mara. Even at midday, a day when the autumn sunshine seeped in through the small window, the place was dark. At night with the shutters closing off that source of light and the tallow candles flickering and flaring, it would be impossible for the alehouse keeper to be sure of who was here or who was not.

'It was different when my wife, God be good to her, was alive. She'd keep an eye on everything, she'd notice everyone. But since she died on me, well, I'm hard put to keep serving drinks. I'd not be any good for giving evidence or saying who was here, or who was not.'

'No, no,' said Mara soothingly. 'What happens here of an evening, Barra? Do people usually sit down, or do they move about?'

'Move about, mainly,' said Barra. 'They'd all be having a word with each other, coming up and asking for a beer, and, of course, I'd be busy writing it on the slate. Not many people here would have silver or copper either to pay for a drink, so I'd put it on a slate and they'd pay me later. You know young Peadar's father, well he used to pay me with a lobster. They were his drinking money, you could say. Some give oats and that's always welcome and others might give a few eggs, that sort of thing.'

'And what about someone like Donal the songwriter?'

'Oh, he'd have to find the money, or else he might give

free entertainment for an evening. I wouldn't have any use for one of his songs myself, but there's some that think he's a good singer. He brings along his timpan and sings away. People drink all the more when they are singing these old songs,' he added with a cynical smile on his battered face.

'Well, that's very useful, thank you, Barra.' For form's sake Mara wrote a few words on the sheet in front of her and dismissed him with a smile before turning to Ciaran.

'You and Emer have made up your differences, is that right?' she asked.

'That's right.' He looked a bit uncomfortable. 'To tell you the truth, I don't think that she ever really wanted to bring me to the court. It was just that new Brehon persuaded her mother into it. He used to spend time in the alehouse picking up cases, in this very place, you know. People used to say that it was no place for a Brehon. You'd never see the old man, the old Brehon, God love him, in a place like this. But the new one was a very different man. Didn't care how low he went if he got a case for himself. That's what Peadar was saying.'

'Peadar is a bit of a leader of you all, is that right?'

'He's a boy with brains,' agreed Ciaran. 'People say that's why he didn't get on with the old man. Too much to say for himself, too many ideas.'

Mara studied the boyish face in front of her. 'Would it be rude of me to guess that you and Emer were talking to the priest about your wedding day?' she asked.

He beamed happily. 'That's right, Brehon. I'm going to be an old married man soon. No more trips out with the lads, I suppose.' He sighed theatrically.

'She'll probably be glad to get you out of the house for a while,' said Mara. 'And if you go off hunting and bring back a fat goose, why, then she'll give you a great welcome. Or do you fish?' she asked quickly. She had seen an unmistakable look of panic in his eyes when she had mentioned geese and his head had swivelled back towards where Peadar was standing.

'No, I'm not much good with the fishing,' he said in a more relaxed fashion. 'Peadar's the boy for the fishing.'

'Someone told me that he is a great shot, too,' said Mara,

wondering whether she was going too far. 'Or was it the knife throwing competition that he won at Coad last year?'

'No, it was the arrow shooting,' said Ciaran and then bit his lip.

'So when is the wedding going to be?' asked Mara hastily.

'In three weeks' time; the priest said that he would read the announcement next week.'

'And Emer is quite happy now to drop the case against you? The king asked me to enquire?'

'That's right, Brehon. It was all her mother, you know. Emer has always been scared stiff of the old . . . We planned all the time to get married before the winter set in, I just wanted to get the house ready, first. Wouldn't want to be living with her mother. It was just pure malice. Why make me pay a fine to Emer? Wouldn't make sense, would it? We'll be sharing every-thing from now on. In fact, don't tell the priest, but Emer has moved in with me. There's a lot of wool sitting there since the shearing in the summer and she's giving me a hand with it, carding it and spinning it, ready for the weaver.'

Ciaran looked very happy and very pleased with himself. Mara made a mental note to get Turlough to give the happy couple a small present, thanked him and moved on to the next person.

'You won't know me, Brehon, but I am Mór O'Connor and I live up there on the cliffs. You might have seen my place when you and your scholars were down there with the body of that man.' The elderly woman plumped down onto the stool opposite Mara.

'Yes, I think that I might have. Do you have some bushes growing behind it? With fishing nets over them? And a wall around your garden?'

'That's right, Brehon. You must come up and see my place some time. I have a great little herb garden there. And I have the bushes netted to stop the birds picking all the fruit. Elderberries are great to make a drink when you have coughs and rheums. I gave some to your husband the king once, God bless him. He said it was the best thing that he had ever tasted.'

'Did he?' Mara suppressed a smile when she remembered Turlough's appreciation of the French wine that Domhnall's father, Oisín, imported from France for her. He was not a man to disappoint any of his subjects, though. Even the poorest of them was spoken to as an equal and he managed to make all feel that he was one of them.

'Well, I must tell him that I met you,' Mara went on and then slipped in: 'So you saw us down there with the body, did you? You knew that there was something wrong, did you?'

'Bless you, I was there before you ever arrived. I went straight down there when I saw the young fellow, Niall, dash away as soon as he saw him. Not that I'm curious, you know, but I just came to see what was wrong. But the man was dead. No amount of medicines would bring him back to life. And he wasn't killed with an arrow either, his throat was cut.'

'You saw the hunters, then, did you? The evening before, just about supper time.'

The woman didn't hesitate. 'No, I didn't. I was busy at my hearth. I would have been making my potage for my evening meal. I didn't go to the window once.'

Might or might not be true, thought Mara, but she moved swiftly on.

'You wanted to see me, didn't you? I saw you ask my grandson to put you here?'

'That's right, Brehon, because I have something to tell you. I was out taking some medicine to a man in Fisher Street on Friday and when I came back there was something missing from my shelf. A pot was missing.'

Mara's interest sharpened. This was unexpected. 'A pot,' she echoed. 'What was in the pot?'

The woman hesitated for a moment. 'I just keep a little of it,' she said. 'It's valerian. It does no harm if just a little is taken. I'm very careful with it, but it was gone. And that gave me a shock. I don't know why anyone would come into my house and steal something like that and take it away. I went out to see if there was anyone around and I saw young Niall down the hill and then I saw him run back, get on his pony and gallop away. And I'll tell you, Brehon, when I went down to see what it was that he had been looking at, well, I got a fright when I saw that dead man and a whole pot of my valerian missing. It's a terrible thing to say, but I was relieved when I saw that the man's throat had been cut. Cruel thing to do to him, leaving him there under the water.'

'Valerian.' Mara repeated the word to impress it upon her memory. She would ask Nuala about that. If it were as dangerous as this old woman seemed to think, then it was worrying to imagine it loose in the community.

'Thank you, Mór,' she said. 'Thank you for telling me about the valerian. I'll come across to see you as soon as possible and you can show me your medicines.'

It was a strange and worrying occurrence, she thought, though she could not think what connection it could have with the murder of Brehon O'Doran.

She dealt with the next two people waiting to talk to her in a fairly mechanical manner. One was keen to impress on her that he could not have been one of the hunters as he couldn't shoot an arrow straight to save his life. 'Ask the priest, ask anyone in the world,' he said dramatically. The other was a friend of Ronan's who said that he saw Ronan just as it was getting dark and then did not see him again for a while. That was interesting, Mara thought, but she was eager to get on to the last person in her line who was Peadar.

By the time he had placed himself on the stool in front of her Peadar, though a strong-looking young man, was trembling noticeably. His knees knocked together as he sat down and he hastily pulled his *léine* and cloak over them to hide the involuntary movements.

'So you came here for a drink with your friends, then you left, and returned later, that seems to be what happened?' said Mara briskly. She felt a little sorry as she saw him stare, open-mouthed at her. He had fallen into her trap easily. Domhnall had so arranged the room that the interviewers were well away from those that waited. It would be very hard for Peadar to be sure that someone had not actually said that about him.

'Where were the bows and arrows left?' she kept her voice crisp.

Peadar's eyes slid to the door.

'Yes, I suppose with all of those thick bushes on both sides of the alehouse, it would be easy to find a hiding place. You left them in the bushes, is that right?' Keep the questions thudding out as quickly as possible, Mara told herself.

He didn't nod, but he didn't deny it. This time he looked across the room, seeking the eyes of his friend Donal the songwriter. Mara looked, too, as unobtrusively as she could, but even in the poor light of the alehouse, she could see how Donal stiffened and for a moment did not notice that Cael was inviting him to sit down. From the quick glance that her girl scholar shot across the room, Mara guessed that Cael had interpreted the exchange of glances correctly. She could rely on Cael, she thought. After Domhnall, the girl had shone last year as the cleverest of the scholars.

'You thought that you would teach Brehon O'Doran a lesson, that was the way of it, wasn't it,' stated Mara in a chatty fashion. 'You had those mummers' hoods left over since the *Samhain* celebrations last year, so when you came out from the alehouse, one by one, so as not to attract too much attention, you disguised yourselves with them. And then you went up to the hillside, just outside the Brehon's house and you shot off a few arrows at the geese, relying on the cackling to attract him out of doors. You knew by now, I'd say, that he would not show the same indulgence towards hunters on his land as the previous Brehon did, and you were not disappointed. He came out, shouted at you all.' Mara tried to visualize the scene. Yes, that was the way Gaibrial O'Doran would have handled the matter. 'He probably threatened to fine you at the next judgement day, demanded that you remove the hoods,' she continued, trying to convey with her voice and assured manner, that she knew exactly what had gone on at sunset on that Friday evening. 'And then,' she continued, 'the five of you manhandled him towards the cliff. Perhaps you merely wished to tie him up, put him in the lobster pot, give him a ducking under the waterspout, but when it came to it, I suppose fear of retaliation, sudden realization of what the man had done to all of your lives, well, the violence escalated, you slit his throat,' she finished and sat back and waited.

'We didn't slit his throat,' said Peadar hoarsely. 'I swear to you, Brehon, we didn't slit his throat. We put him under the waterspout, that's right. We did that, but no one killed him.'

'I'll need to talk to you five a little more about this,' said Mara. She looked around. Most of the people in the room had now given their evidence and were standing in groups, quite relaxed now and chattering animatedly. Cael had finished with Donal and was now interviewing Ronan who suddenly banged his fist on the table causing a sudden silence in the room.

'You're putting words in my mouth,' he roared and Cael made a careful note. Mara left Peadar. Turlough's men were outside the door and had instructions to allow none through until she gave the order.

'Would you like to tell me again,' said Cael politely. 'You went out for a breath of fresh air; that's right, isn't it? And you did hear geese overhead, that's right, too, isn't it? I have a note here that you said that. And you wanted to get a goose for your mother's pot. I think you said that, didn't you?'

'It was nothing to do with the new Brehon,' he muttered.

'Perhaps, you could tell us a little more about that, Ronan, when the room is a little quieter,' Mara intervened. Domhnall was having a quick word with Art and Cian and then he came across to her. 'Nothing much, except for these five,' he said in her ear and she nodded.

Aloud, she said, 'The king has issued a pardon for all sentences on Friday. Could the five men concerned: Donal, Ciaran, Ronan, Seán and Peadar please come outside with me and I will explain this further. As for the rest of you, thank you very much for your help in this matter and now I will not trouble you any further.'

Seven

Cáin Adomndáin
(The Law of Adomndán)

It is an offence to set a trap on common land unless the trapper issues a warning in the usual places such as an alehouse, a mill and at the church door. If failure to do so results in injury or death to any person or domestic animal, then the trapper is legally responsible to pay the correct restitution.

'Show me where the bows and arrows were hidden,' Mara said once they were outside. The five men looked at her and then at each other with a mixture of guilt and resentment on their faces. Mara gave them a moment to think, but stood quite near. She was not going to leave them alone to cook up some story between them. They were all, she was sure, very aware of the armed presence of the king's men and none ventured to move away. Seán looked towards Niall and he scowled. Niall flushed a dark red and appeared embarrassed and uncomfortable. Donal muttered something to Ciaran about peering out of the window and Ronan agreed enthusiastically.

'Come on,' said Mara after a minute, allowing a hint of exasperation to enter her voice. 'It's a simple question. Where were the bows and arrows hidden? Donal, you answer me.'

'Underneath the blackthorn,' said Donal after a minute.

'Good choice,' said Mara crisply. Inebriated men usually knew enough not to urinate up against the long sharp thorns of that bush. They looked at each other slightly embarrassed at her comment but said no more.

'And they were in the old lobster pot, is that right?' asked Domhnall.

Peadar gave a despairing shrug of his shoulders. 'That's right.'

'And you brought it from your father's farm.'

Another nod.

'Tell me about it.' Mara allowed a hint of a threat to enter her voice. She turned elaborately as though to check the king's men were still there and the captain of them moved his hand to his belt and touched the short sword that hung from it. The eyes of the young men followed hers and then they turned back.

'The basket was just to carry the bows and arrows,' said Peadar hurriedly. 'We didn't think about putting him into it. We just wanted to get him out following us and then we were going to grab him and shove him under the waterspout just to teach him a lesson.'

'And the rope?'

'That was there, already. That was lying coiled up in the bottom of the basket. That was my father's rope. He kept it there.'

'I suggest that your plan was to tie up the man and to leave him under the waterspout,' said Mara crisply. 'In that way, he would get much more of a punishment. Pushing him under the waterspout would be just a small child's trick.'

They said nothing, just looked at each other. Not very ready with their tongues, she thought and was glad of it. It would mean that she could get at the truth more quickly.

'Bring out a small table from the inn, will you, Domhnall?' she murmured in his ear and then, very quickly, in order to distract attention from him, she asked brusquely, 'Who was the man who suggested squeezing Brehon O'Doran into the lobster pot?'

'I did,' said Peadar. He lifted his head and looked straight at her. 'As you say, Brehon, pushing him under the water was not enough of a punishment. Even if we tied him up, he'd probably roll away as soon as we turned our backs on him, and we couldn't afford to have any witnesses to the deed. We kept our hoods on, but if a few lads from the alehouse came up they could snatch these off if he commanded them to do it. So we gagged him and we tied him up and then, well, you know, Brehon, this man had ruined our lives. Mine most of all, of course. Until the king, God bless him, pardoned me, I was an outlaw, a man who had no right to set foot in his country for ten years, a man who could be killed without penalty by anyone in the kingdom. And there was Ciaran. His life was spoilt. The Brehon had set his woman against him. And Seán's family would have been ruined with that fine for something that was not his fault, just an accident with the wind turning direction so quickly and the same went for Ronan and as for Donal, he just didn't know what to do. He has no family here in the kingdom. He would have had to leave a place where he was happy, sell his timpan to pay the fine and go back across the sea to his homeland.'

'And so you made another plan.'

'That's right, Brehon. We thought that he could wriggle away if we just tied him up, so we managed to stuff him into the basket and we decided that we would go back to the alehouse and that when the alehouse shut for the night and when everyone had gone home, then we would come back and set him free.'

'Just like that.' Mara allowed a questioning note to come into her voice and she saw them look at each other.

'Well, no,' said Peadar after a moment. 'We thought that we would take his gag off and get him to promise to have another judgement day and to say that he had made mistakes with his punishments. We thought we could get him to promise that, if we threatened to put him back under the water for another few hours.'

Mara considered this. It was possible that had been the plan. Though they would all have had to be naïve if they thought that Gaibrial O'Doran would have kept that promise extracted from him in those circumstances. It was, she thought, more likely that one, or all of them, had been responsible for his death.

'And did you?'

'We came back,' said Peadar evenly. 'We came back and we meant to set him free, but it was no good.'

Mara waited.

'It was no good,' echoed Donal. His brown face turned sallow under the sunshine and his voice was husky and broken. 'We brought a pitch torch with us, Brehon. We didn't light it until we were a good step away from the alehouse. There was a bit of a moon that night and you know, by the sea, it's never completely dark. The sea shines the moonlight back onto the land. Well, we walked up. We could hear the water splashing, and the waves, we could hear them, too. It was high tide about that time, on Friday night, and the waves were smashing against the cliffs. And when we came up to the top of the cliff, well, there was just a sheet of foam there in front of us. And we had to light the torch to see where he was.'

'And I said, "Christ, I hope we haven't left him too long",' said Ciaran. 'You know what it's like, Brehon. When you're drinking the time goes quickly. But when we came up there, I could see that the moon was much higher in the sky than I had expected.'

'We all rushed into the spray, all except Peadar. He was holding the torch. And we picked the Brehon up, carried him out. He was a dead weight; we expected that because we had put a stone, a big boulder, in the bottom of the pot to keep it upright.' Donal stopped for a moment and then said, 'I had a feeling, though, that something was wrong. Something about the weight, something about the way he was so still.'

'But anyway, we got the basket out; we managed with the four of us, two of us on either side,' put in Ronan. He was anxious to get the story finished.

'And then I shone the torch on his face,' said Peadar sombrely.

'And Ciaran said, "He's fainted" and Peadar shone the light a bit closer and then he said, "Sweet Jesus. The man is dead." And he was shining the light of the torch on the neck. We could see that his throat had been slit, from ear to ear.' Donal looked at her pleadingly.

'Did you think of reporting this death?' put in Mara.

'There was no one to report to, was there. No Brehon, nobody. Donal thought that we should get the priest, but Peadar said that his soul would have well and truly gone. The man was stone cold – I know that the water would have cooled him, but even so he was stiffening. He had been dead for hours. And I was saying that we would be blamed for it. I knew what it was like to be blamed for something that was just an accident,' said Seán bitterly.

'So we lifted him up again and carried him to the same place where we had put him a couple of hours ago,' said Peadar.

'How did you know it was the same place?'

'We could see the hollow in the grass, Brehon, just near to the blowhole, just where the water would go over him.' Ciaran looked a little uncomfortable. 'He must have struggled a bit, rocked it from side to side; that was all that he could do with the weight of the stone that we had put into it.'

'Wish we had never thought of it,' said Donal.

'We must have been mad,' said Seán.

'We were mad,' said Peadar in an undertone. And then when Mara looked at him, he said earnestly, 'Our lives had been ruined by that man, Brehon. I was thinking of throwing myself over the cliffs. I had no life left. It was only the thought of that cousin of mine, that Clooney, that stopped me doing it. I made up my mind that in the twenty-four hours left to me I would get even with a few people. I was the one that planned putting the new Brehon under the waterspout and then I planned that I would destroy as much of my father's farm as I could before I left. I planned it all out. The lads were going to help me. We were going to turn the cattle into other people's lands, and the hens too. And then I was going to set fire to the hay ricks and to the turf stacks against the house and let the house burn down with them.'

'But if Brehon O'Doran had given in to your demands, then you would not have needed to do all this. You would have inherited your father's farm and have defeated your cousin's malice. You would not have needed to do anything else.' Mara considered the strong resolute face in front of her. 'But did you really think that he would have been able to go back on his judgements, judgements given in front of the king?'

His glance wavered and he looked at the others. They said nothing. Mara looked at the small table that Domhnall had carried out from the inn.

'Place your knives on this table,' she said abruptly. She watched carefully as the knives were pulled from the sheaths that hung from their belts and were placed on the table. Domhnall, Cael, Art and Cian stood on the opposite side of the table and Niall moved hesitantly forward and then stepped back as Cian glared at him. The October sun was bright at this hour of midday and the knives sparkled in its light. Mara watched carefully. Both Peadar and Donal were left-handed, but the other three were right-handed. It was surprising to find two out of the five to be left-handed, but she remembered that Fergus had once told her that a high proportion of the people of this area were left-handed and he guessed that they were all descended from one ancestor.

Domhnall and the scholars handled the knives with care, passing them from one to the other, turning them over and holding them close to their eyes. After a few minutes, first one, then a second and a third was replaced on the table and the fifth knife was passed from hand to hand. Cael took it over to Mara, holding it carefully at the very base of the handle. Their eyes were doubtless better than her own, but Mara could see quite clearly what had caught their attention.

The fifth knife had a line of dark, reddish brown caught in the join between blade and hilt. The knife itself was suspiciously clean, the blade shining and the wood of the handle was pale in colour, considerably paler than the other four knives. It had, she reckoned, been recently rubbed down with wet sand.

'Whose knife is this?' Mara looked keenly along the line of faces that had turned towards her. They all looked guilty, confused and worried. But what did that prove? There was a moment's silence. They all knew, of course. A man's knife was a most important possession, something which never left him, day or night. These five were close friends, they would know each other's knife almost as well as they knew their own.

'It's mine,' said Ciaran after a moment.

'You're sure? Look closely,' said Mara, but she only spoke to give herself time. This had been a surprise. If blood had been found on any knife, then she would have expected that it would have been on Peadar's, the leader of the group and the man with most to lose because of the unjust judge.

'It's mine, all right.' Ciaran stretched out his hand, but Mara did not relinquish it. This might be important evidence in a murder trial, but even while she thought that, she wondered. Was Ciaran capable of murder? Ciaran, she thought, might have had less motive than the other three, and certainly far less than Peadar. All this business with Emer was just malicious nonsense on the part of her mother. However, she gathered that he and Emer had been quite drunk that night when they went into the bushes outside the alehouse, and a man who drinks heavily can often commit a crime which he would not have done in his sober moments.

'Have you lent this knife to anyone recently?' Mara still held it, gripping it by the well-cleaned handle.

'No,' said Ciaran.

'But you have cleaned it recently, sanded it, that's right, isn't it?' Mara held the knife up to the sunlight, but she kept her eyes fixed on Ciaran and saw his lips tighten. He had now seen the telltale evidence of blood.

'That's right,' he said after a minute. 'Caught a few bass off the rocks the other night, so I cleaned them and took them back up to my mother to cook for our supper.'

'I see,' said Mara. It was, she thought, a reasonable explanation. Art was looking at her closely and she nodded permission to him to ask a question.

'Where did you clean them, Ciaran?' Art's voice was perfectly natural, a question from a boy to a young man only a few years older.

'Just down by the rocks,' said Ciaran warily.

'In one of those big rock pools, I suppose.' Art seemed to be thinking about that.

'That's right.' Ciaran seemed to decide that Art as a fisherman's son was interested in his method so he went into a long description of the bait that he had used, and of the length of the line. He had caught, it appeared, ten fish and they all had a great supper from them.

'And you cleaned your knife afterwards.' Gently Art brought him back to the subject of the knife.

'That's right,' said Ciaran cheerfully. 'Strung the ten of them on a piece of twine from my pocket, small ones, you know, about the size of my foot, but these are the tastiest. And then I cleaned my knife and my hands and went back up.'

'And the handle of the knife?' Art leaned over slightly to examine the knife in Mara's hands.

'That's right,' repeated Ciaran. He was slightly less sure of himself this time. 'Must have missed that bit there, between the handle and the blade.'

'Well, that seems to be an explanation for the blood on your knife, Ciaran,' said Mara. Art, she was pleased to see, immediately ceased to question Ciaran. It was time, she thought, to wind up this meeting. There was, however, one more question to be asked.

'The law,' she said formally, 'distinguishes between a murder committed on the spur of the moment, in the heat of anger, but then repented and confessed to. It is slightly after the twenty-four hours since the body was found, but I am sure that I can persuade the king to extend the period of mercy and allow for just half of the fine to be paid. So now, I ask each one of you whether you had any hand in the unlawful killing of Brehon Gaibrial O'Doran.'

Her eyes went along the row of young men in front of her. Even if one owned to the murder now, the penalty would still be three milch cows, or three ounces of silver added to the honour price of the newly appointed Brehon which would, she thought, amount to seven *séts*, three-and-a-half ounces of silver, or four milch cows. Only Peadar would be able to find that fee to pay to the family of the dead man, and it would leave him with nothing to graze the fields of the small farm that he had inherited from his father. Even as that thought crossed her mind, Peadar himself spoke up.

'Like we told you, Brehon,' he said. 'We found the man dead. It was none of our doing.'

'How do you know?' asked Mara. 'Surely it was possible for one to slip away while the others drank. The cliffs are only minutes away from the alehouse.'

'We stayed with each other,' said Peadar doggedly. He cast a quick glance at Ciaran standing with his knife in his hand and then turned his eyes back to Mara. 'The man was dead when we found him,' he repeated. 'None of us is a killer.'

'Well, you know where to find me if any of you recollects anything that will be of use in finding out the truth about the death of Brehon O'Doran. In the meantime, Ciaran, I would like to keep this knife. You will get it back when I have finished with it. You others can take your knives now. Thank you all

for your help. You may go now,' said Mara and nodded to
Domhnall who returned the knives, one by one to Peadar,
Ronan, Seán and Donal. They stood awkwardly for a few
minutes and then with muttered words of farewell, they went
soberly down the road.

'Interesting that they went off like this; that they didn't go
back into the alehouse like the rest of the parish,' said Cian
looking after the five figures.

'Makes one think that they have something to talk about,'
observed his sister and earned a nod of approval from Domhnall.

'What did you make of Ciaran's explanation, Art?' asked Mara.

'I don't think that anyone cleaning fish, just beside a rock
pool, would get blood on the hilt of his knife, not to the
extent of having to sand it off afterwards,' said Art, examining
the knife again. 'He'd just slit the fish, flick out the innards
into the sea and then do the next one. Even if a drop of blood
got onto the handle, he'd just dip it into the salt water. He
wouldn't need to sand it down. That would only happen if
there was a lot of blood and if it had soaked into the wood
before being cleaned off.'

'They're coming back,' said Cael in a low voice.

They had been talking hard, in very low voices, with several
glances over their shoulders towards the Brehon. Now Peadar
had turned on his heel and was marching back up the hill
followed by Ciaran. The other three lagged a little behind.

'Ciaran wants to tell you something, Brehon,' said Peadar
when he reached the small garden. He nudged Ciaran. 'Go on,'
he said. 'Nothing will happen. The Brehon will understand.'

'That's not my knife, Brehon,' blurted out Ciaran. 'I took it
from the sands down by the harbour. It was just lying there.
It's a good knife, much better than my own, so I just took it.'

'I see,' said Mara. She took the knife and held it up. 'Did
you make any enquiries about whether someone had lost this
knife?'

'No.' Ciaran looked uncomfortable.

'And where is your own knife?'

'I threw it away, threw it into the sea. It was useless. I had
broken the blade of it. I broke it last week. It wasn't worth
keeping.'

Mara studied him. He had a hangdog and rather hopeless look on his face.

'I know you don't believe me,' he said after a moment.

'Should I?'

That simple question seemed to embarrass him hugely. He turned helplessly to Peadar.

'He found it this morning, Brehon,' said Peadar in a low voice. He, too, sounded hesitant. 'We were coming to Mass and Ciaran just spotted it. It was lying there on the sand, just where the tide had left it. We reckoned that it had been lost from a boat and that it came ashore with the tide.'

'And it was just the two of you?'

'That's right. I stayed last night with Ciaran. I had twenty-four hours before I had to leave the kingdom.'

A strange explanation, thought Mara. Still, perhaps it was true. It was natural that these five young men who had been involved in the death of Brehon O'Doran would cling together, whether guilty of the ultimate death, or not.

'I see,' she said eventually. 'Thank you, Ciaran. I will return the knife to you when I have finished with it.' She waited until they had gone back down the road before laying the knife on the small table in front of her scholars.

'It's a good knife, not fancy, not much used, I'd say,' said Cian bending over it. 'May I pick it up, Brehon?'

'Alder wood, what do you think, Art?' he said after a minute.

'Definitely. It's very white. Looks a good knife, not much used, I'd say, not like a fisherman's knife, but then Ciaran works mainly herding his father's cattle. I'd say it could be his knife. He could have whittled the wood some time while he was up in the mountains, picked a branch of alder and shaped it. They get very bored these herdsmen. Perhaps he did it last winter.' Art sounded dubious, running a finger over the handle.

'New, or not very much used,' said Domhnall, taking it from him.

'Could it have been in the sea, washed up on the beach? It doesn't seem to be waterlogged.' Cael reached out and touched the knife. 'Yes, the wood is quite light,' she said.

'Well, that's the thing about wood from alders; it doesn't absorb much water,' said Art. 'That's why people use it for buckets and for boards to chop fish on. My father swears that you can't beat a pair of oars made from alder wood. They'll last you a lifetime. That's what he always says.'

'It still could have been a group decision to cut the man's throat,' said Domhnall. 'But they would have had to choose one man and one knife. Not necessarily a knife belonging to the man who slit the throat. None of the other knives were as good as this one. The blade on Peadar's was chipped and the handle was very worn. Donal's was fancy but didn't look strong and Seán's knife and Ronan's knife were both in a bad way with very thin-looking blades.'

'So Peadar to do the deed and Ciaran's knife to do it with.' Cael made a grimace. 'It feels wrong, somehow. And yet, perhaps, they saw it as justice, passed sentence on him, not too far from the place where he passed judgement on them.'

'What we haven't considered is that four out of the five could be speaking the truth,' said Mara. 'I know they said that they were together all of the time, but is that likely? Surely one might go outside to the bushes, or go up to get another drink, without any of the others even noticing. Barra was explaining to me that the majority of his customers get drinks put on the slate so that they can pay later with goods, so getting a drink would not be a quick process. And certainly a man could run to the clifftop in the time that his friends might reasonably expect him to be missing in order to relieve his bladder.'

'If we put the matter of the knife aside . . .' said Cael tentatively.

'I agree with you,' said Domhnall. 'Let's put that aside. A knife can be lent, can be picked up from a table in the semi-darkness. They would have been eating bread and cheese, slicing an onion, I know what these alehouses are like; they would have all had their knives in their hands or else lying on the table. It would have been possible to pick up the wrong one. So if we do forget about the knife, then I would say that the most likely person to kill would have been Peadar.'

'He had the most to lose,' said Art thoughtfully.

'And we must remember that on Friday night he was still under a sentence of banishment. Once the twenty-four hours were up, then he had to be gone out of the kingdom or else

he could be killed as a fugitive. I think that you are right,
Domhnall,' said Cian. 'What do you think, Brehon?'

Mara took her eyes from the knife. It puzzled her. The
plainness and simplicity of the handle and yet its quality, and
its lack of wear all added to the conundrum. Who did it really
belong to? She picked it up and looked at the blade. Well-
honed, but again without any visible signs of wear. A knife
that might have sliced an onion, or cut a chunk of cheese, the
lack of wear pointed to that sort of use, not a knife for a
farmer or a fisherman where it would be in constant use for
all sorts of purposes. Aloud she said, 'Cian, go and collect
Niall from the alehouse. It's time that we made our way back
up the hill to the Brehon's house. Brigid and the cart will be
arriving soon.'

Eight

The Wisdom Triads of the Judge Fithail

There are three things that ruin wisdom:
1. Ignorance.
2. Inaccurate knowledge.
3. Forgetfulness.

An odd boy, this Niall MacEgan from Ossory, Mara thought as they all went back up the hill towards the Brehon's house. Her scholars did not like him much, she could see that. Art, Cian and Cael cast sideways glances at him, answered a question from him with perfect politeness, but volunteered nothing. What was it about him that they didn't like, she wondered. He was the same age and had the same background. She would have expected that they would have been eagerly comparing notes about his experience at a MacEgan law school, questioning him about the place of Brehon law in that alien territory of Ossory, but they did not. Cael had made one remark about the weather, and then said no more. Even Domhnall, the poised and courteous Domhnall, eyed the boy speculatively as he climbed onto the borrowed pony and said nothing. She was not tempted to enquire, though. Over thirty years of dealing with scholars had taught her that boys liked to sort these relationships out for themselves. If anyone was to speak, it would be Cael, and, though they quarrelled and argued, Cael was intensely loyal to her brother. Mara turned her thoughts back to the murdered man.

This knife, she thought, as they rode up the hill, this knife, not a working man's knife, not a rich man's knife, the knife was a puzzle. She wished that she could make time to ride over to Rathborney and to show it to Nuala while the corpse was still viewable. Nuala had a room, more of a cave, really, chipped out of the rock over which the stream flowed.

She had it built at the same time as her hospital. A corpse could be stowed there in the icy chill for a week at least at this time of year. Nevertheless, there was bound to be a subtle deterioration in the condition of the flesh as the days passed. Mara compressed her lips. It was not a new feeling: the wish to be in two places at once; but now it was very strong. She had promised that she would be here at the Brehon's house and the people of Corcomroe had to feel that she was there to listen to them and to act as though this was her kingdom. They could not be left without a Brehon and Sunday afternoon was a traditional time for making calls. No, she would have to stay. She half-turned and beckoned to Cian, waiting until he was beside her before she spoke to him quietly enough not to be overheard by Niall.

'Cian, I want you to ride back to Cahermacnaghten with Domhnall and then to go on to Rathborney. Show Nuala this knife and ask her to consider whether it could have inflicted the wound on Brehon O'Doran's neck.'

No need, she thought, to send a request to Nuala to examine it carefully. Nuala did everything carefully. She would have slightly preferred to ask Cael who was the more intelligent of the two, but Cael would be best for befriending Niall and finding out a little more about him. In any case, Cian, though lacking the superior judgement and brain power of Domhnall and Cael, nevertheless, possessed an excellent memory and could repeat a conversation, almost word for word, hours and even days after it occurred.

Brigid and the cart had already arrived when they reached the Brehon's house at Knockfinn. Mara smiled as she heard her high-pitched voice directing someone to fill up the pot because gallons of hot water was needed and someone else to find the bars of soap and the bag of sand. In a couple of hours, the grimy, dusty house would be shining with cleanliness and smelling of lavender-scented wax polish. In the meantime, she thought, she would keep out of the way after a quick greeting. Brigid, she thought with compunction, was getting too old for this sort of work. She must be almost seventy. She had been a young girl in the household when Mara's mother died and it was Brigid who had brought up the baby, cared for the little girl, looked after Mara's own daughter while the adolescent Mara coped with a bad marriage, with the death of her father, with her studies and her struggles to become Brehon in his place, to take on the school and the affairs of the kingdom. She had worked hard, but she would not have managed without Brigid at her side.

'Dear Brigid,' she said going into the kitchen, 'now don't you go tiring yourself. The girls will do everything. And I see you have brought Seánín and Aodhan with you, too. That's good,' she added as a couple of boys came staggering in with buckets of water.

'Now you just go for a walk, Brehon,' said Brigid decisively. 'This place is not fit for you. I don't know what's being going on here at all. The poor man, God help him. How could anyone let this place get into a mess like that? You can hardly see out of those windows. Covered in dust and salt and God knows what. You might as well not have glass. Shutters would be as good.'

'We'll help,' said Cael. 'Come on, Art. Get rid of your cloak. Roll up your sleeves. Give us a couple of aprons, Brigid. Me to sand down that table. I love doing that. It will be fifty shades lighter by the time that I am finished with it, Brigid. Give me that scrubbing brush, Art. Slosh a bit of water onto it, Seánín.'

'Let's go for a walk, Niall.' Mara seized the opportunity. He was looking dismayed at the prospect of being pushed into this scrubbing and brushing that was going on around him. There was no sign of Orlaith so either she had not turned up or else Brigid had rapidly got rid of one whose standards of housekeeping and cleanliness had fallen so far beneath her own.

'Ríanne should have seen to all that,' muttered Niall as they walked across the grass. It was still thick and green and their feet made track marks on its mist-covered surface. 'That was her place.' He sounded defensive and annoyed.

'Or you, perhaps, or Brehon O'Doran. I suppose you were both older than Ríanne,' said Mara. He seemed taken aback at that so before he recovered she said rapidly, 'You don't like her much, do you?'

He turned to face her, almost defiantly. 'No, I don't,' he said. 'She's stupid.'

'But you grew up together. You must have been friends at some stage. And,' added Mara with a smile, 'you told me she was quite clever.'

'When we were young.'

Mara did not smile. There was something false about his manner. She caught his sidelong glance at her. He was trying to gauge the effect of his words. She kept her face blank. He was older than Cael and Cian, too old for a silly statement like that. And he would not be stupid. The MacEgan law schools had a reputation for very high standards and, judging by what she had heard, they were quick to weed out any unsuitable boys at an early age.

'I don't have too much to do with her these days,' he added after a few moments. He was one who liked to fill a silence, she noticed. A sign of guilt, sometimes, but, on the other hand, the boy was young and it had been a difficult few days for him. She would reserve judgement until she probed a little deeper.

'You must have got a terrible shock when you discovered the body,' she said sympathetically. 'It was quick-witted of you to see that the man was dead. It must have been difficult with that seawater pouring down like that.'

'Oh, it was dead tide, then,' he said. 'There was no water coming from the blowhole. It only comes out when the tide is in.'

'Goodness,' said Mara, exasperated with herself. 'I hadn't realized that. No one has mentioned that before. So it only spouts out at high tide.'

'About an hour each way,' he said relaxing a little at the prospect of enlightening her. 'The tide turns every six hours, in and out, so you get a high tide every twelve hours,' he explained.

'So on Friday night, on the night when Brehon O'Doran was murdered, what time was high tide, on that night?'

'Eight o'clock,' he said promptly. 'Just about the time that bells rang for compline.'

'How are you so sure?' she asked. She had thought of suppressing the question but then decided to ask it. It would be interesting to see how he accounted for his knowledge.

He looked a little taken aback. 'We, I . . . well, there wasn't anything to do so I used to walk up to the cliffs and have a look at the blowhole. I'd never seen anything like it. I've seen the sea at New Ross and at Waterford, but it's different here. Much wilder, the waves are much higher and more violent and there aren't those big holes in the cliffs, back in Ossory. Not so windy, either.'

He was talking for the sake of talking, Mara decided. Again the comments were naïve, were those of a younger child. Was the flow of remarks an attempt to cover up the word 'we' that he had used?

'When you say "we", do you mean yourself and Ríanne?' she asked.

He thought about that for a moment and then said hesitantly, 'I meant myself and my master, Brehon O'Doran.'

Unlikely, thought Mara. Somehow she could not imagine Gaibrial O'Doran wasting time looking at the tide. From what she had heard, he had spent that week talking to people, accumulating cases for his first judgement day.

'Let's walk down to Bones' Bay,' she said. 'I want to see how Fergus is getting on. The king said that he was very upset after the judgement day. People will carry stories to him as though he were still the Brehon and could do something about it. It upset him badly, apparently.'

'He's doddering, isn't he? Does he ever make sense these days?'

'Sometimes,' she answered the question but felt that he might have been better not asking it. 'In fact,' she went on, 'there are times when he can be very sensible. He forgets so much, but some things stick in his mind. I've been surprised from time to time about how sharp he can be.' She looked sideways at Niall. 'I'm sure that I have no need to tell you to treat him with the utmost respect.'

'I think that I'd throw myself over the cliff if I were he,' he muttered and she pretended not to hear him. Honesty compelled her to admit that she shared his feeling. However, Turlough, a sensitive man despite his loud voice and blunt manners, thought that Fergus was, in the main, happy. He has changed into a different way of life, was how Turlough put it.

He had become fascinated and thrilled by wild flowers, by the herbs that grew on the wayside, by the tiny birds that sang in the hedgerows and the jolly little puffins that nested in Crab Island just across from the house where Turlough had placed Fergus, just above the small bay. The woman who looked after him encouraged him to go out for daily walks, to gather leaves from the bushes, herbs from the cliffs, berries to make into preserves, nuts from the hazel grove in a hollow near to Fisher Street and seaweed to boil for winter coughs and colds.

'Be polite and courteous to him when you talk with him,' she said sharply. 'Remember that he was a highly esteemed Brehon for many long years, not just before you were born, but before I was born. He deserves our respect now, as well as our protection.'

No need to lecture Ríanne, she thought with satisfaction when they went into the small cottage overlooking the bay. The girl was sitting, literally at Fergus' feet, her large dark eyes fixed on him, her hands folded on her knees as he chanted.

> Refection according to rank,
> Contention in the host,
> Cudgels in the alehouse,
> Contracts made in drunkenness,

And then, Fergus, not even noticing the arrival of Mara followed by Niall, leaned over and said confidentially in Ríanne's ear, 'Of course, you must remember that this doesn't count when they are making a contract to help each other with the mowing. Everyone is always drunk then!'

Ríanne giggled appreciatively at this and Fergus sat back in his chair with a pleased smile on his face.

'This is the best scholar I've ever had,' he said to Mara. He showed no surprise at her presence and seemed to think that she had been there for some time.

'Passed every examination with top marks,' he continued beaming proudly at Ríanne. 'Tell . . .' He hesitated for a moment, staring intently at Mara, and a distressed look passed over his face. He had obviously forgotten her name. He whispered in Ríanne's ear.

'Mara is her name,' said Ríanne with a beaming smile and then a slightly apologetic look. 'I call her Brehon, of course.'

'So, you're learning the law, Ríanne,' said Mara, seating herself. There was no sign of the couple who looked after Fergus, so she supposed that he had been left in the care of Ríanne for the moment. She had thought to ask the girl to accompany them back to the Brehon's house, but it appeared that would not be possible, just now. Fergus might not be safe to be left alone with a fire burning in the hearth, although, from what Turlough had told her, the old man was still able to go on unaccompanied walks. Perhaps, she could put a few questions here, but she would have to see how talking about the murder would go. Ríanne might be upset and that would upset Fergus, also. For the moment, however, she would just chat to the girl.

'Yes, Brehon MacClancy is teaching me a lot,' said Ríanne and Mara warmed towards the girl. 'We've been going through all of the wisdom texts and I am remembering more and more of them, aren't I, Brehon?' she leaned across and touched his hand. Dear old Fergus was beaming with delight. 'Though I did know some law already, didn't I?' she added. Niall gave an amused snort of laughter and Ríanne's face changed. 'Though Niall will probably tell you that I am stupid and know nothing.' She looked with dislike at the boy and he scowled back at her.

'No, you don't know much law. You're just making it up,' he said angrily.

'The penalty for a secret and unlawful killing is twelve *séts*, or six ounces of silver, or six milch cows, in addition to the honour price of the victim,' she said. She uttered the maxim, not in the sing-song manner of a scholar, but slowly and deliberately, looking not at Fergus, but straight at Niall's eyes.

He flushed angrily. 'And how about the penalty for telling lies about someone,' he said.

'What's he saying to you? What's he doing? He's upsetting you, isn't he? Where did that boy come from? Get out of my house,' roared Fergus and Niall started with alarm. Mara placed a soothing hand on the old man's sleeve.

'No, Fergus, don't distress yourself. These two are friends. They were brought up together. You know the way that scholars just make jokes and tease each other. Don't let it bother you. Niall, why don't you go for a walk on the beach for a little while?'

'Go on,' said Ríanne impatiently. 'Can't you see that you are upsetting him? It's just like you to stay where you are not wanted.'

'You're one to talk,' scoffed Niall, but Fergus rose up from his chair and Niall moved quickly to the door.

But before he reached it, the door swung open and in came – not Gobnait nor her husband, as Mara was hoping – but Boetius MacClancy.

'What are you doing here?' snapped Mara. She was alarmed to find him confident enough to stride into the old man's house without even the courtesy of a knock. Fergus was in no condition to defend himself from his grasping and devious nephew.

'I've come to see my dear uncle,' said Boetius smoothly. 'You do remember that he is my uncle, don't you, Brehon?'

'I remember everything about you, Boetius,' said Mara eyeing him steadily. 'I remember your conduct, I remember how you allied yourself with the enemies of Ireland and of your king. And I remember that I banished you from the kingdom.'

'Ten years ago,' said Boetius. 'And, may I remind you, ten years have now passed. So here I am again, coming for what is owed to me. I am the only living relative of Fergus. I should have been summoned before now to take command of his affairs.' He cast a look, half-pitying, half-contemptuous in Fergus's direction. Niall had, by now, sidled out of the doorway, going, no doubt, in search of Gobnait and her husband. Fergus gazed back placidly at his nephew. The presence of Boetius had not disturbed him in the way that the presence of Niall had interrupted his peaceful time with Ríanne.

'You see,' said Boetius, assuming a false air of puzzlement, 'you see, I must acknowledge myself to be bemused. You, Mara, are the wife of the king. But you are also Brehon of the Burren, one of the three kingdoms of King Turlough Donn. Now, no doubt because the people of the Burren had known your father and were prepared to accept his heir, even though that was a mere daughter . . .' Boetius eyed Mara, but she gazed back at him steadfastly. Nothing that man can say will move me, she promised herself, thinking back to that terrible time when Boetius had had her at his mercy.

'As I say,' resumed Boetius, 'it does seem very strange to any student of ancient laws that you can be both the wife of the king and his servant the Brehon. After all, it was always said that if the Brehon gave a false judgement, then the people could appeal to the king.' Boetius paused dramatically and then said in a loud clear voice, 'Appeal to the king against his own wife! Expect the king to give judgement against one that shares his bed and his board? Surely that is inconceivable!' He gazed at her with triumph and Fergus looked from one to the other with a bewildered expression.

'But, when it comes to taking command of the land of Corcomroe, of the ancient territory where the MacClancys fulfilled the laws of their king, right back into the ages, well, now, I, Boetius MacClancy, nephew of the last Brehon, descended from the same great-grandfather, now I say, this Brehon of this land here is a MacClancy and I, the heir to the MacClancy clan, say that you, Mara O'Davoren, are a usurper in this land. What do you say, Fergus?' he said turning to his uncle. 'I am right, am I not? The MacClancy clan have been and are the lawful Brehons in this land of north-west Corcomroe.'

'You're right, indeed,' said the quavering voice of Fergus. He was looking at Boetius with a slavish smile of admiration.

'And I am your heir, am I not?' questioned Boetius.

'You are my heir, Boetius,' confirmed Fergus.

'You see, Brehon,' said Boetius, 'there is no coercion, no force, no bribes. Fergus, my uncle, a man without wife or without sons, he confirms that I, Boetius, son of his late brother, am now the lawful heir to his goods, his lands, and his position as Brehon of north-west Corcomroe.'

'That's right,' said Fergus, nodding his head. 'It goes down from father to son,' he explained to Ríanne, 'and since I have no son, so it goes sideways to my nephew Boetius.' Once again he beamed happily at Boetius. 'I'd trust him with my life,' he said.

'There you are, my lady judge,' said Boetius grinning maliciously at her. His small green eyes twinkled and his red beard, cut into the spade-like shape popular among the English, jutted forward aggressively. 'There is no reason why you cannot tell the people of the kingdom that I am now their Brehon, is there, Fergus?'

Fergus looked a little puzzled but nodded obediently.

Ríanne looked from one to the other, her eyes sharp with interest.

Niall said, 'But . . .' And then stopped.

'Don't worry about anything, Fergus,' said Mara trying to keep the note of anger from her voice. 'You know that the king will settle everything. You do not need to concern yourself.'

'I assure you that the king is perfectly happy that I take over the legal affairs of this place.' Boetius continued to smile.

'I don't believe that the king has said a word on the subject,' said Mara stonily, though the recollection of the way in which Turlough had filled the vacancy for Brehon by appointing Gaibrial O'Doran made her slightly uneasy. But then she remembered.

'The king told me himself that he had rejected your application,' she said.

'The king!' Boetius raised the almost invisible pale ginger lines of his eyebrows. 'The king!' and then with a false laugh, he said, 'Oh, you are talking about your husband, your bedfellow, Turlough Donn. "Captains" they are called now. We don't call them "kings". No, I was speaking of His Grace, the King of England, Henry the Eighth.'

'King of England,' said Mara vigorously, 'but no king of here. Whatever he might pretend to lay claim to in the way of lands in the east of Ireland, we here in the west have our own kings, our own kingdoms and our own laws. Now that the Brehon of north-west Corcomroe, Gaibrial O'Doran, has been secretly and unlawfully killed, then it is up to King Turlough Donn O'Brien to appoint his successor. That's right, Fergus, is it not?'

She expected him to agree with her immediately, but he turned large wistful eyes towards his nephew.

'Blood is thicker than water,' said Boetius. 'That's right, Fergus, isn't it?'

'That's right,' echoed Fergus obediently.

He had been working on the old man, thought Mara with a flicker of annoyance. Why had Gobnait allowed this to go on? Perhaps she hadn't really listened. Or perhaps she didn't think that it was her place to check a fine gentleman like Boetius. She would probably have only taken notice if Fergus had become upset.

'And you'll start up that . . . what do you call it . . .? You know what I mean . . . you know that . . . you'll start it up again . . .' Fergus' voice quavered as he sought for an elusive word.

'The school, that's right. You want the law school set up again, don't you? Never you worry, Fergus, I'll see to that, too.' He nodded towards Niall. 'This young man can be the first pupil.'

Niall said nothing. Somewhat surprisingly he made no mention of King Turlough's offer to send him back to Ossory. He looked across at Ríanne and for a moment Mara thought she saw the beginnings of a grin twitch at the girl's lips. A moment later, her face grew solemn and sweet again and she leaned over and picked up the rug that had slipped from Fergus' knees and replaced it tidily. The sunlight from the window lit her face and Mara could see that there was a purple and yellow bruise on the girl's face, just under her left eye, an old bruise, fading back into the tanned skin around it, but the mark was still there. It must have been a heavy blow, Mara thought. Not Niall, she reckoned. The girl's attitude to him was quarrelsome, but there was no fear in it.

No, it was probably the husband.

Gaibrial O'Doran, when alive, had possessed a cold eye and an autocratic manner. Ríanne might have challenged his authority and he would not brook that. Mara wished that she could have had him up before her in her court. A heavy fine and a lecture from her, as well as an explanation of the rights of a wife to look for divorce, might have dissuaded him from this form of bullying. She looked a little more sympathetically at Niall. A man who treated his young wife, little more than a child, like that, would have no compunction about beating a scholar. Niall had a wary look.

But the man was now dead and her task was to solve this murder. She had to admit to herself that she would prefer the perpetrator to be Boetius. He was the man who had most to gain if greed were to be a motive. He had been rejected once by Turlough, but Mara knew her husband well enough to know that he would have cloaked his refusal in several kind words about Boetius who might then have been hopeful that if the first choice of the king were to be found dead, then a man like himself, well-qualified, the nephew to the former and most popular Brehon, might well be the king's second choice.

Possible, but would Boetius have risked it? Would he not, rather, have returned to London where he was probably still in the favour of Stephen Gardiner, secretary to Cardinal Wolsey of England? It was possible, but she doubted that he would have risked Turlough's anger for a second time by becoming involved in a murder.

But now she found her mind dwelling on Niall. He was young, but boys of that age had intense feelings, were prone to fits of intense hatred and of falling into intense fits of despair.

But would that be enough to form a motive for murder?

She thought it was possible.

The boy could have gone up to the cliff, seen his master sitting in discomfort, wet, cold, bound and gagged, and it might have crossed his mind to get rid of this man and then he would be able to return to Ossory. It would be a clever murder and Niall, she was sure, was a clever boy. She recalled his tentative guesses about the hunters who had lured Gaibrial Doran out of doors and enticed him to cross over the land towards the cliffs. He had pretended not to know them originally and had then hesitantly put forward the possibility that it might have been Peadar. Yes, looking back at it, she admitted that it had been cleverly done and her suspicions had been diverted from him to the five men who had appeared in court on the day when Gaibrial O'Doran had been killed.

'No,' said Fergus suddenly. He had been sitting very still with a brooding expression on his face when suddenly it sharpened and the eyes focussed. 'No,' he said again, almost shouted it this time. 'No, not that boy, that's a wicked boy. He's a violent boy. I don't want him in my school.' Leaning over he took Ríanne's hand and patted it in the way that a man would pat a frightened dog. 'You stay with me,' he said. 'I'll look after you. There's murder in the air. It's not safe. Gobnait thought it was thunder, but I know better. I learned the law long, long ago. It's murder. There's been one murder and there will be another. Get out of my house, you boy! Get out of my house immediately.'

'Go, Niall,' said Mara. 'Wait for us outside.'

'I'll give him a drink of his mixture. Gobnait showed me what was brewed for him. It's valerian and it calms him,' said Ríanne. She was on her feet, cup in hand and had poured something from one of the flasks on the shelf. She offered it to him with a smile and no trace of fear, but Mara wondered whether Fergus was safe. There appeared to be no reason why he should have taken such a dislike to Niall and now he was not sipping from the cup, but glowering at Boetius. Mara was glad when the door opened and Gobnait came in. A tall, strong-looking woman, thought Mara with relief. She should be able to cope with Fergus if he started to do something dangerous. She had a kindly air about her and Fergus' face lit up at the sight of her. He smiled at Ríanne.

'The visitors will all be gone in a minute,' he said reassuringly. 'We'll be comfortable together again then.' He drained the cup and lay back in his chair, his eyelids drooping.

'I gave him some of the valerian,' said Ríanne to Gobnait.

'He'll sleep now,' said Gobnait. She looked anxiously at Mara. 'I was just gone for a few minutes, Brehon. My husband's niece had a baby and we went down to see the new child. We shouldn't have left the Brehon, perhaps, but he goes on very well with the little lady here.'

'No harm done,' said Mara rising to her feet. So that accounts for the theft of the valerian, she thought. She wondered whether to say something but decided that the matter wasn't worth her interference. Valerian grew wild amongst sheltered heaps of stone and a new batch could be made with no expense. As for its administration to Fergus, it was probably useful. Fergus in his younger days had himself well under control, but occasionally his temper would flash out when goaded by a badly-behaved scholar. Gobnait had a difficult task and Mara found it hard to blame her for ensuring a few hours of quiet for herself from time to time.

'We'll all leave you now,' she said aloud. 'I'll speak to the king about getting someone else in the house so that you and your husband can go out together from time to time. I'm afraid that I must take Ríanne, now, but she will come and visit again. Come, Ríanne, come, Boetius. We will leave him to sleep in peace.'

And she stood by the door and waited until Boetius had gone ahead of her before she went through it.

'I don't want you to visit Fergus again except in my presence,' she said to him bluntly.

He raised one of his narrow eyebrows, his head tilted to one side, the left eye slightly closed and the right squinting at her.

'He is my uncle, Brehon,' he said.

'I am placing Fergus under the protection of the court,' she snapped. 'I'm sure that even your long years in the courts of London have not completely wiped your native law from your mind, but just in case it has, then I'll spell it out for you: "the rights of the insane precede all other rights. A contract with a person of unsound mind is invalid." Let me not hear of you trying to inveigle him into bestowing any of his lands, his possessions or his property to you. Now, I suggest you untie your horse and follow me up to the Brehon's house. There are some questions that I need to ask you.'

Nine

Colc Conara Fuqill
(The Five Paths of Justice)

A judge must be prepared to give a pledge worth five ounces of silver in support of his judgement. His judgement is not valid unless he swears on the gospel that he will utter only the truth. If he refuses to do so, he is no longer regarded as judge with the tuath *and the particular case is referred to the king.*

If a judge leaves a case undecided, he must pay a fine of eight ounces of silver.

'Did it ever occur to you, my dear Mara,' said Boetius as they moved slowly up the steep hill, riding side by side. 'You don't mind me calling you Mara here with just the two of us, do you?' He said the words with a false air of concern, peeping at her from under his pale ginger-coloured eyelashes.

'I prefer "Brehon", that is my title and that is what I am addressed as by all except my family and friends,' she added. He made her skin crawl with dislike and disgust, but she was pleased to hear that her voice sounded clear and confident.

'Very well, my dear Brehon,' he said cheerfully. 'I was about to remark, in fact to interrogate you, if I may be so bold, to question you in fact on your knowledge of the law.'

He was spinning this out on purpose so she ignored him. Her eyes were on the cliffs. She had seen from the doorway of Fergus's house a long expanse of golden sand on Bones' Bay and beyond it the sea just rippled at its fringes. And now there was no sign of the waterspout above the sea from the place of broken rock and caves known to the people of Doolin as 'Hell'. It doesn't spout up at low tide, she thought. I must get Niall to work out a timetable of the tides. That will keep him busy. She half turned in her saddle to look back at the boy and was pleased to notice that Ríanne seemed to be talking to him, at least her head was bent down and his turned up towards her.

'I was thinking about *Colc Conara Fugill*, those five paths to justice.' The unctuous voice of Boetius interrupted her thoughts. 'I'm sure,' he continued, 'that you know every one of them very well, have trodden every inch of them during all those years when you have been the king's judge in the kingdom of the Burren. And I was thinking about that line which says that if the judgement of a Brehon is questioned by the people of the kingdom, then that particular case is referred to the king.'

'Yes,' she said shortly. 'That is true. And the king can change the judgement when it appears that the sentence is unjust. As happened last Friday,' she added wondering what he was getting at.

'But what I was going to remark, my dear M . . . my dear Brehon, was that you being the wife of the king, this seems to invalidate this law, to make it, at any event, extremely unlikely that it would be evoked by the king's subjects. It is well known, of course, that the king thinks very highly of his clever wife. And that, I suppose, is the reason why he has permitted you, though you have no *locus standi* to act as investigating magistrate in a murder that is outside your own jurisdiction.'

'No one has expressed dissatisfaction,' she said shortly, and then despised herself for answering him. He had, however, she thought, brought up a valid point. It had not occurred to her before now. By the time that she had married the king she had felt very secure in the estimation and confidence of the people of the Burren.

'No one ever questioned my judgements during the sixteen years in office before I became the king's wife,' she added.

'I can see that it is a new idea to you and that you are taken aback by my words,' he said with a pleased smile. 'I apologize if I have caused you any distress. I just felt that it was an interesting point. Of course, after thirty years in your position I suppose you feel that you are the law, that you can pass judgement, even without the formality of a law court, as you did just now when you classified my uncle as a *druth* and said that he would be placed under the protection of the court.'

'I classified him as a *mer*. I used the word *mer*. Fergus is not,
and never has been a *druth*. He was a man of keen intelligence
for all of his life until the last year or so. He is now suffering
from senility due to his age. The brain, like the limbs, slows
down and wears out, in some more quickly than in others.
You should reread your copy of *Berrad Airechta*.'

'Oh, but I have, my dear Brehon. And I know the law. If
Fergus is classified as legally incapable due to his mental condition, then his lands should be divided up amongst his heirs.
Now that Corcomroe north-west has had a temporary Brehon
appointed to it by the king, as he calls himself, though in
England, they prefer to call them captains, chieftains, if you
like.' He eyed her keenly but she said nothing and he continued,
'Then surely this case should be heard as soon as possible. I,
as the only living heir to Fergus, demand that it should be.
As I said to your husband, Turlough Donn O'Brien, "My
lord," I said, "I come but for my own". I would be pleased if
you would arrange to hear the case as soon as is convenient
to you. I'm afraid that I shall want to move from that primitive
alehouse into my uncle's house, which, I understand, you are
now occupying.'

He was right, of course, that was the galling and infuriating
part of it. Turlough, in his impulsive way, had made a quick
assessment of Fergus' needs, had settled him in that comfortable
little house, and had appointed Gobnait, a woman wise in
nursing and in the use of herbs, to look after him with her
husband to help him in his task.

But, of course, it should all have been done through the
courts, at Thomond, for preference. Still, she was not going
to make any concessions to Boetius.

'You realize that with inheritance comes responsibility,' she
said coldly. 'The court, when the case is heard, will expect
the inheritor of Fergus' lands and property to take full care of
him. If you fail in that, then you must pay a fine of five *séts*
and forfeit part of the land. The court, I feel, will want the
present arrangement for the happiness and security of your
uncle to remain in place while it is appropriate for him. Rest
assured that all such legal matters will be arranged. Now let
me turn to a matter of more immediate concern. Could you

tell me when you came back to the Burren?' He would have
come up the Shannon to the kingdom of Thomond, in the
first place, she reckoned. But Turlough had mentioned his
application to take over the place of Fergus. Was that what
had prompted Turlough to take such hasty action? 'Don't think
to lie to me,' she added. 'Whether you came by land or by
sea, I can find people who will let me know. You would not
go unnoticed here.' She glanced down the hill towards the
alehouse. Barra would be quick to find out all possible details
about his visitor. He had the name of being a gossip.

'There is no secret about my movements,' he said loftily.
'But shall we postpone our conversation until we are indoors.
May I help you to dismount?'

To her relief, Art emerged from the doorway and held her
bridle after she had guided the horse to the mounting block.
She took her scholar's proffered hand with gratitude. She could
not bear the thought of Boetius touching her with his slimy
damp hands, which she remembered so well. She was beginning
to be seriously worried about him. He was, she supposed, an
adversary worthy of her steel, but she could not forget the last
time that they had encountered each other, a time when she
had been lucky to escape with her life. Nevertheless, he was
now within his rights and she would have to deal with him.

'Thank you, Art,' she said. 'And here's Ríanne come to join
us. Will you take her in to Cael and Brigid? Come into the
parlour with me, Boetius.'

She decided against asking Art to bring in some refreshments.
This was to be no social visit. This was to be an interrogation.
She led the way without a backward glance to see whether he
followed. She could feel that familiar rush of strength and of
confidence and she held her head high as she opened the door.

The parlour, she noticed, had been transformed. The floor
shone with cleanliness and smelled of that mixture of lye and
rosemary that Brigid concocted every summer. The table, after
Cael's ministrations, was many shades lighter in colour and still
slightly damp. The window was open to the sea breezes and
its diamond-shaped panes of glass glinted in the autumn
sunshine. As Mara went to pull the frames closed, she could
still smell the verjuice mixture that Brigid always used on glass.

'Sit down, Boetius,' she said, indicating the stool by the table while she herself took the padded chair by the fireside where dear old Fergus used to sit. Its cushioned back and seat gave out a whiff of wormwood when she sat on it, but at least it wasn't damp.

'You arrived in Doolin Harbour by boat once you had left Bunratty Castle,' she asserted. Turlough had not been sure, but he had thought that Boetius had gone off with some fishing men.

He eyed her warily, but said nothing and his silence emboldened her.

'Was it Peadar who took you?' she asked and before he could prevaricate, she said quickly, 'It's pointless to lie. I can find out these matters so quickly and if I find that you have lied, why then, I will wonder why you needed to do so.'

He smiled at her. It was a forced smile and she did not respond.

'You have spies in every nook and cranny, do you?' he suggested.

'Answer yes or no,' she said sternly. Peadar, she knew, was not an ocean fisher. According to Setanta, Art's father, he had never been able to afford an ocean-going boat, and as he didn't belong to a fishing family, he had not been offered a place on one of the big boats that set out from the harbour. When he was rejected by his father, he had built himself a small, light, skin-covered canoe and used it to fish trout and salmon from the rivers of Corcomroe. When Boetius failed to persuade Turlough to appoint him as Brehon, then he would have taken an available boat back to Corcomroe.

He shrugged. 'As you please. The answer is "yes". No crime in that, is there? I made no secret of the matter. You saw me at Knockfin. You heard me trying to teach that man from Ossory a little of the law. I was surprised that you did not intervene, my lady judge, but since you did not, I felt that I should say something.' He had dropped into English and she replied to him in the same language.

'And you would have been friendly towards Peadar, you would have commiserated with him when he received that harsh sentence?'

'Of course.'

'You were at the alehouse, that night, were you not? In the company of the five young men who were feeling aggrieved and angry after those severe sentences.'

She could see him reading her mind. His small green eyes were weighing up his position.

'There is no law against a friendly drink, a few words of commiseration.'

'But there is a law against incitement to a crime. You know the text that is interpolated in *Di Chetharslict Athgabaála* and what it says about "a culpable onlooker at an offence". Would you like me to give you the whole text?'

He made no reply but a frown creased his forehead and his pudgy lips were folded together. Secretly, she was surprised how much knowledge he had retained after ten years' of banishment. Turlough's contacts in London had related that Boetius was studying law at one of the Temple Inns and was acting as a secretary to Stephen Gardiner and advising Cardinal Wolsey on Irish affairs.

'Well, then you will just have to take my word for it.' She kept her voice crisp and assured and her eyes steadily on him. The stool where he sat was a little lower than the easy chair and she relished the advantage that it gave her. She had half-wondered about sending Art over to the alehouse to bring back one of Turlough's men, but decided against it. The house was full of noise and bustle, girls' and boys' voices, the shrill commands from Brigid. She felt quite secure.

'So now,' she went on, 'let's get back to that conversation in the alehouse. What did you discuss?'

'They wanted my opinion on the sentences,' he said after a moment's thought.

'And . . .'

'And I gave it to them, my poor best,' he said. The mock humility in his voice annoyed her, but she did not let it show.

'Was there any discussion about revenge?'

'My dear Brehon, you don't surely imagine that I was part of that schoolboy trick of placing the man under the wave spray.'

'But you were there when it was discussed.'

He said nothing for a moment, but she kept her eyes fixed on him and tapped impatiently with a fingernail on the newly scrubbed arm of the chair. It gave out a low, dense sound and this seemed to startle him. He looked towards the window and then back again.

'I was,' he said.

'And you did nothing to discourage them.'

'It was not my place.'

'And you didn't think of having a word with the alehouse keeper, with Barra.'

'Why should it? How did I know whether it was just talk?'

'But you saw them leave?'

'No,' he said. 'I had left the table by then. You can ask Barra or anyone else. I was not with them at that stage.'

'And where were you?'

He thought about it for a moment. She could see him wondering how good her sources were and then he said, 'I had tired of the company and tired of the smell and the lack of air. I went for a walk.'

'Towards the cliffs, is that right?'

He shook his head. 'No, not towards the cliffs. I went in the opposite direction, down the hill and towards the harbour. I went to watch the sea. I used to come here as a boy when I was at law school in Duniry in Galway. I liked to watch those enormous waves rolling in from Crab Island. They were marvellous on that night, even more impressive than I had remembered them.'

'So it was full tide when you left the alehouse.'

'Thereabouts, I'd say.'

'And did anyone see you on the road downhill, or perhaps at the harbour watching the waves coming in?'

He did not hesitate, which was, she thought, perhaps his first mistake. Surely a man who was telling the truth about a walk, a walk after he had swallowed some of the local ale, surely he would stop and interrogate his memory, try to visualize the night, but Boetius came straight out with a flat 'no'.

'There was no one on the road, no one at the harbour,' Mara confirmed.

'I didn't say that.' He grinned at her. 'I'm too much of a

lawyer to make an assertion such as that. What I said was that, I saw no one.'

'And if I were to make enquiries, you would guess that I would find that no one saw you, would that be correct?' asked Mara.

'Very likely,' he said. 'On the other hand, it may be that someone was looking from a window, was standing in the shadow of a house, was sitting in a boat tied to the pier, or perhaps looking across from Crab Island. I wouldn't like to discourage you from making your investigations. Obviously, there is a death that you have to solve. Equally obviously, you would like to get rid of me, like to declare me an outcast from the home of my ancestors, so it would make sense, would it not, to tie the two affairs together. The only problem is that I did not kill Brehon O'Doran.'

'I would possibly believe that if it were not for my prior knowledge of you and of what you can plot, of the evil which you could bring about in order to have your own way. I wonder why you came back. There is little for you here, you know. Most of the land is *Tuath Clae* land. It was given for the use of the Brehon of this area, they were to take the produce. But it is O'Brien land and it remains O'Brien land. It did not belong to Fergus. Therefore, unless you were to be declared Brehon, then the only part of your inheritance is this house and the seven acres that surround it. And that will only become yours if a court declares that Fergus is incapable of managing his own affairs and has to be cared for. I would imagine,' she continued thoughtfully, 'that, in that case, the court would make it a condition that Fergus should live here and that you should care for him. Or else that you should use the revenues from this property to finance the present arrangements.' He was not looking downcast, she noticed. He still had a half smile on his lips and a speculative look in his eye. 'After all,' she continued, watching him closely, 'you must have a much more glittering future ahead of you at the court of King Henry. Why leave that to come back here for such a small return?'

He said nothing and she began to think hard. He was not stupid and he had demonstrated that he still had an excellent knowledge of the law which he had acquired at Duniry Park in Galway twenty years ago. Why had he come?'

'Stephen Gardiner sent you, I suppose,' she said after a minute. 'You were to be the advance party, the thin end of the wedge. You were to get the position of the Brehon here, and then you were to undermine our laws by gradually introducing English law in its place. You will become known as a man skilled in both laws and there will be respect for your learning. And then you will start to change matters according to the instructions that you have received. Small things, first, small people who might not have the confidence to appeal to the king, but who would find themselves paying the penalties like our neighbours across the sea. There will always be a possibility of whipping up anger in families who have lost a son or daughter. They will want a death to pay for the other death and, who knows, the priests will tell them that this is God's law; that Deuteronomy says: "Then all the men of his town are to stone him to death. You must purge the evil from among you". And then, little by little, the penalties of hanging, drawing, quartering, cutting off the right hand of the petty thief, executing a person for a larger theft, building prisons, all these customs which have been successfully introduced into the east of Ireland, will come to the west and our ancient laws will be lost. That, I think, was the plan and I tell you, Boetius, that while there is breath in my body, you shall not bring these laws here.'

'Goodness, how eloquent you are!'

'There was just one thing in your way. The king, our king, King Turlough Donn O'Brien, did not appoint you but rather chose Brehon O'Doran, the man from Ossory. So you had an obstacle to your master's commands. There was a man in your way and so you removed that man. I do believe that you are capable of doing this and I shall investigate the evidence and expect no mercy from me, Boetius MacClancy, if you were the one who killed. The last time you were here, you conspired; over ten years ago, you were content with stirring up bad feeling; this time, I suggest to you that you have gone a step further.'

'I suggest to you that you have not a single shred of evidence to connect me to this murder. You have, on the other hand, five angry men, five men who saw their lives turned upside down, five men with bows and arrows in a creel and murder in their hearts, perhaps.'

'So you knew about the bows and arrows,' said Mara softly. 'But how did you know that, Boetius, if you merely chatted to them in the alehouse.'

'Strong drink loosens tongues. I'm sure you remember Fithail on that subject.' He made an effort to recover, but his pudgy lips had tightened and there was a spark of anger in his eyes.

Mara leaned back against her cushions.

'I think,' she said softly, 'that it was you who set up the whole affair. You would be friendly with Peadar, you intervened on his side during judgement day, you devised the punishment, you would remember all about the blowhole from your days here. It was all a slightly silly affair and would have done them no good, but it made them feel better. But when they were safely back in the alehouse, drinking and reminiscing, exulting in the discomfort of the unjust judge, then you, Boetius MacClancy, you slipped out of the alehouse, went through the bushes, stole up the hillside, keeping to the shadow of the hedge. You knew this place here very well, you could calculate the tides, or ask a fisherman, you would have known that the blowhole only operated for around high tide and so you stole up there, found the water to have subsided, slit the man's throat and then returned to the alehouse.'

'Except that I didn't,' said Boetius. 'Don't think that you can pin this on me. The burden of proof lies with you, remember.'

'Let's take this step by step,' said Mara. 'You agree that you knew of the plan?'

'Yes,' he said shortly.

'You suggested it?'

'No.'

Mara let that pass. She would talk with the five young men, but it might be difficult to be sure. Boetius was clever enough to drop subtle hints and then to overwhelm someone as naïve as Peadar with admiration of his cleverness at thinking out such a revenge. It was a silly scheme, almost too silly for anyone except a schoolboy, but these young men may have been drinking steadily for most of the day. Days of Judgement

normally took place on some day of a festival, but on the few
occasions when they were on ordinary working days, the
custom of repairing to the alehouse held good. Five angry
men, lots to drink and a subtle and clever man at their side.
A man, she thought, who might just have seen the possibility
of having another chance of seizing the traditional MacClancy
post of Brehon.

'Could you show me your knife,' she said, holding out her
hand.

He took it out with such readiness that she guessed it would
not be revealing. It was a very elaborate knife, purchased in
London, she thought. There was some gold wire twisted around
the pommel between the handle and the blade. Difficult to
clean completely, she thought and took it to the window. The
October sun was setting in the south-west and a long, low
gleam came through the window. She pushed open the frame
and stood examining it as carefully as she could. She could see
no traces of blood on it but she would need to ask one of her
scholars in order to double-check, she thought. One of the
drawbacks to being fifty years old was the deterioration of her
sight. However, she would not give Boetius the satisfaction of
admitting to any weakness.

'I'll keep this for the moment,' she said, and then quickly
whirring around to catch him off guard, she said rapidly, 'You
can use your other knife for the meantime.'

There was no change in his face, however. He said with a
trace of amusement in his voice, 'That is my only knife, Brehon.
I am not a soldier.'

And yet, she thought, this is a very elaborate knife. Does
he really cut and spear his meat, his cheese with this knife. Or
was food cut to bite-sized portions in the circles where he
lived just now?

'Well, I'm sure that you will manage,' she said. 'Thank you,
Boetius. That is all, you may go.' She did not accompany him
to the door, but nodded curtly at his farewell greeting. She
stayed where she was at the window and watched him mount
his horse and ride away. It was hard to judge, but she had a
feeling that there was something jaunty about his carriage. His
back was very straight and his beard stuck out aggressively

which seemed to indicate that he held his chin high. She pushed open the window and the sea breeze swept back the sound of a very merry tune, not one that she knew, probably one that he had picked up at the court in London. She felt her own lips tighten. There was no doubt but he felt that he had got the better of that exchange and she was honest enough to admit to herself that he might well have been right. She stayed very still for a moment. This, she thought, was a very clever man. It was nonsense to think that he had come all the way from London just to claim the few acres that Fergus owned and this poorly maintained house. He would, she suspected, have known that any revenue that he got for this would, according to the law, have to be used to maintain his elderly uncle and, although the man was weak in his mind, his body was still active. Fergus, surprisingly, was a strong, fit-looking man. He was able to go for long walks and to scramble around the cliffs. He might live for many years yet.

No, she thought, Boetius came for the prestigious and lucrative post of Brehon, and what was more, she felt certain of this, he came with instructions from his master, Stephen Gardiner, to replace the ancient laws of Ireland with their English equivalent. She had a momentary vision of the ancient mound at Knockfinn being used as a place for men to be hanged and swore that she would do everything in her power to frustrate him.

'You're looking very angry,' said Cael coming quietly into the room with a pot labelled lavender polish in her hand and a piece of threadbare linen over one arm. 'What do you think of my table? Good, isn't it? Brigid thinks that it didn't have a proper scrubbing for ten years. She keeps muttering about giving a piece of her mind to that Orlaith.' She felt the table carefully and then shrugged her shoulders, getting to work, energetically rubbing in the polish. 'Might be a bit damp, yet,' she observed, 'but at least it will smell nice and I hate leaving a job half done. What have you got there, Brehon?'

'I've been wondering whether there are any bloodstains on this knife. Come to the window where the light is good. Have a good look at it. It's the knife belonging to Boetius MacClancy, the nephew of Fergus.'

Cael put the pot and the linen rag on the table and came across to the window, holding the knife carefully by the end of the handle and scrutinizing it with care, turning it over in her hand.

'Can't see anything. I'd have expected there might be something between the blade and the handle, but there is nothing there. It doesn't look as though it has been cleaned, either, does it? The handle is quite polished. Speaking as an expert in scrubbing, I can say quite categorically that no one scrubbed this. It's not like the knife that you took from Ciaran, is it? That had definitely been scrubbed.' She handed the knife back and returned to her polish.

'No, it isn't, is it,' said Mara thoughtfully. Boetius, she thought, was too clever to have kept a bloodstained knife on his person. And despite his words, it was quite common for a well-to-do person to have more than one knife. She checked herself, though. It would be easy to be blinded by her dislike of the man and focus too much on him in this early stage of the investigation.

Cael hadn't repeated her question and Mara was glad that the polishing of the table was now engaging all of her attention. If Cael had asked her why she was looking so angry, she would have had to tell her that she was furious with herself at allowing that corrupt and evil man to have found her in the wrong. It was true, she acknowledged to herself, she was high-handed in her dealings. She made decisions quickly and no one ever challenged these decisions. Fachtnan, her previous assistant, had always agreed with her and now, her new assistant was her own grandson. Perhaps, she thought, she should ask Turlough to send another Brehon from Thomond to investigate this murder. Boetius had mentioned this and she had not really replied to the insinuation, but he had, she admitted, right on his side.

'I'm wondering whether I should get another judge to work with me on this case,' she said aloud.

'I wouldn't,' said Cael pausing for a minute. 'After all you have us to help you. You don't want a stranger coming here and having to explain everything and argue about everything. It would slow everything down and I don't think it would suit you. Cian is offering Niall two to one that you will have it solved by the end of the week,' she added. She had turned back to her task and once more was rubbing vigorously. She did not look at Mara, but her tone was decisive and Mara took a certain amount of wry comfort from the fact that her scholars believed in her abilities.

'And what did Niall say to that?'

'He took the bet. Cian is very pleased. He pledged half an ounce of silver and he's already making plans to spend his winnings on a new bow and set of arrows when we go to Coad fair.' Cael had a grin on her face.

'Do you like him, Cael? Niall, I mean.'

'I can't make him out,' said Cael frankly. 'There is something odd about him. He's like someone acting a part. And Rianne is the same, you know. They're both pretending that they hardly know each other, but then they look at each other when they think that no one is noticing, and it's like as if they are sending a message. Cian and I used to do that when we were young.'

Mara got to her feet, tucking the knife into her satchel. 'I'll have a word with them both, and I'll look to see whether they do that when I am talking to them,' she said.

Ten

Cáin Lánamna
(Law of Marriage)

Heptad 3

1. *A wife is free to leave her husband if he repudiates her for another woman, although she may stay in the house if she wishes.*
2. *If a blow from the husband leaves a mark, she may leave him and obtain her share of the property.*
3. *She may divorce him if he fails to support her.*
4. *She may divorce him if he is impotent for any reason.*
5. *She may divorce him if he is indiscreet about the details of their sexual life.*
6. *She may divorce him if he becomes a priest.*
7. *She may divorce him if he lies with boys.*

Ríanne, to give the girl her due, was joining in heartily with the housework, cleaning the pewter with a mixture of sand and lye. Art was sitting beside her, working busily on the kitchen knives. Niall, however, was standing by the window, with a frown on his face, dubiously eyeing a goose wing which had been thrust into his hand by Brigid.

'Climb up on that chair and get those cobwebs from out of the corners, Niall. Come on, boy. That's not a hard task. We all have to help, you know.'

Brigid usually managed young people well. Over thirty years of experience of caring for the welfare of the young scholars at the Cahermacnaghten Law School had honed the mixture of authority, flattery and genuine warmth with which she ensured that they respected and obeyed her. Mara stood back, unwilling to interfere until appealed to by her. Ríanne, she noticed, did not look towards her friend and companion, but ostentatiously worked harder, keeping her head bowed down over her task, even exchanging a surreptitious smile with Art. Cian came across, muttered something into Art's ear and the pair of them dissolved into giggles. Niall glared at them. He had a very unhappy look on his face and Mara began to feel sorry for him. It was always her policy to give scholars a way out without losing face so now she addressed herself to R1anne.

'When you and Niall have finished your tasks, could you come into the parlour, R1anne? I have a few questions to ask you both about Ossory and about Brehon Gaibrial O'Doran.'

It was true, she thought, noticing a flash of relief on Niall's face. It would be part of her usual procedure to explore the background of anyone who was not from the kingdom. But there was something very tense about that boy that worried her slightly. There was no doubt in her mind that he had not told all that he knew.

'You're making a good job of that fireplace, Cian,' she said approvingly. 'Goodness, Brigid, look at the shine coming through!' Cian was scraping the soot from the crane that hung over the fire and using a mixture of his own spit and some verjuice to polish the sections that he'd cleaned.

'Hasn't been touched for years,' said Brigid with a sniff. 'As for that cellar! God only knows when it last saw a scrubbing brush. And the food press! And I could swear that the bread basket hasn't had its crumbs removed in a month of Sundays.'

Now that Brigid's attention was deflected from Niall he had climbed onto the chair and was flicking at the cobwebs with the goose wing. Mara withdrew hastily and went back into the parlour. She was touched to see how Brigid had put all her energy into getting that room fit for her before tackling the kitchen which harrowed her housewifely soul. Cael's table was still slightly wet with polish so she sat by the fire and sorted through her impressions.

This murder, she thought, has almost too many suspects. Each one of the five young men sentenced had a motive perhaps, but Peadar had more reason to kill than had any of the others. So he had to be the prime suspect.

But then Ciaran was the one who had the knife bearing traces of blood.

A knife that, he said, he had picked up from the beach.

A fairly unlikely story. She bent down and took the knife from her satchel. There was no doubt that it had been recently scoured, probably with sand and seawater. But why abandon it?

She compared it with the knife belonging to Boetius and was holding the two, one in each hand, when Cael came in.

'Brigid said to tell you that there would be a meal ready in about an hour,' she said. And then: 'Are you still looking for traces of blood?'

'That's right,' said Mara with a sigh. 'On this one, anyway. Even I with my old eyes can see the blood on Ciaran's knife.'

'Do you believe that Ciaran found it, or do you think that it is really his own knife?' asked Cael.

Mara grimaced. 'I just don't think that this is the sort of knife that Ciaran would have. And I keep thinking that of all of these lads, he was the one that would have suffered least from those punitive verdicts. He and Emer were on the verge of making up, anyway, according to him and since the fine was to be paid to her and her family, the *Tuath* might have agreed to count it as a wedding present to set up the two young people. Ronan, Seán, Donal the songwriter, and especially Peadar, who was faced with banishment, well, all of these had more reason for revenge and more incentive to remove this Brehon and hope that the next one appointed would not insist on the payment of these huge fines.'

'So your suspect, your prime suspect, would be Peadar,' said Cael seriously.

'Not really. Not at the moment.' Mara hesitated. She found it hard to talk about this man, but her scholar deserved a frank answer.

'I'd prefer it to be Brehon Boetius MacClancy,' she said. 'And I am busy building up a case against him in my mind and perhaps neglecting other suspicions in the meantime. That's wrong, I know, but I find it hard to stop myself.'

'You don't like him, do you?' asked Cael. 'You've met him before, is that right?'

Ten years ago, thought Mara, ten years ago Cael was only three years old, then. The story of Boetius and Stephen

Gardiner, sent over by his master, Cardinal Wolsey, was now ancient history.

'A long time ago,' she said aloud. 'He was banished from the kingdom of the Burren by the king, banished for ten years. Of course, he has a right to come back now. Brehon law always says that when retribution has been made, then the wrongdoer resumes his place in society. So Boetius has a right to come back here. Presumably, he heard about the senility of his uncle and he came across hoping to gain his place, but was refused.'

'And so he might have murdered Brehon O'Doran to ensure that he didn't have a wasted journey. Seems a bit of a chance to take, doesn't it? After all, if the king had turned him down once . . .'

She broke off as there was a tap on the door and then Ríanne came in, smiling sweetly at Mara. She left the door open behind her, but otherwise did not acknowledge Niall who followed her.

'All the pewter is as clean as I could make it,' she said gaily. 'Art is putting it on the shelf now.' She gave a sidelong glance at Cael and a slight giggle and Cael grinned back as she went out of the room. There was no doubt that it was obvious to the sharp-witted Cael that Art was smitten by this pretty girl.

'Sit down, Ríanne, sit here. Niall, you take this stool. I just wanted the two of you to tell me a little about Brehon O'Doran. Perhaps you could start, Niall.'

'I don't know much,' said Niall. 'I think that my uncle knows more about him. In fact, I think he was at my uncle's law school. He became an *aigne* when he was with my uncle and then he went on to a school in Galway to take his examinations of *ollamh* and Brehon.'

'I see,' said Mara. It was a common practice and a good one, she thought. A young man would gain extra experience by moving to a new school for his higher qualifications. It was good for everyone and kept the links between the schools and helped to ensure that the law remained consistent, no matter which part of Ireland it was practised in. She had recommended that course for many of her scholars.

'And how did it come about that he came back to Ossory?'

'He came to marry her,' said Niall with a slight jerk of his head. 'If it wasn't for that he would not have come to the place ever again. My uncle helped to draw up the marriage contract.'

'Did you know him, Brehon O'Doran, did you know him before then?' asked Mara turning towards Ríanne.

'Never saw him before in my life,' said Ríanne cheerfully.

'Were you married against your will?' asked Mara.

Ríanne shrugged her shoulders and grimaced slightly. 'Not really,' she said. 'It was a matter for my parents. My sisters have all been married and I knew that they would find someone for me. I thought he wasn't too bad when I saw him. My eldest sister was married to an old man with a sore leg. I didn't want that. Gaibrial wasn't too bad.'

'But you didn't find being married to him was pleasant,' suggested Mara. 'Was that because you would have preferred to marry someone else?' She cast a look at Niall, but he didn't seem, or perhaps didn't want to seem, to be interested in the conversation and was engaged in plucking tiny shreds of cobwebs from his rather grubby *léine*.

'I certainly did not.' Ríanne shook her head emphatically and looked around at her audience. 'I didn't particularly want to get married, but then I didn't want to be a nun either and I suppose that you have to do one or the other.' She sighed heavily and . . . and dramatically, thought Mara. There was a sense in which this girl seemed almost as though she was playing a part – sweet and affectionate with old Fergus, affable and helpful with Brigid, and now, with Mara, she seemed to be subtly inviting sympathy from a woman who had found a different way, who lived an independent life as Brehon and *ollamh* of a law school.

'So you were married, when?'

Ríanne counted on her fingers, her eyes abstracted. 'Fifteen days ago. Goodness, it seems longer than that,' she said. 'It was on Michaelmas Day.'

'So, on the 29th of September?'

'That's right,' agreed Ríanne. 'We got married and we came across here and as soon as he saw the house, he wasn't too

pleased. Started wishing himself out of it.' She hesitated for a
moment and then said, tentatively, 'But then a few days later
he cheered up. He told me one night that he had a way of
getting rich quick and then as soon as he got the money we
would leave this place.'

'Through the law cases, was that it?' From the corner of her
eye Mara noticed a contemptuous smile on Niall's face.

'I don't think so.' Ríanne shook her head. 'He was a very
impatient man. When he said "quick", he meant quick.' She
touched the yellow-brown marks of bruise under her eye and
grimaced slightly. There was, thought Mara, something slightly
contrived about the gesture.

'Did he hit you?' she asked abruptly.

Ríanne flushed. There was a flash of anger in her eyes. She
tightened her lips for a second, and then forced a smile.

'Don't all men hit their wives?' she said.

'Not if they don't want to be divorced,' said Mara bluntly
and added, 'I'm surprised that you don't know the law, or that
Niall didn't tell you.' Her eyes went to the boy sitting silently
gazing at the window. He didn't move or acknowledge her
remark, though, and she decided not to pursue the matter.
She turned back to Ríanne.

'Tell me how you think that Brehon O'Doran planned to
get rich quickly,' she said.

'I thought that he was going to get a big sum of money
from someone,' she said.

A big sum of money. Mara thought about it. Was it from
Fergus? The fact that Gaibrial O'Doran had made that remark
after he had arrived in Corcomroe seemed to point that way.
But how? Had Fergus got a store of silver somewhere? No
one had investigated that matter. And yet it was possible. Ever
since the death of his wife, Siobhán, about ten years ago, Fergus
had lived very simply. Perhaps he had accumulated some money
and had stored it somewhere. It was, she thought, a possibility.
The old man had become distinctly odd during the last few
years. He had even avoided replacing his elderly housekeeper
when she had retired and made do with a couple of hours'
work a week from Orlaith.

'He was clever at finding out things about people,' said

Ríanne dispassionately. 'He would find out secrets and then he would chuckle to himself about it.'

There were, thought Mara, some people who liked secrets for the feeling of power that it gave them. But there were others who used secrets as a means of blackmail. Which one of the two was Gaibrial O'Doran? The latter, she suspected.

'And do you think that Gaibrial had succeeded in getting that money?' she asked.

Ríanne shrugged, her eyes raised to the ceiling and her mouth screwed into a grimace.

'Oh, for goodness sake!' Mara was beginning to get irritated with this pair of young people. Sighs and shrugs were in the experience of all teachers of adolescent scholars, but that was no reason why they should be encouraged. 'Come on, Ríanne,' she said bracingly. 'A man has been murdered. There's no doubt about that fact in my mind. No one cuts their own throat. So now my task is to solve that murder and I am asking for your help. Forget that you disliked the man, he's not going to come back to life now and I am asking you a few simple questions which you don't seem to be keen to answer. Is there any reason why you should not help me?'

Ríanne looked startled and almost slightly afraid. 'No, there isn't,' she said. 'But you're asking me questions that I don't know the answer to.'

'Well, then, just say that you don't know. Stop shrugging your shoulders and sighing. It's getting on my nerves and I have enough to do,' said Mara with a smile to take the sting from the words. 'And, you know, Ríanne, the sooner that this murder is solved, well, the sooner you and Niall can go back to Ossory. I don't think that I can let you go until I have an answer to the question of who killed Brehon O'Doran. You do see this, don't you?'

To her relief Ríanne grinned at this plain speaking. 'No, I don't think that he had found any money. He was in a really foul mood after the judgement day. I think that he probably noticed the king's face after he had finished and he was looking very worried and annoyed. I noticed that.'

'And what was Gaibrial's reaction to that, do you think?'

'He came over to me after he had finished and he asked

me how it had gone. And I told him that the king didn't look too happy. The king was looking over at us. He was pretending to smile at me, he was holding my hand, but he whispered: "Wait until I get you home. You'll suffer for this." But I ran upstairs and locked my door when we came in and Orlaith was there serving the meal and so he and Niall ate it and didn't leave anything for me.' Ríanne turned her head and looked accusingly at Niall who continued to stare at the window.

'And when the hunters came?'

'I saw them from my window. There were five of them. I couldn't see them very well, just the back of their heads. But I was glad to see them. I was saying to myself: "Let him work off his temper on them", so I came out and went downstairs to see whether there was anything left to eat, but there was hardly a crust left on the table and Orlaith had gone home.'

Now, thought Mara, we come to the interesting bit.

'So you and Niall sat down by the fire and waited for Brehon O'Doran to come home,' she suggested.

'That's right.' Niall joined in the conversation.

'And what did you do? How did you pass the time?'

'Nothing much,' said Niall.

'I asked Niall what he thought of the judgements that day,' said Ríanne.

'And what did he reply?' asked Mara with interest. After all, she thought, these two young people may have listened together to law lectures. Niall had said earlier that Ríanne had lived next to the law school. It was natural that she was interested in the law.

'He told me to shut up. He was scared of our master.'

'But he had gone out, had he not?'

'He had a habit of sneaking back in and listening at doors,' said Ríanne and there was a note of sincerity in her voice. There was little doubt, thought Mara, that the dead man was very unpleasant. The murder had to be solved and retribution exacted, but she told herself that all of the facts that she was uncovering about the life and character of Brehon O'Doran would have to be taken into account if it proved that one of his victims had killed him.

But Boetius MacClancy will pay the full penalty of the law and will be sentenced to banishment, if I have anything to do with it, she thought fiercely and then softened her voice.

'You sat there all by yourself while Niall went up to his room to study?' she queried in sympathetic tones. An assertion, she found from experience, often elicited more of an answer than did a question.

'No, he didn't. He had a dice and he was tossing it up and down on the hearth. He was betting his left hand would win against his right hand.' Ríanne sighed in an exasperated way. 'He just went on doing it over and over again. Even when I got up to light the candles, he didn't take any notice of me, just went on throwing the silly things and making notes on the hearth floor with a burnt stick.'

'So you went off up to your bedroom and left him to it, did you?' Mara looked swiftly at Niall, but no expression crossed his face. He looked bored.

'No, I didn't. I stayed in the parlour. You see there was a fire there, but none upstairs in the bedroom. I was forbidden to light that until just before my master wished to go to bed,' explained Ríanne and Niall's face showed no flicker of a change, no glance of query or of disbelief.

'And this went on until when?'

'Well, it was getting dark and I said to Niall, "Surely he's not still out there, chasing after those hunters?"'

'And what did Niall answer to that?'

'I don't think that he said anything,' said Ríanne, frowning slightly, 'but then I said, "Niall, you'll just have to go out. If he's had a fall or something, he'll kill us both."'

'And so?'

'So he went.'

'Just like that. Did he say anything?'

'No, I don't think so.' Ríanne frowned as though searching her memory. 'He took his cloak down from the nail behind the door,' she added helpfully.

'And a lamp.' Niall spoke for the first time in a slightly husky voice.

'That's right,' agreed Ríanne. 'He went into the kitchen and came out with a storm lamp.' She shut her eyes, screwing them up in an effort of concentration. 'I remember now. He pushed a twig into the fire and when it was burning, he lit the lamp.'

'All without saying anything?'

'He doesn't talk much.'

Mara sat back.

'And what time was that?'

'About midnight,' said Niall, speaking for the first time.

'As late as that? Have you a clock? How did you know the time?'

'By the stars,' said Niall.

'You did wait for a long time? He must have been gone for hours. It gets dark about eight o'clock.'

'We were scared of him,' explained Ríanne. 'I had been thinking that perhaps he went to the alehouse after he had chased the hunters. He would have been furious if either of us had come looking for him then.'

'Midnight.' Mara thought about the matter for a while. The man would have been dead, certainly by then, according to the story told by the five men drinking at the alehouse. 'Midnight,' she repeated. 'And where did you go, Niall?'

'Out through the gate and into the field. I walked a bit along the edge of the field. It had oats in it last summer so I kept to the side by the hedge.'

'And what did you do, Ríanne?'

'I stood at the door and watched him.'

'And then?' queried Mara.

'And I couldn't see any sign of him for a minute. I called out, but there was no answer. And then after a while I saw him. I saw that he was coming back.'

'After a while? How long?'

'I don't know,' said Ríanne and added, 'I can't read the stars, but when he came back he said, "There's no sign of him. I'm off to bed." And he pushed past me and he went up to his bedroom.'

'Didn't you think to search a little further, Niall, go to the alehouse, or down to the village?' asked Mara.

'I didn't want to,' said Niall sulkily. 'I had gone far enough and shouted enough and I tripped over something and the lamp went out. I came back in and went upstairs and went to bed. Why should I go stumbling around on the cliffs at night looking for him? I don't suppose that he would bother if I went missing? So I came in and I went upstairs and went to bed and to sleep.'

'And you, Ríanne,' said Mara, 'did you go to bed, also?'

'No, I didn't,' said Ríanne. 'I stayed there in the parlour with the door open to the passage way so that I wouldn't miss the sound of a bang on the door if I fell asleep.'

'And did you fall asleep?'

'No, I stayed awake all night. I was frightened,' explained Ríanne.

'And did Niall come downstairs again?'

'No, he didn't,' said Ríanne resentfully. 'I was left there all alone wondering what had happened to my husband.'

'Did you sleep, Niall?' Mara turned quickly, but the boy was just looking at the floor, his eyes hidden and his face blank and without expression.

'Yes, I did.' He looked up then and seemed to see a doubt in her face. 'I sleep very well, Brehon. Nothing ever keeps me awake,' he said awkwardly.

'But when Ríanne woke you up, what time was that?'

'After sunrise. So then I went out. At least I could see everything, then, not like the night before, stumbling around in the dark. The sun was up. And I went to the cliffs and I found him, all trussed up in the lobster pot.' There was a slight choke in the boy's voice, almost as though he suppressed a fit of giggling, but Mara ignored that. It's a funny age, Brigid would say when discussing the behaviour of one of the fourteen- or fifteen-year-old scholars. There had been no doubt that the boy had been deeply shocked by the finding of the body and shock in that age often ventilated itself in nervous laughter. That fit of vomiting had shown that the boy was deeply upset by the discovery of the dead body of his master. She would ask no more about the lobster pot or the predatory birds.

'And you came across to find me, then.' It was very odd thought Mara, that the boy had not gone straight back to Ríanne. Or was there a possibility that he had been involved in the murder of Brehon O'Doran? Had he gone back out again that night? Could he have done this? Did Ríanne really stay awake all night? Could Niall have gone back out, found the body of his master, tied up and helpless, and then had slit his throat. And, yet, unless Ríanne and Niall had a very poor sense of time, when he went up to his bedroom must surely have been well after the finding of the body by Peadar and his friends.

'That's right,' said Niall. 'I went up to Ballinalacken Castle first of all, but a man in the stables told me that you had already gone so I just went after you.'

'I see.' Mara rose to her feet and went to the window looking out, thinking and speculating. There was, she noted, a dead silence behind her. What were they thinking, these two young people. Were they exchanging glances, wondering whether their stories were believed? She turned her head, but both were gazing into the fire.

'Go back and help Brigid, now,' she said. 'Tell her that we'll have dinner as early as it suits her, will you?'

Both of the young people were very white-faced. A cup of Brigid's ale and some hot food would be good for both, she thought as she watched them go from the room with bent heads and then turned back to the window again, looking over the smooth green grass and the ploughed-up surface of the small field beyond it. Niall had got as far as there the night before. He had a lantern in his hand and that would have made him very visible to Ríanne. He could not have gone further without her knowledge. Were they both telling the truth? If they were, then neither could have been involved in the murder of the man whom they both named as master. As she watched, Cian came into view, carrying a leather bucket and he upended it over a small weedy patch where some lanky onion leaves straggled through the surrounding vegetation, spilling out a bucket-load of soot. The vegetable patch did not look as though there had been any attention paid to it for a long time. Poor Fergus, he had been neglected, she thought with a stab of compunction and then she put him from her mind and returned to the fate of his successor.

'Cian,' she called. 'If Brigid can spare you, would you walk to the cliff with me?'

He gave her a grin. 'Be with you in an instant. I'll hand over the honour of chief bucket man to Niall. That will please his lordship.'

Mara waited by the gate. The sun was warm on her back. It had been a wet summer, but the autumn seemed to be making up for it. There was a sparkle on the sea and the three Aran islands, normally so misty, were now clearly outlined against the skyline, even showing here and there the long, low shape of a whitewashed cottage, distinct against the grey stone.

Cian was back in an instant as he had promised, pulling up a bunch of coarse blue grass and scrubbing the soot from his hands with it.

'You should have seen Niall's face when I handed him the bucket and the scraper,' he chortled.

'You don't like him, do you?' queried Mara. She was careful to keep her voice non-judgemental. It was important, she always felt, that her scholars could be open and honest with her.

'I think that he's a fraud and a liar,' said Cian bluntly.

Mara turned to look at him. Art, she had observed, did not like Niall, but she had put that down to the fact that he was missing his foster-brother, Cormac. Now it appeared that Cian was strongly opposed to him, also. Was it because they both suspected that she might invite Niall to join the law school and, with the conservatism of boys who had grown up in one small community, they did not want that.

'Why do you say that?' she asked with interest.

'This vomiting business. I don't believe it.'

'He did get sick, violently,' said Mara.

'Yes, but did you look at it?'

'I smelled it.'

'Yes, so did I and I looked at it, too. I could see what he had for breakfast. And perhaps what he had for his supper last night, too.'

Mara turned to look at him. 'And why does that make him a fraud? He didn't pretend to vomit, he really and truly did vomit.'

'Easy to make yourself vomit. Stick your fingers down your throat. Or drink saltwater. Probably, though, he stuck his fingers down his throat just after he came through the gate.'

'But why should he do that?'

'Sympathy,' said Cian. 'He probably thought you looked as if you'd be sympathetic when he saw you at Judgement Day.'

'But why should he want me to be sympathetic?'

'So that you wouldn't accuse him of murdering his master. It makes sense.'

'Sounds a bit far-fetched to me,' said Mara dubiously.

'No, it's not,' said Cian holding the gate to the oats' field open for her. 'Think about it. When are you most likely to throw up? When you see something disgusting and horrible like a dead man and birds pecking his eyes out – or two hours later? Wouldn't you have expected him to have spilled his guts when he saw the dead body?'

'But perhaps he did. And then when he was faced with telling his story, the horror overwhelmed him and he got sick again.'

'No,' said Cian impatiently. 'I told you, Brehon. I looked at it before Cumhal got the lad to cover it over. I'm telling you. He got up his last meal. There's no chance that he had thrown up an hour or so earlier. It would have been just bile in that case.'

'I see,' said Mara slowly. 'That's rather clever, Cian. You are going to make an excellent lawyer. You know, that did not occur to me. And, yes, you are right. It did make me feel sorry for him and it did make me feel that he had had a terrible shock and that the discovery of the dead body had shaken him badly. But would that have been enough to make him do that?' She thought about it for a moment. If Cian was right and Niall had voluntarily made himself sick, what did that imply? 'But why should he need sympathy from me? He was doing all the right things, reporting a murder. He didn't need sympathy, just action. He couldn't have been afraid of me, for any reason, could he? He was not a small child, though he did behave a little like one.'

'What if he did the murder,' said Cian energetically. 'Then he would want to deflect suspicion from himself. He would want to give the impression that he was a poor fellow who just stumbled on a body.'

'Why come and fetch me at all? Surely it would have been more sensible to have allowed someone else to find the body?'

'On the other hand, he might think that it would assure his innocence. When did he say that he had found it?'

'He said that he went out last night, urged by Ríanne, but he just got as far as about where we are now and then he dropped his lamp, it went out, so he decided to go back.'

'Hmm.' Cian sounded sceptical.

'I don't think that his heart was in it. Ríanne thought that he should, not because she wanted, what she calls her master, back but because she thought that he might wreak vengeance on them if he had fallen and no one came to look for him – he, Brehon O'Doran, according to Ríanne, had a habit of punching her. She has the marks of a bruise under her eye.'

'I noticed that, too,' said Cian. His lips twitched in a smile. 'When I brought my bucket back into the kitchen, I threw it at Niall, just fooling around, and a smut came out of it and went onto Ríanne's cheek. Cael did the usual girl business of "Oh, Cian!" and all that sort of thing and she got a rag and dipped it in the water and washed Ríanne's cheek.' He paused looking at Mara expectantly and she looked back at him pretending to be puzzled as she did not want to spoil his story.

'And a miracle cure! You can have me canonised as a saint. I throw a flake of soot at a girl, say a quick prayer, and the big bruise on her cheek disappears.'

Mara laughed. 'You're sure?' she queried, but he was quick and observant. She had little doubt but that he was reporting the truth. And that had been a very interesting point about Niall's attack of vomiting.

'Easily done,' said Cian. 'Bit of blackberry juice, I'd say. Cael noticed, too. I saw her look at me.'

'So you think that both of them are lying, openly or tacitly?'

'I do,' said Cian bluntly as they passed through the gate that led from the oats' field to the cliff side. And then, he said quickly, 'Look, Brehon, there's Brehon MacClancy.'

The tide was fully in, the waves crashing against the cliffs and there was a jet of seawater spurting up through the blowhole. Fergus stood to the side of it, but the sea wind blew the spray inland and the old man's hair and beard were soaking wet with seawater. He was not alone. Donal the songwriter was there and Fergus was holding his hand.

Eleven

Berrað Airechaca
(Shearings of the Court – Court Procedures)

The old term for a witness is Fiadu, *meaning one who sees. A witness must be sensible, honest, conscientious and of good memory. A person can only give evidence about what he has, himself, seen or heard and must be prepared to swear in support of this evidence. What does not take place before a witness's eyes is deemed to be 'dead' and he may only swear about what he has seen or heard.*

Mara's first instinct was to breathe a sigh of relief that the young man was there in order to protect Fergus from absent-mindedly stepping into the blowhole on the cliff. The ground around it was probably not too safe either, it was littered with rock and broken stone, making it very possible that the elderly man might trip and break his leg or worse. But then a glimpse of Donal's face showed rather a different story. The young songwriter looked embarrassed and angry and seemed to be struggling to release himself from the grip on his wrist.

'I saw you, Donal. I saw you,' the old voice quavered on a high note. 'I saw you, boy. I was up on the hillside. I saw you. I saw you creep up there and I saw the knife. I saw the knife flash in the moonlight.'

'What did you see, Fergus?' Mara had reached the old man's side in a couple of quick strides. Cian, fingering his own knife, was standing beside Donal.

It was one of the old man's good days, apparently. He recognized her instantly.

'I've got a problem on my hands, Mara. And in this lovely peaceful part of the world. Do you know, Mara, I could count on the fingers of my hands the murders that I have seen in my long life.' Fergus's voice took on a sing-song note. 'Drunkenness, oh yes, plenty of that, especially at the time of

the fairs, fights, trespass . . .' Fergus laughed on a high, shaky
note but then bit his lip and looked sternly at Donal. 'But,
murder, and the murder of a stranger to our kingdom. You
must make full and open confession, boy,' he said severely. 'You
must confess to me now, and then you must repeat your confession to the people of the kingdom. And then you must pay
retribution. I will have to fine you, Donal. That man left a
widow, a little girl, a nice little girl. She's left without her
husband now and you will have to give her . . .' Fergus searched
his memory and then came triumphantly out with: 'You'll
have to pay her six milch cows and . . .' This seemed to be
the end of the spurt of energy. His hand fell away from Donal's
sleeve and he stared at the ground, mumbling to himself.

'I didn't do anything, Brehon,' said Donal in a low voice to
Mara. 'I didn't come up here with a knife. I wasn't the one
that killed the new Brehon. I swear to you. He must be
mistaking me for someone else.' His handsome, highly coloured
face was now pale in patches and there were beads of sweat
on his forehead. 'He's just a daft old man,' he said angrily. 'He
doesn't know what he's talking about.'

'Don't speak of Brehon MacClancy in that disrespectful
manner,' snapped Mara. There was, she noticed, a sound of
panic in the young man's voice and she wondered why. Most
people in the area knew quite well that their Brehon's wits
had been wandering for some time. Why was Donal worried
about that? And, of course, there were times, increasingly fewer
in number, when Fergus made perfect sense. She decided that
she could not ignore this.

'Where were you when you saw Donal with the knife,
Fergus?' she asked in a low voice.

'Up there.' Fergus turned and pointed without hesitation.
'Up on the Pooka Road.' He looked slightly embarrassed and
then said in her ear, 'I like to climb onto the big stones up
there. I like sitting up on high and watching the world go by.'
He half-sang the last few words in a trembling falsetto.

Mara tightened her lips. The Pooka Road was a flat stretch
of limestone pavement on the cliff beyond the harbour. From
where they stood, it towered high above them, a pale grey
expanse of stone, littered with enormous stray boulders. It was

rumoured that the Pooka had used fairy magic to roll those stones along and to crush all of their enemies beneath them. Whether Fergus was still agile enough to climb on one of those rocks, well, she doubted that. But even standing up there on the limestone pavement he would have had a clear view of the cliff on the opposite side of the harbour. Yes, she thought, the cliff with its waterspout would certainly be visible to him. But would he have been out that night? This was something that she would have to check. She saw Cian's eyes thoughtfully scan the Pooka Road and then turn back to Donal with a tough look on his young face. It did seem to him, as it had seemed to her, that if Fergus had really been up on the Pooka Road he could definitely have seen something if he had looked across at the waterspout.

And it had been a night of a full moon.

And that made her think of something else.

Why had a lamp been so necessary for Niall when he was sent out by Ríanne to see where Gaibrial O'Doran had gone? She shelved that query at the back of her mind and turned back to Fergus. 'You saw a young man, Fergus. Could it have been him?' She pointed straight at Cian.

Fergus smiled gently. 'That's only a boy, Mara. That's one of your boys.' He hesitated for a moment, his eyes troubled as he searched for a name and then sighed as he gave up the struggle. 'That's your boy,' he repeated. 'He's a good boy. And so is this young man here.' He patted Donal on the shoulder.

'Young men make mistakes,' he said. 'They do things that are evil, but they are not evil themselves. The law gives them a chance to pay and to . . .' His voice faded out and Mara realized that whatever had been in his mind had fallen into the void.

'Let's all walk together up to the Pooka Road,' she suggested and his old face lit up.

'I'm a great walker,' he said.

'You'll come with us, Donal, won't you?' suggested Mara and he nodded. There was a sulky irritated look on his face, but the initial panic seemed to have subsided and his colour had come back.

'Do you need someone to give you an arm, Fergus?' she asked.

'No, no I'm a great walker,' he repeated and strode out.

'Go after him, stay with him,' said Mara authoritatively to the songwriter and Donal obediently caught up with the old man.

'Cian,' began Mara.

'Go down to Gobnait and check whether he was out that night,' put in Cian quickly and she nodded, pleased as always at those signs of independent thinking and quick wits when shown by her scholars. He was off instantly, taking the small blackthorn shrouded lane, which would shield him from the sight of both Fergus and Donal.

Mara waited until he was out of sight and then moved quickly ahead to join the other two on the way down to the harbour. There was no doubt that Fergus was, as he had claimed, a very good walker. She would almost have had to run to catch up with him. However, she was happy to walk behind and leave to Donal the burden of making conversation with Fergus. After a few minutes she heard the sound of a favourite song:

> Beidh aonach amárach i gContae an Chláir
> Cén mhaith dom é? Ní bheith mé ann.
>
> A Mháithrín, an ligfidh tú chun aonaigh mé?
> A stóirín-ó, ná h-éiligh é.

Donal sang the old song well and to her amazement, after a minute, Fergus joined in with his high quavering voice, singing the lines where the lovesick girl pleads to be allowed to go to the fair with her beloved, the shoemaker, while Donal sang the mother's refusal in a pleasant baritone. The song lasted until they reached the harbour and then Donal began it all over again. They had hardly gone more than a few yards when a deep bass voice joined in, singing the words in English:

> There's a fair tomorrow in County Clare
> What good it's to me, I won't be there!
>
> Oh, Mother, will you let me go to the fair?
> My dearest dear, I do not dare!

I'm in love with a shoemaker.
If I don't get him, I won't live!

Oh, Mother, will you let me go to the fair?
My dearest dear, I do not dare!

'I've entertained a whole table at Hampton Court with that song,' said a voice from behind her and Mara turned around to see Boetius smiling affably at her. 'The Cardinal, himself, was very taken by the tune when I sang it in Gaelic and he urged me to change the barbarous and uncouth words. And so myself and Thomas Wyatt got together and hammered out a few simple words to match the tune. We all thought it was a great improvement to hear it in English.'

'*We*,' queried Mara. 'So you count yourself as an Englishman, now, Boetius?'

'England, Ireland. It's going to be like England and Wales, you know. After all the Welsh struggled for a while, but now most Welshmen count themselves as English, the civilised ones, anyway. You, my dear Mara, I beg your pardon, my dear Brehon, could almost pass for an Englishwoman with a few alterations in dress and perhaps a hood and veil, for modesty's sake. I have heard you speak in English to my friend and patron and I can assure you that you do it very well. I remember—'

'I think it would be a grave mistake on your part, Boetius, to remind me, or to remind the king of the time when you brought that man, Stephen Gardiner, into Ireland. Let him never show his face here again. And I can tell you this, Boetius,' said Mara, pleased to hear how firm and dispassionate her voice was sounding. She allowed a pause to intervene, waited until he had turned an inquiring face towards her and then repeated, 'I can tell you this, that if it turns out that you have had anything to do with this matter, then I shall immediately request the king to banish you from his three kingdoms and to make it a lifelong banishment this time.'

She gave him a moment to digest this and then she said affably, 'If you are at a loose end, why not accompany us up to the Pooka Road. Fergus, your uncle, was telling us that he was up there, on that moonlit night when Brehon Gaibrial O'Doran was murdered.'

He gave a start. She could have sworn that. And there was a short, but a very noticeable silence before he said, in a voice which he strove to keep even, 'I don't suppose that his testimony is too reliable.'

'All testimony is of interest to me,' said Mara. 'Even a dumb animal can sometimes give testimony. I remember a case where I convicted a man of stealing a cow on the evidence of a dog. The dog,' she explained, 'did not bark. He was a savage guard dog, half-wolf and he barked at everyone, all except at his owner and at the man who bred him and that, of course, identified the thief.'

'You are trying to divert me,' he said with his unpleasant smile. 'We were talking about Fergus. There is no way that his testimony can be worth anything.'

'As I explained to you, earlier, Boetius, Fergus has not been assessed by any court and therefore I will look at any testimony from him just as I would look at testimony from, say yourself. I would assess the words, assess the person who spoke the words, look for corroboration and in the end, I would use my judgement. And now, could I ask you to join the singers ahead. My scholar is just coming and I wish to have a private word with him.'

He was not best pleased, but he moved on and caught up with Fergus who hailed him with great delight and presented him as his nephew to Donal. Mara stayed where she was, waiting for Cian to catch up with her. Out here, in the open air, voices carried easily and the further she was away from Boetius the better. She could see the jutting beard as he looked over his shoulder from time to time, but Donal, probably dreading a repetition of accusations, started singing the song again, urging Boetius to sing with him, this time repeating each line three times in the traditional way and Fergus joined in with him.

'Did you see her?' asked Mara quietly as Cian slowed to a stop beside her.

'Yes, I did,' he said. 'And yes, Brehon MacClancy was out that night. And he was where he said he was. So he could have seen Donal. Gobnait sent her husband out after him. And Fergus was perched on one of those boulders. Gobnait said, "Himself got the fright of his life when he saw him up there, just for all the world like one of the Pooka come back to the earth again.'"

'I see,' said Mara. There was no doubt that Fergus had the slightly strange, fey look of a denizen of the otherworld. It was getting near to the season of *Samhain,* that time when spirits from the underworld passed readily into this one. There were always a lot of superstitious fears and horrors being aired at *Samhain.* She made up her mind to have a word with Gobnait and to impress upon her that Fergus must be kept indoors on that night. If he was seen up there on the Pooka Road or emerging from one of the many caves around the cliffs, then there might be trouble with some drunken young people. She nodded her thanks to Cian and moved quickly to catch up with the singers.

Fergus, she noticed, now seemed to be on great terms with Donal, patting him on the back, congratulating him on his singing, telling him what a good kind lad he was, someone who would not hurt a fly.

'No, he wouldn't!' Fergus turned to Mara, his face puzzled and upset all of a sudden. 'That boy wouldn't hurt a fly,' he said, pointing to Donal, who had taken out a small wooden pipe from his pouch and who was blowing it energetically, stamping the time with his boots on the limestone flags of the roadway. 'No,' repeated Fergus with the air of one who had made a great discovery, 'that boy wouldn't hurt a . . . wouldn't hurt one of those things . . . you know those things that . . .' He made a flying motion with one hand, looked dubiously at Cian and muttered something to him and then went on ahead of them.

'What did he say?' Mara asked the question in a low voice, though she doubted whether Fergus would take any notice.

'Well, he was just raving, saying, "But I saw the knife. I saw it cut through the man's throat . . ." I don't suppose he knows what he is saying or whether he could really remember even if he did see something.' Cian's voice had a compassionate note in it. Mara nodded at him and then moved up to join Fergus.

'Don't worry about it, Fergus,' she said reassuringly. 'You are retired now, aren't you? Just leave it to me, won't you?'

Fergus looked at her with a puzzled air, and then his face lit up.

'Boetius MacClancy, that's the man that I saw,' he said triumphantly and Donal took the pipe from his mouth and stared incredulously from one man to the other. 'That was the man that I saw that night. He had a knife in his hand. It was bright in the moonlight.'

Mara sighed. There was not the slightest resemblance between Donal the songwriter and Boetius the lawyer. Donal was probably no more than about nineteen years old, slightly built, very slim, not tall, with dark hair worn quite long and the merest beginnings of a moustache. Boetius must now be in his middle thirties, heavily built, a great mountain of a man with red hair and a red beard, cut like a short spade in the English fashion. His clothes, also, were different. He was dressed in a doublet and hose, wearing the colours of scarlet and green while Donal wore the usual cream-coloured *léine*, made from the flax that grew locally and his cloak was woven from the grey wool of the sheep that grazed the mountains at their backs. He looked different, he walked differently, his voice was light and musical and he spoke rapidly, quite unlike the slow, pompous delivery of Boetius. It would have been difficult to find two men less alike.

Still the accusation had been made and they might as well go ahead and see where Fergus had been perched that night. And who knows, she thought, with a moment's hope, Gobnait's husband, she could not remember his name, but could visualize him, a quiet, sensible-looking man, who knows, but he may have seen someone on the headland or by the cliff edge. Somehow, she had a feeling that Fergus did see someone and that the sight of Donal on the cliff had resurrected that memory. He had sounded very convinced about the knife.

The mid-autumn sun had moved into the south-western sky above the sea by the time that they climbed the steep slope leading up to the Pooka Road. A bar of thick, jagged black cloud ruled a line across the setting sun, concealing half of it but allowing a vaporous orange haze to escape below and to light up the sea so that water and sky seemed to merge. The dry limestone pavement shone in patches of pale and darker grey and the setting sun threw black shadows to the sides of the enormous boulders making them look almost as though they were slightly raised from the ground.

Ahead of them, Mara saw Fergus look over his shoulder a few times and then he detached himself from the others and came back to her.

'I'm so glad, Brehon O'Davoren, that you have come to assist me in this secret and unlawful killing,' he said in formal tones. 'I must say that it is one of the most difficult cases that I have dealt with during my years here. And the fact that the murderer may be a relative of mine, well, that makes everything very much more difficult, does it not?'

Mara watched him carefully. Did the confused old man now imagine that Donal was a son or nephew? But then she followed the direction of his eyes and saw that they were fixed on the podgy figure of Boetius. She looked back at Fergus and saw him frown.

'He's putting on a lot of weight, isn't he? I don't think that he used to be like that.' His tone was querulous and he twisted his hands before him in an uneasy fashion, scowling at his nephew in a puzzled fashion.

Mara considered what to reply. Her memory of Boetius on the first day when she had seen him, over thirteen years ago, on the day when her son Cormac was born, was that even then he was quite an overweight individual. He had just graduated from law school, she remembered, so was a young man then. Perhaps he had been slimmer in his boyhood, she thought, and then noticed that Fergus's eyes were moving between Boetius and Donal and his brow was wrinkled into lines of indecision and doubt.

'But I saw him,' he muttered, more to himself, than to her. 'I saw him, I saw his knife. I saw him cut the throat of the man tied up in the creel.'

'Who put him there?' asked Mara and he whirled around as though startled, as though he had forgotten that she was there.

'I don't know, Mara,' he said. 'I don't know at all. I came

up onto the Pooka Road and I looked out to sea and then I looked over at the water . . .' He hesitated, visibly struggling to find the word, and then shook his head. 'You know, the water . . .' He jerked his hand upwards, miming the action of the waterspout. 'And that was when I saw him.' This time he definitely pointed towards Boetius, not to Donal who was trying to teach Cian to sing a two-part melody. They were both laughing, but Boetius hung back, looking, from time to time, over his shoulder at his uncle and at Mara.

'What was he doing when you saw him?' asked Mara.

'Creeping,' said Fergus, his voice now quite definite. 'He was creeping along with a knife in his hand. Yes, that was what he was doing.'

'Did he do anything else?'

'He . . . you know . . . he . . .' Fergus mimed bending over. He moved his hand from left to right as though slitting a man's throat and then went on quite fluently, 'I saw his knife. I'm sure that I saw that knife. I saw it move. I'm sure that I remember how I saw it flash in the sun, no in the moonlight, that's what it was,' he repeated with satisfaction, 'it was moonlight. I remember now. Sometimes, my memory isn't too good, but then it just comes back in a flash.'

'What was he doing?' asked Mara.

'He was fishing, I suppose,' said Fergus dubiously. 'No, I'm wrong. I know that now. Fishing is not the right word. There was a killing, Mara, did you know that? Gobnait told me. There was a killing. She tried to frighten me, she tried to tell me that I can't go out at night because there are men with knives around at night and they are looking for people to kill. She's a kind woman but very silly.'

Mara looked at him. Each year, during the month of August, the Brehons of Ireland met to talk over cases and to ensure that the law, as administered in one kingdom, did not deviate from the law in other kingdoms. There had been an interesting discussion about witnesses and how much reliance could be put on the evidence. She remembered that the elderly Patrick MacBerkery spoke fluently about the unreliable witness. 'Beware the man who is too fluent, who has an answer to everything. Give me the honest man who hesitates and says from time to time: "I am not sure." What, she wondered, would Patrick make of dear old Fergus? He was honest, but could any reliance now be put upon his evidence?

'Yes,' she said aloud. 'Yes, you are right, Fergus. There was a killing. But don't you worry about it. You are having a holiday now. I'll take care of everything. The king has decided that would be the best thing. He didn't want to trouble you on your holiday.'

'God bless him,' said Fergus and to her relief that seemed to make him quite happy. 'Look, Mara, do you see that over there?' He pointed to one of the boulders. 'Look, that's mine,' he said. 'I climb up there and I sit up on top of it and I can see everything. I feel very well when I do that, Mara. My head gets very clear when I sit up there.'

'Cian,' called Mara and he came back to her instantly.

'May Cian climb up there?' she asked Fergus and he nodded eagerly. 'Cian, yes, that's his name,' he said with a certain childish pleasure as though his memory had identified this boy. 'Come around the back of the stone and I'll show you how to get up.'

From a distance the giant boulder had looked smooth, but when they came nearer they could see that the surface was deeply fissured, cut with lines where the rainwater had explored weaknesses and had dissolved the limestone. And at one spot, there was, indeed, a line of small hollows, deep enough to hold small puddles of water in wet weather, but now in this dry spell almost seeming like roughly chipped-out steps leading up to the summit of the huge rock.

In a moment, Cian had scrambled up, agile and sure-footed, he did it without even touching a hand to the stone, but Mara could see that even old Fergus, if he kept a hand ready to clutch some of the protruding knobs, could easily climb this boulder. So far his story seemed to be true.

'I sat up there and looked at the moon. It was very peaceful and then I looked over at the water flying up from the cliff,' said Fergus, smiling at the memory.

'It was high tide, wasn't it,' said Mara. Never lead a witness, just encourage him to tell his story; make some innocuous remark about the weather or the surroundings. Her father used to say that and she had passed on those words of wisdom to her scholars.

'And then I saw him.' This time Fergus pointed directly at Boetius who looked back with a heavy frown on his face.

'Saw me do what, you old . . .?' Boetius caught back the word, but his face was purple with fury.

'So it wasn't me after all; it was the *stráinseir*,' said Donal. He gave an exaggerated sigh of relief. 'I was a bit worried for a while,' he confided to Cian who nodded in a neutral fashion.

'That man is not a *stráinseir*,' said Fergus severely. 'That is Boetius MacClancy and he is my nephew and he's going to be the new Brehon of the kingdom. That's right, Boetius, isn't it?'

Mara looked from Boetius to Donal. The young songwriter seemed to be looking quite carefree, now, and Boetius nodded vigorously.

'That's right, Fergus, now you are making sense, aren't you?'

'But you can't be a Brehon if you have murdered a man, can you? What do you think, Mara?' said Fergus. He sounded quite indifferent and then, leaving his stick on the ground, he climbed with great agility up to the top of the boulder and gazed across to the cliff on the other side.

'I can see a fox, Mara,' he called down. 'A young fox, I'd say. He's a beautiful sight with the sun on his fur.'

In an instant, Cian, sharp-witted as ever, had scaled the boulder. 'Yes, I see him, Brehon MacClancy. You're right. He's a very fine fellow, isn't he?'

Mara nodded as Cian came rapidly down again. Two questions in her mind had been answered: Fergus could climb that boulder and yes, he could have seen a man on the other cliff on that moonlit night. His eyesight had remained to him as his mind crumbled. The third question was, however, still unanswered: who did he see?

'I think that we have to try to settle this matter now,' she said, addressing herself to Boetius and to Donal. 'Brehon MacClancy thinks he saw someone on that night and I am afraid that I must ask both of you to go over there with my scholar, Cian. At least, let's get this matter sorted out and don't worry, either of you. I do realize that Brehon MacClancy's memory is not good so his evidence would not be accepted in a court of law. Nevertheless, I think that it is fairer to both of you not to leave this matter as it is. Cian, will you go across with Boetius and Donal? I'll wait here and see what he says.'

It didn't take them long to cross over by the harbour and after a few minutes she saw Donal approach the area where the water burst through the cliff. He had a knife in his hand and he was making threatening gestures with it, as though mimicking the slitting of a throat. Fergus stayed perfectly still and eventually Mara said, 'Was that what you saw that night, Fergus?'

He looked down at her in a startled fashion. 'No, no, not at all. What put that into your head?'

'I must have made a mistake,' said Mara apologetically. 'You do remember seeing a man coming and the cutting of the throat, don't you?'

'Of course I do,' said Fergus indignantly. 'I know my memory is not good, but that's not the sort of thing that anyone could forget, is it?'

'No, of course not.' Mara looked across. Really, even on the ground where she was standing there was a very good view of the other side. She saw the red hair and even the jutting beard of Boetius as he approached.

'Was that the man, Fergus?' she asked. And then, when he did not answer and a moment later Donal followed, she continued, 'or that young man there?'

Fergus looked very carefully. He spent some time, even raising a hand to shield his eyes, although the sun was behind him. After a minute, he gave a long sigh.

'I'm sorry, Mara,' he said. 'Do you know, I just can't remember.'

'Don't worry about it, Fergus.' Mara tried to make her voice as reassuring as she could. 'It's of no consequence, really.' No judge in the land could convict on the evidence of this poor man, she told herself, and yet, there was a niggling feeling that there had been a ring of truth and of conviction in his earlier statements.

His face brightened as he took in her words.

'Do you know, Mara,' he said in a low and confidential tone, 'I think that we should drop this matter. After all, he's no loss, is he? He was a bad husband. That poor little girl! Did you see that terrible bruise on her cheek? He did that to her, you know. And poor Peadar! What a terrible sentence. There's no worse fate, is there, to be banished from your kingdom. I would go mad if anyone took me away from here and shut me up where I couldn't see the cliffs and the sea. Don't let anyone shut me up, Mara, will you?'

'You're happy where you are, Fergus, are you?' Mara moved her thoughts from the murder. That could wait. The poor old man, her father's friend, had to be reassured.

'Yes, I am.' He watched her anxiously. 'I heard Boetius though. He said that I should be locked up.'

'Boetius will have no say in the matter. I can promise you that, Fergus. The king is the one who gives the orders and he wants you to be happy and comfortable. You will stay in that little house by the sea for as long as you want to.' She would ask Nuala to come and see him, she thought. Nuala would be able to predict the future and see what was needed. 'It would be nice, though, wouldn't it, if you had someone to go around with you when you go on walks, someone who would talk to you and then you could get that person to remember things for you. That would be useful, wouldn't it?' She had thought that she put it rather well, but he looked offended.

'There's nothing really wrong with my memory, Mara,' he said. 'And I remember now who it was that I saw with the knife. I just can't think of his name. I don't think that I ever knew it. It was that lad who was with the new Brehon.'

Twelve

Do Brethaib Gaire
(On Judgements of Maintenance)

It is the duty of the kin group in particular, and of the people of the kingdom in general, to care for its incapacitated members. The aged, the blind, the deaf and the sick have all to be cherished as do the insane. With reference to the insane, there is also a duty of care to the people around so that none may be injured.

Mara found it a little difficult to tackle Gobnait. They were alone together in the neat and tidy room, but Gobnait kept jumping up and attending to various household tasks. Cian had good-humouredly walked down to the harbour with Fergus at her murmured request, but they would be back soon and in the meantime Gobnait seemed to want to avoid any discussion of her charge. There was no doubt that the woman's position was a hard one. She would have an ingrained respect for the Brehon MacClancy whom she had known for her entire life. It would be hard for her to gainsay him in any way. Added to that, she was, it appeared from the well-polished flagstones and the gleaming furniture, a very good housewife. The house that the king had bestowed on Gobnait and her husband in exchange for taking care of Fergus seemed to be her pride and joy. It must be tempting for her to allow the old man to wander around the cliffs while she scrubbed and polished and, of course, prepared tasty meals for him, thought Mara.

'So, I was thinking that there might perhaps be some boy who could be employed to go on walks with him. Perhaps somebody who enjoys the countryside, just as Brehon MacClancy does, someone who could pick herbs with him, and perhaps catch a fish, but above all keep him company. The king will pay him a wage,' finished Mara.

Cora Harrison

'Well, he did take very much to the little lady,' said Gobnait dubiously. 'But I don't know about a boy.'

'Ríanne will be returning to her kingdom,' said Mara briskly. 'I think a boy, a strong boy, not too young, someone who could manage him if he wanted to do something dangerous, could restrain him if necessary. I would worry about those caves and the broken cliffs over there near Doon MacFelim.' It was, she felt, a little below her dignity, to refer to the place as 'Hell' but after a momentarily puzzled look, Gobnait nodded wisely.

'Just what I was saying to Pat,' she said. 'I do be worrying about him sometimes, but you know what it's like, Brehon, there's the fire roaring away and pots boiling on it and his food to make and the drinks for him and all that sort of thing . . .'

'That's right,' said Mara. 'So if you had a good strong boy who would be a companion to him on his walks, then you wouldn't worry, would you?'

'Would this boy have to live in the house?' Gobnait cast a glance down at the shining pale grey of her flagstones, seeming to envisage them covered with muddy footprints.

'No, that wouldn't be necessary. Just a local boy who would live in his own house, but come over here a couple of times a day and go for a walk with him. The days are getting very short now, so two walks would be enough and, of course, Brehon MacClancy wouldn't go out at night, would he?' Mara said the words carelessly, but kept her eyes on the woman's face.

'Oh, no, no, I'd stop him doing that,' said Gobnait hastily.

Mara waited. It had crossed her mind that the whole story might have been a figment of Fergus's imagination, but the detail of the knife blade flashing in the moonlight had had a ring of truth about it. She looked across at Gobnait interrogatively.

'Of course it must be very difficult to keep an eye on him all the time. I suppose that he would just slip out when your back is turned, is that right?'

Gobnait flushed guiltily. 'Well, he has got out once or twice. And, of course, on that night of all nights. Perhaps you heard that . . . Here comes Pat. He'll tell you.'

Pat was a slow-moving, thoughtful man, a fisherman without a boat who made a living by fishing along the shore with lines and nets. To Mara's relief, he was enthusiastic about the idea of a boy and could immediately think of a couple of names.

'Don't suppose that he'd settle to watching anyone fish, though, Brehon,' he said decidedly. 'I tried it a few times, but he's restless-like. He'd want to be off in five minutes and that's no good with fish. You have to wait for them. They're cautious creatures.'

'I was saying to Gobnait that I'd worry about him going out when it gets dark,' said Mara. 'Could you lock the door once the light goes?'

'The very thing that I was saying to Gobnait. In fact, we've done it during the last few evenings. Once we have our supper, we just lock up. I was that worried about him last Friday night. And when I heard about the murder, Saturday, it was, when I was coming home for my dinner, I heard the news, well, as soon as I got in the door, I said to Gobnait that we'd lock up every night from then on. It gave me the fright of my life to think of him around the cliffs and someone with a knife up there across the way.'

'Not that anyone would hurt him, the poor, misfortunate man,' said Gobnait hastily.

'They might do if he saw something,' said Pat. 'Feelings were running very high on that Friday, Brehon. Everyone was hit, one way or another, by those judgements. Even people like us who haven't much, well, young Seán is Gobnait's sister's boy and we would have been asked for something just to pay that fine. We'd have been the first she'd turn to. We've got the name of being well-off now, you know.'

'Did Fergus go anywhere near Doon MacFelim on that Friday night?' queried Mara.

'No, thank God,' said Pat readily. 'I was in the alehouse, just having a drink and seeing what the word was about those judgements and when I came home, Gobnait sent me straight out to find him. I tried the Pooka Road, first, because he's got a great *grá* for the Pooka Road. Gives people a fright sometimes, sitting up there on one of those rocks, for all the world like one of the Pooka himself, so that's where I went,

but then I found him down on the beach, just sitting on a
rock and looking out to sea.'

'And when you were up on the Pooka Road, did you see
anything over on the other cliff, over near to Doon MacFelim?'

Pat shook his head. 'No, I didn't, Brehon. Next day when
I heard about the killing, Gobnait was asking me that very
same question and I told her that I hadn't seen a soul or a
sinner.' He looked straight across at Mara and she thought,
I wonder if he is lying? The community, she thought, would
close ranks if they imagined that one of their own, one of
the five young men who had been sentenced on that night,
had murdered this stranger, this unjust judge who had
imposed such harsh sentences on their young men. In any
case, her question had been answered. Even if Fergus was
not on the Pooka Road when Pat discovered him, there
was a likelihood that he had been there earlier, perhaps even
minutes before.

'Was busy with looking for *himself*, making sure that he
hadn't slipped and fallen and then when I found him down
on the beach, well, I was chatting to him, you know, keeping
him in good humour.' Pat seemed to find her silence troubling.
He had added the words in a careless manner, but his face was
anxious.

'Of course,' said Mara. She rose to her feet. They were
coming back, she could hear the click of the gate and the
shuffle of feet on the path of sea pebbles.

Cian's voice rose up: 'No, I'm Cian, Brehon MacClancy,' he
was saying. 'I think Moylan was a boy who was at the law school
a very long time ago. Perhaps I look a bit like him, do I?'

God preserve me from becoming like that, thought Mara,
like a small child to be humoured and to be coaxed along,
and yet it wasn't like that either. Children took such things
for granted, took them as their due. Fergus, she was sure,
suffered. He was like a man lost in a thick fog, trying to grope
his way to an understanding of his position, trying desperately
to identify some landmarks which would help to orientate
himself.

'So I'll leave it to you, then,' she said addressing both husband
and wife. 'You find someone who will go for walks with him

and keep an eye on him. You agree a fair price and I'll have a word with the king and he'll be happy to do this for such a valued old friend of both of us. And we are very grateful to all that you do in order to keep him safe and happy.' She laid a slight emphasis on the word 'safe' and hoped that she had said enough.

And yet, she thought, as she went outside, was it any real kindness to keep Fergus safe? She thought of Turlough's words about going over the cliff if he got into that state and in her heart she agreed with them. If she were honest, she told herself, there would be little sorrow in news of the death of Fergus, only relief that he had been saved worse disintegration.

But in the meantime, she told herself, there was a murder that had to be solved and although Fergus was in a muddle a lot of the time, there were other times when he was quite clear and lucid. He looked calm and clear-eyed, she thought as she went outside and his mistake of confusing Cian with her long-gone scholar, Moylan, was a natural one. They were, she herself had thought from time to time, quite alike physically and in manner. In the meantime, though, she had to consider his statement and bear in mind that, although his feeling that he had witnessed the murder might be a delusion, nevertheless it was possible that he might well be remembering something that really happened.

'So when you were up on that boulder, Fergus, you could see where the water was spouting out of the cliff, couldn't you? Did it go up very high?'

'Very high,' said Fergus eagerly. 'It must have been high tide, Brehon.'

Mara looked around. There was no one on the roadway so she chanced a question.

'And that was when you saw the knife?'

Fergus nodded, but there was a slight hesitation in his manner.

'And the man, you saw the man.'

Fergus seemed to think about this for a moment, but then he shook his head.

'No, you're wrong, Mara. I didn't see the man. No, I didn't see him,' he repeated creasing his forehead in a puzzled way. And then, quite formally, he nodded to her. 'Thank you for

your help, Mara, but I think we'll leave this matter, now.
It was a lawful killing; I've decided that. The man deserved
to die.'

And then he walked past her and pushed open the door.
Mara heard him making eager enquiries about dinner.

'What do you think, Cian?' she asked as they walked back
up the roadway.

'I think, to be honest, Brehon, that the old man is cuckoo,
completely, well, I don't mean that exactly . . .'

'I know what you mean,' said Mara with a sigh. 'But, you
know, for just a while, I thought that he might be making
sense, I still have an uneasy feeling that he did see a knife; that
just seemed a very clear image in his poor old mind.'

'Yes, but he would probably have heard that the man had
his throat cut. He'd be trying to visualize it, so he would see
someone . . .' Cian broke off. 'And yet,' he said dubiously. 'Yes,
I remember the way that he said it. Yes, he did seem much
more clear-minded then, didn't he? You could be right, you
know,' he said more enthusiastically. 'Yes, I think you are right.
I think that he did see someone. It would be great, wouldn't
it, if he did see someone and somehow we managed to get it
out of him. He's funny, you know. Sometimes he seems to
remember something and sometimes he doesn't.'

Mara nodded in agreement. 'After all, Fergus *was* out there,
that night. At least we know that. Gobnait sent her husband,
Pat, after him. It definitely was dark, was moonlight when Pat
went out. Unfortunately Pat didn't see anything, but that says
nothing. The person with the knife, well he wouldn't stay too
long, would he? And he would have the sense to move into
the shadow of the hedge as quickly as possible, especially if he
heard voices from the other side and on a quiet night voices
would carry for a long distance. And Fergus did seem very
sure, when we met him first, that he had seen who killed
Gaibrial O'Doran.'

'Just a pity that he didn't stick to one person,' mused Cian.
'But he was very confused, later on, wasn't he?'

'What do you think, Cian? You heard Fergus? What did
you make of it all?' She would not normally have used the
elderly man's first name to one of her young scholars, but there

seemed to be too many 'Brehons' in this case and this was beginning to irritate her.

'I think it was probably Niall that he saw,' said Cian promptly. 'And I'm not saying that because I don't like him much, but it does make sense, Brehon, think about it! It wasn't really likely to be Donal. He's not the type to use violence. And although he was fined heavily, I'd say that he'd have wriggled out of it some way, packed his pipe and wandered off, not committed a murder. And then there's the old man's nephew, Boetius from London. Somehow I don't see that fat fellow wandering around the cliffs in the dark. He'd probably trip and fall over and hit his head against a rock. And all the others that he mentioned, no, I don't think so. I think by then he had forgotten who he had seen and he was getting so muddled that he was just mentioning anyone that he could think of or that he caught sight of. I half expected him to accuse me of the murder. But Donal was his first choice. And, you know, Brehon, Donal is not unlike Niall in appearance so it might be easy to muddle them if your mind is confused. I think he saw Donal, up there on the cliff, and he thought, there's the man who cut the throat of the new Brehon and then after a while he began to be unsure and he started throwing out names.'

Mara thought about it. It did seem to make sense. The sight of Donal at that fatal spot had roused a memory, a recollection of seeing a slight, dark-haired youth with a knife in his hand. Fergus would know young Donal very well, but wouldn't be too sure about Niall who had only come into the kingdom so recently.

'You have a point, Cian. But you know, Niall has a very poor motive for murder. After all, to cut a man's throat just because you want to get home to Ossory doesn't really make sense, does it?'

'You never know with someone like him,' said Cian in an elderly fashion. 'He's a strange fellow.'

'And he has an alibi,' Mara pointed out.

'Ríanne? Well, she's just a girl. She would have been in a dream. Or, just telling a lie.' And then Cian stopped abruptly in the middle of the roadway.

'What do you think of this, Brehon? They plan it between them. Niall goes out to see what has become of Brehon O'Doran. He doesn't drop the lantern, or anything like that. In any case, it was the night of the full moon. So he goes on, right up to the cliff, it isn't too far, after all. He goes up there and he finds his master tied up in the lobster pot and he comes back and he tells Ríanne.'

'Why didn't he release him?'

'Because he was scared of him,' said Cian without hesitation. 'Brehon O'Doran was the sort of a man who would kick the dog if he were in a bad humour. He would definitely have taken his fury out on Niall. He'd be angry and he'd be humiliated, wouldn't he? Anyway, Niall probably thought that it served the man right. He crept back and told Ríanne and they got to hoping that he would never come back, perhaps hoping that he would fall over the cliff or down the blowhole. And while they were talking about how wonderful that would be . . .'

'I see what you mean, Cian.' Mara nodded. 'The wish became the father to the action.'

'Perhaps the plan was to push him over the cliff while he was tied up, but Niall is the type who might lose his nerve. In any case, Brehon O'Doran was a heavy man. And Niall is a lightweight. It might have been too difficult for him to haul him over. After all, it took all of my strength and of Art's to drag him away from the water and we're both heavier and stronger than Niall is. And so I think that he lost his nerve, panicked, pulled out a knife and slit the man's throat. It doesn't take much strength to do that.'

'And then he went back . . .'

'And told Ríanne what he had done, told her that they would both be free of Brehon O'Doran, that they could both go back to Ossory and he warned her to say nothing. And then they probably talked it over, planned that Niall would go out in the morning, find the body and then go straight over to fetch you.

'And it never really made sense, did it, that he wouldn't take the trouble to go back and tell Ríanne that he had found the body of her husband. What was the terrible rush to get to you? He would have practically passed the doorway of the house at Knockfinn.'

'I wonder why pretend that she didn't know?' asked Mara. Cian, she thought, had made the case very well. Though not an academic like his sister, he had a shrewd and logical brain and he could put his thoughts into words very well. He would make an excellent lawyer for defence or for prosecution when his time came.

'That was probably her idea.' Cian pursed his lips with a disdainful expression. 'She probably liked the thought of a bit of drama, and all the accusations that Niall hadn't bothered to come and tell her that he had found the body distracted any suspicion from her. If you come to think of it, Brehon, it all did add up to the impression that they did not like each other, that they had nothing much to say to each other. And, of course, that made it unlikely that they were partners in a crime.'

'Why did he go out in the morning, and pretend to discover the dead body, though? Why not leave it for someone else to find?'

'Because if he was the one who told you the news, then he could slip you all the information of the hunters, and about the masks. He got you very quickly onto suspecting Peadar and his friends, didn't he? And, of course, because you are the king's wife, he could hope to get the king to offer to send the two of them, Ríanne and himself, back to Ossory as soon as possible, if between them they got you to be sympathetic towards them. That was their aim, if I am right,' concluded Cian.

'I must say that you have made an excellent case, Cian,' admitted Mara. 'And so you think that the last person that Fergus named, in fact, the person with the knife that gleamed in moonlight, was Niall?'

'I rest my case,' said Cian with a grin.

'I think that I'll have a chat with them both,' said Mara. They would shortly be at the house door, but she decided against going inside. Brigid would be scrupulously careful that no one interrupted the Brehon when she was in the parlour, but the house was full of the noise of exuberant young people, banging dusters, scraping chimneys, pumping water from wells and dashing in and out of the fuel shed. It was difficult to know what question to put to them, she mused unhappily. She needed some more evidence, some witness who saw something, not just a strong inner belief that both girl and boy were lying.

Cian, she thought, had made a very good case. There had been something odd, something slightly theatrical – her mind went to some Greek plays that she had read with her father when she was a scholar – yes that would be the word for the way that the two of them had behaved. And if Rianne had smeared a blackberry over one cheek bone in order to simulate a bruise, well that did seem to show that they had planned the approach to Mara, Brehon of the Burren and the wife of the king of the three kingdoms.

'No,' she said aloud, 'on second thoughts, I think that I will leave that for the moment.' She narrowed her eyes. There was a distant sound like that of marching feet and then she saw a flutter, a glimpse of blue and saffron.

'It's the king, the king's banners,' said Cian joyfully. Cian and Cael were fostered by the king and he lavished gifts and praise on them continually, admired their prowess, laughed at their jokes and enveloped them in the warmth of his personality.

'Well, that's good,' said Mara. 'I was just thinking about him. I have a few questions for him.'

'About the secret and unlawful killing of Brehon O'Doran?' queried Cian.

'That's right,' said Mara. 'You know the way I always tell you scholars that in order to understand the present, you need to go back into the past. Well, the king was involved in this matter before we were and now I think that we need to take a step backwards and examine what was going on before the murder occurred.'

Thirteen

Bretha Comaithchesa
(Judgements of the Neighbourhood)

A king carrying building material to his castle has the same and only the same claim for right of way as the miller carrying material to build his mill; the poorest man in the land can compel payment of a debt from a noble or can levy a distress upon the king himself.

Even before the emblem on Turlough's banner, the silver shield held aloft by an arm placed against the blue and saffron background, had come properly in to view, Mara had formulated a series of questions for her husband. Fergus had been Brehon of north-west Corcomroe in the time of her father, he had been her own sponsor for the position of Brehon of the Burren after her father's death. She remembered clearly how he had taken her to the castle of Turlough's uncle, the then king, the Gilladuff (dark-haired lad) as he was known and argued the case for her to be allowed to take over her father's post. He had demanded that questions be put to her by a whole swathe of lawyers, gathered there at Bunratty for the unusual event of electing a woman Brehon and had beamed happily at her fluent answers. Dear Fergus, she thought, he had such confidence in me that he gave me confidence. She had heard her voice ring out in the great hall and had seen the astonishment on the faces of the lawyers who had questioned her and who had put to her as many complicated legal issues as they could have devised.

So Fergus had always been a father figure to her and she had never questioned him about his affairs or doubted his judgement until his memory problems began to get too bad to be ignored and a certain unrest and riotous behaviour among the young people had been whispered about, even over in the Burren. Cormac's foster father, the fisherman, Setanta, brought some stories and others were carried by Brigid's husband, Cumhal the farm manager.

'I'm glad to see you, my lord,' she said formally when Turlough drew his horse up with a flourish beside her.

He beamed happily as he vaulted from his saddle, like a man of half his age. 'I thought you might be needing a bit of help,' he said, boisterously kissing her with a loud smacking of his lips that drew grins from his escort. 'Need a man with brains around, don't you? That's right, isn't it, lad?' He winked at Cian and then turned back to Mara. 'We're staying the night up in Ballinalacken Castle; you'll come, won't you? You won't leave me alone, will you?'

'Well, I've my scholars over here at Knockfinn and then there's Niall, Brehon O'Doran's scholar, and there's Ríanne, his wife. They're there, also. I probably should stay at Knockfinn. Brigid is getting a bit old to expect her to manage everything.' In Cian's presence she did not like to mention the antagonism between her boys and Niall, but it was in the forefront of her mind.

'They'll be all right. Cumhal is following us over with a cartload of turf and logs,' said Turlough. 'Terrible damp house, that place in Knockfinn. As soon as Cumhal told me that you were staying there and that you'd sent for Brigid and her crew to clean the place up, well, I said to him immediately, "Who cares about a few cobwebs? What she needs to do is to get fires going in the place, get the place warmed up." We had a good laugh, myself and Cumhal, about women fussing over things like cobwebs. "Bring some charcoal and some braziers too," that's what I said to him. Only one bloody fireplace in the whole house. No wonder the poor old fellow went a bit off his head. I would if I was living there alone with the mist seeping in through those draughty old windows.'

'Oh well, if Cumhal is coming, then I suppose I could come back to Ballinalacken for the night,' said Mara. Cumhal, she knew, was a tough customer. Cian and Art would obey him instantly and Niall, she guessed, did not have too many reserves of courage.

'That's my girl,' said Turlough enthusiastically. 'Let's go for a walk down towards the cliffs and you lads,' he called to his riding party, 'you lads go back to Ballinalacken and tell the steward that the Brehon and I will be along in an hour or so and to get the pots boiling for a good supper. Cian, you be a good lad, and take this horse of mine up to the house. Give him a drink and a rub down and then you can turn him loose in that little meadow where the oats were. He'll have a bit of fun picking up anything that was left behind after the reaping.'

Turlough, thought Mara as she strolled at his side towards the cliffs, managed men and boys very well. He was a tireless leader and no detail was too small for his attention. Another king might have given commands for an elderly and senile Brehon to be removed from his post; Turlough had come across himself and had been involved in every minute detail. She listened to him with a quiet feeling of deep love for this second husband of hers.

'So I said to him, "Fergus, old lad, a house with only one fireplace is no place for a man like you!" So do you know what I did, Mara. Well, I got the lad who does the building work for me, and I took him down to that little beach down there, Bones' Bay, is that its name? I took Fergus with me, too, poor old fellow, and when we got down I found a stick and I drew a house in the sand, there in front of them both. "See, Diarmuid," I said to him. "One big square chimney in the middle of the house." And I drew it there, Mara.' Turlough eyed her to make sure of her attention. '"And then," I said to him, "put a fireplace into each side of the chimney. Now you have four fireplaces, Fergus. Well, I'm going to give you four rooms, one on each of the four sides of the chimney." And then I drew it out for Diarmuid, the parlour overlooking the sea, a bedroom for Fergus facing the south so that he gets plenty of sun, the kitchen facing north to keep the food nice and cool and then a bedroom for Gobnait and Pat at the back facing the east. But do you know, Mara, the poor old fellow, poor old Fergus, he was staring at me as though I was talking Greek or something, he just couldn't understand a simple drawing, so do you know what I did. Well, I got down on my hands and knees and I built up the walls out of wet sand and I made nice little openings for the doors and I sent one of the men to get pebbles to make the fireplaces. Well, you

know, Mara,' Turlough roared with amusement, 'it was like I
was six years' old again, out on a beach on Arran, wearing
nothing but a *léine*. You'd have split your sides laughing if you
had seen me, Mara. But the great thing was that Fergus really
did understand after a few minutes and he knelt down beside
me and took up some sand and made a seat by the fire, like
a bench, you know. And I made another on the other side of
the fire and we both cackled like a pair of children.'

'So that was the beginning of the house, was it?' Mara joined
in her husband's laughter, but she felt very touched to think
of the king of three kingdoms on his knees building a sandcastle
in an attempt to make a senile old man understand.

'That's right. And I said to Diarmuid, "Take every man you
have available. They're to work from morning to night." And
it was great weather, wasn't it, Mara? You were in Galway
when we were doing it, but I bet that even there you had the
sun. And I said to Diarmuid, "No excuses! The stone is all
there on your doorstep and there's a good well on the site.
Bring in the lime, use all the carts you need, but just get it
built and ready to live in before the end of September." And
we did,' said Turlough with simple pride. 'It was whitewashed
on Michaelmas Day and I thought it looked a little beauty of
a place.'

'And how did you find Gobnait and Pat?' asked Mara, tucking
her arm into his.

'Oh, the priest recommended Gobnait. He said that she
knew all about herbs. He said that the pair of them were very
poor and that the house they were living in was only made
from turf. He said that she was a very pious woman.'

'And they were pleased?' Mara thought of the snug little
house and the shining silver on the dresser. Moving into that
from a house made from sods. What a change.

'And the furniture?'

'That was me, too,' said Turlough beaming with pleasure.
'Let's have everything new, that's what I thought. So Diarmuid
brought a few carpenters along and they made it on the spot
so everything fits. And I got them to make the two seats, one
on either side of the fire, just the way that Fergus had done
them out of sand.'

'And the silver on the dresser?' queried Mara.

'Oh, that's probably their own; they brought their own things with them, I suppose,' said Turlough. 'And I suppose Fergus might have brought some plates and knives and things from his own place. Don't know whether he had much. I was there myself and I could see that there was nothing but rubbish. They burned most of it, my men did – old clothes and broken chairs and sticks and a few mouldy wall hangings . . . well, it was in a fine old mess. Rats, too. We had to get a few cats in, I remember one big tom cat with only one eye. He caught three rats on the afternoon after we moved Fergus out.'

'It's odd, though, that there wasn't anything but rubbish, isn't it? I know he let the school go about ten years ago so he hasn't had the income from that. But then there was the stipend that you paid him. And he had the lands of Tuath Clae free of rent for his lifetime, is that right? I think he told me that, or it may even have been my father.'

'That's right,' said Turlough. 'I think that he was granted that by one of my uncles, either Conor na Shrona, the chap with the big nose, or perhaps it was my father, one or other of them. Before my time, anyway. And it was granted to him personally, not just to whoever held the office of Brehon.'

'So the new man, Brehon O'Doran, had no right to the land, did he?'

'That's right. Strictly speaking he had no right to the house, either, but I thought that he could have it for a while until he had enough silver accumulated to build himself a home. I got my steward to go through it and make sure that there wasn't anything valuable left in it.'

'It's strange, Turlough, though, isn't it? There he was, Fergus, just himself for the last ten years, and even before that it was just himself and Siobhan. He had no children ever. And when Siobhan was alive he had the fees from his law school as well as the rents from the farms and the sale of the produce of his own farm. What on earth did he do with it all? The house is like a place occupied by a very poor man. It's a miserable place.'

'I suppose that it is,' said Turlough uncomfortably. 'I don't think that I ever really visited it much. I would call to see him and he would come to the door and propose that we visit the alehouse and I was quite happy with that. I wouldn't have seen him short of silver; if he had wanted anything then he could have asked, but, you know, these lands are quite extensive.'

'Yes, I know. About the same size farm as my father got from your father and then when I was given the position of Brehon, the farm was mine. It was my father's own personal property and he left it to me. I know how much it brings in and it's quite substantial. I've never wanted for anything. But I asked your uncle for a yearly stipend and he paid it to me. And so did you when you inherited twenty-four years ago.'

'Funny, I remember that day when I met you for the first time. I was scared stiff of you before you came in. I thought you might ask me some tricky question about the law and I'd look a fool. I had heard that you were very clever. But then you admired my dog; you got down on your knees and stroked the old fellow and we were friends from then on.'

'And Fergus?' Mara steered him back. Turlough could take a long time once he started on romantic memories.

'Fergus had the same arrangement as you,' said Turlough promptly. 'That was the arrangement I inherited and I left it at that. The silver was paid every year on the eve of Bealtaine, just in the same way and at the same time as yours was paid.'

Mara thought about this for a moment and then shelved the thought at the back of her mind. There was another more important matter to discuss with her overlord, the king.

'We have to talk about those lands of Tuath Clae. You see, Turlough,' she said, 'Boetius has been talking to me and, though I didn't admit it to him, he does have a point. He is, as far as I know, if we go back to the great-grandfather of Fergus, the only living relative in the *derbfine*. He asserts that and I think that it is true. I remember Fergus saying something about that to me, something about how Boetius was the only male relative that he had.'

'Funny the way that happens in some families, no boys born. There are too many of them in the O'Brien family. I trip over possible male heirs wherever I go, these days. They're all bringing themselves to my attention all the time. I suppose they think that I am getting to be an old man, now,' said Turlough cheerfully.

'Yes, you do look a bit decrepit. Now, could we come back to Boetius? He has brought up the matter of Fergus and I had to admit he has a point. There is little doubt in my mind now that Fergus should be the subject of a court investigation into his mental state. Boetius, as his only male relative, is quite within his rights to demand this. But you see, Turlough, the position is that if Fergus is classified as legally incapable due to his mental condition, then his lands should be divided up amongst his heirs.'

'And that means that Boetius gets the lot.' Turlough gave a whistle. 'Worth coming back from London for that. I suppose that all in all, he should perhaps be Brehon, as well. I can't offhand think of anyone more suitable. The last one wasn't a great success, was he? Got himself murdered a few weeks after he arrived in the kingdom.'

'I don't agree about that. There must be someone more suitable. Don't rush into it, this time.' Mara felt a great wave of irritation rise up within her. The law mattered more to her than it did to Turlough, who, deep down, felt that most disputes could be settled with a sword, but she had not expected him to envisage, so cheerfully, the prospect of having Boetius as a Brehon.

'You see if he is here, living on the spot, and if his uncle, dear old Fergus, was Brehon, and his grandfather, Hugh MacClancy, before that and his great-grandfather, Conor Oge MacClancy was Brehon before that, going right back into ancient times. You can't get away from things like that, Mara. If Boetius comes back and takes over the house and the lands at Knockfinn, it would be very hard to exclude him from the post of Brehon. You could almost say that he has a blood right to it. If I hadn't had young Gaibrial O'Doran in mind, I might have appointed him in the first place. Don't worry about it, Mara. I'll keep a close eye on him and make sure that his judgements are fair. I'll tell you what I'll do, I'll attend every one of his judgement days for a year until he settles back into our way of doing things. And I'll make sure that there is none of this hanging and drawing and quartering of that King Henry. What a way to treat a fellow human being!'

'And you are prepared to forgive and to forget what he did ten years ago?'

'Well, he explained all that to me. He was under the influence of some drug or other. I blame that Englishman, that Stephen Gardiner, myself. He was a nasty piece of work. Just like his royal master. Boetius told me that he was out of his head half of the time and really did not know what he was doing. And I believe him,' added Turlough with a touch of defiance in his voice.

'So Boetius comes back from England, finds that the position of Brehon has already been more or less promised to Gaibrial O'Doran of Ossory, he comes over here to his uncle's lands, appears at the judgement day hearings, and then, that night, Gaibrial O'Doran is found dead,' said Mara trying to keep her voice neutral and judicial.

Turlough stared at her in dismay. 'Don't say that you've discovered that it was Boetius who cut the man's throat,' he said.

'I am in the process of investigating a murder,' said Mara stiffly, 'and yes, Boetius has to be a suspect, if I take into account, as I am sure that he has, the possibility, even the probability, that he might well obtain the very lucrative post of Brehon, then he certainly had a motive. It might well be, that he would reckon that the deed was worth doing if it results in him being appointed as Brehon of north-west Corcomroe. And that, as we both well know, would please his masters at the court of the English king. And it would be a very sad day for us who want to preserve our ancient ways. Boetius may not have planned it, but when he found that these stupid, probably drunken young men were chortling over tying up Brehon O'Doran and placing him under the waterspout – and Boetius admitted to being in the alehouse that night – well, he might well have seized the opportunity of getting rid of a rival. The death would be put down to one of the five young men. And then he would have it all, the position, the lands and the fees, as well as approbation and support from London. And he could open the law school again, gradually switching over to teaching more English law than Brehon law and then he would have the fees from the parents of the scholars, also. He could be a rich man quite soon. I wouldn't be surprised to find after a couple of months have elapsed that he'll be building himself a fine new castle here at Knockfinn.'

'Great place for it.' Turlough looked appreciatively at the view across the cliffs to the churning waves of the Atlantic and to the misty outlines of the three islands of Aran. 'He should do it just the way that you planned it up in Ballinalacken, put in those three big windows on the first floor where you can look down at the ocean.'

'And if he played foul to obtain the post? If he was the person who drew the knife across the throat of a helpless man trussed up in a basket?'

'Oh, if that's the case, then I'll have nothing to do with him,' said Turlough decisively. 'That was a cowardly act and I'll have nothing to do with a coward. I'll expel him again and then he'll not have land nor plate nor position. He can go back to his friends in London. But the sooner you get this affair tidied up, the better. I'd like to get this part of my kingdom settled down. You wouldn't like to have it, would you? It would be something for young Domhnall to do, wouldn't it? You'd like to have your grandson set up as Brehon in a kingdom of his own, wouldn't you? He's a clever lad. He'll pass all of his examinations, won't he?'

'It will be another four years or more before Domhnall can possibly even qualify as a Brehon and then he should probably get some experience first,' said Mara firmly. 'And I am hoping that he will take over the school of Cahermacnaghten and the law affairs of the Burren when I feel too old for it all. That will be enough for him. There must be plenty of young Brehon lawyers in the country who would be interested in the position.'

It was not, though, she knew, the most desirable of posts. For judicial purposes, Corcomroe, the most westerly of the three O'Brien kingdoms, had been divided into two parts and the smaller of the two had been this one in the north-west. Fergus had been happy there and had stayed for his entire working life, but Fergus had not been ambitious. Once again she puzzled over his life. Siobhan, his wife, had been a strange woman, far more occupied with her own family, and especially with the children of her numerous sisters. She was missing from the side of her husband for three days out of five. She obviously had little interest in the house or the farm around it. Perhaps she had given them all numerous presents too. She thought of Turlough's words: *land or plate or position.*

'There's land here, yes,' she said aloud. 'Not well looked after, but nevertheless, it is all here. The position is here, too; it's in your gift and you have a right to bestow it on Boetius. So he may well get land and position, but as to plate, well that's a mystery, isn't it?' Every *taoiseach*, Brehon, physician, blacksmith, wheelwright, carpenter or wealthy farmer that she knew of, did routinely convert spare silver into plate, to be displayed on shelves of a dresser, or kept locked safely away in a strong box or chest. She frowned with puzzlement.

'Poor old Fergus,' said Turlough compassionately. 'I hope that he's happy. He has a very lost look sometimes.'

'Let's drop in and see him,' said Mara on an impulse. 'He seemed a bit upset when I saw him last. He thought that he might have witnessed the murder, but really he was quite incoherent and he named about four different people. It will do him good and cheer him up to see you.'

Fergus, though, seemed almost unaware of their presence when they came in. He was comfortably ensconced on the padded bench built by Turlough's carpenters and his head was nodding, his eyes when Mara looked at them, seemed dead and unresponsive. There was a pewter cup on the hearth beside him and Gobnait removed it hastily.

'He always has a little doze around this time,' she said. 'It brightens him and then when he wakes up, he has something to eat and a drink of ale or whatever he wants and then he's out and about, as energetic as a boy. Oh, and that reminds me, Brehon. You were talking about someone to go on walks with him and to make sure that he didn't come to any harm, and I thought of young Conn Bacach. He's lame, God bless him, but he can walk well if it's slow and that's all that himself can do anyway. And he's a big strong lad. And he's not slow in his mind, no, not in any way. Would you like to meet him, my lord?' she said to Turlough. 'He's a nice lad, and mind

you, it's not easy to get a lad who has nothing much to do
and yet would be big enough to turn back a man who wanted
to do something dangerous. Come with me, my lord, and
we'll go and see him. He's doing a bit of digging for his
mother to get the winter cabbages in, but he's not too good
at it. "In fact," she said to me, behind his back, like, "Gobnait,"
she said, "I'd be better off and quicker far to be doing it
myself, but he's a bit depressed like with his younger brother
out driving cattle."'

Talking vociferously, Gobnait ushered Turlough out through
the door. Mara hesitated for a moment, cast one eye on the
sleepy face of Fergus, then picked up the pewter mug and
sniffed at its remains. It had a strong smell of valerian. Gobnait
probably administered some to Fergus whenever he got tire-
some, or, to be fair to the woman, whenever he got agitated
and restless. She looked around the room for a long second
and then followed Turlough and Gobnait out into the strong
sea wind.

'I won't go down with you. I mislike leaving himself alone
when he's by the fire like that. Look, it's that small place down
there, by the beach. His father is a lobster fisherman. Hasn't
a boat, though, and that's a pity because young Conn Bacach
has nothing wrong with his arms. He could row fine, but that's
the way it is. They haven't a boat and they have to go out on
the rocks to float the creels and Lord knows, it's not a great
living. The younger boy picks up a bit of work here and there,
but the husband he's obstinate, like. He's stuck on the idea
that one day he'll start having great catches, though the lobster's
not a creature to come in too near to the rocks. That's what
Pat says, anyway.'

Amazingly, there was a small, neat vegetable garden behind
the tiny shack, its soil probably made from well-rotted seaweed
and pulverized rock. Not difficult to dig, but the boy with the
spade had one foot twisted sideways, a birth injury, thought
Mara and wished that this kingdom, like her own, had the
services of a good physician, and he balanced awkwardly on
it as he pushed the shovel with his good foot.

'God, lad, you have a fine pair of shoulders on you. Have
you ever tried shooting with a bow?'

Conn Bacach flushed scarlet at the king's words. He dangled
the shovel awkwardly from one hand and looked around for
help.

'No, my lord,' he said after a minute. 'I've never had my
hands on a bow, but I'm a good shot with a stone. I can bring
down a bird for the pot if I manage to get myself balanced.'

'Yes, there would be that, of course,' said Turlough. 'You'd
put a lot of power behind a shot, I reckon. What do you do
about balance? Sit down, or would that spoil your aim?'

His curiosity was genuine and Mara watched how the boy
visibly relaxed.

'I find it best to get myself wedged into a slot between the
stones,' he said. He pointed down to the beach and said, 'I
usually climb down there and stand there between those two
piers and wait until the birds have forgotten about me.'

Turlough turned and looked. 'Quite a climb, that! You have
no problem with your foot when you're climbing, do you?'

'I'm used to it,' said the boy stoically. He did not flush or
look embarrassed, but seemed to accept the king's interest as
genuine. 'I suppose my arms and my shoulders take the weight,'
he added thoughtfully after a moment and Mara felt an immediate liking for the boy. He looked intelligent and courageous.
And he found words when they were needed. She thought he
would be a good companion for Fergus and would be sensitive
to the poor old man's needs.

'We were looking for a companion for Brehon MacClancy,'
she explained. 'We want someone who would walk around
with him, talk with him, help him to gather herbs and fruits
and . . .' She looked around; it was difficult to know what
exactly Fergus spent his days doing.

The boy nodded. He had obviously been told of the possibility by either Gobnait or his mother. 'He'd probably like
gathering seaweed, too,' he said. 'He's in a sort of second
childhood, isn't he? I've seen him picking up shells on the
beach. Never minds the weather, either, does he? He's out and
about whether it rains or shines. And, of course, he's a great
man for the caves. I've seen him climbing down the stone
platforms. I've been a bit worried about him once or twice.
I followed him one time, but he wasn't best pleased. I've seen

Gobnait out there, too, searching for him. But I'd try to keep him away from there. It's a bit dangerous for him. I'd distract him with going somewhere else.'

'I can see that you would be a very good person to look after Brehon MacClancy,' said Mara. The boy sounded mature and sensible.

'I've been thinking about a present for you,' said Turlough, to Mara's surprise. She had thought this part of the business would have been conducted with the boy's mother, but Turlough had taken a fancy to Conn, she could see that. 'I was thinking that if I gave you a nanny goat you could bring it around with you on a rope and it would feed on the herbs and the grasses around the cliffs.'

'They eat seaweed, too. Goats love seaweed,' said the boy. His fair skin had reddened again, the freckles almost lost in the tide of colour, but this time it seemed as though excitement called the colour into his cheeks.

'Is that a fact,' said Turlough. 'Well, you live and you learn. My old uncle used to say that and he never spoke a truer word.'

'And Brehon MacClancy will be interested in the goat, too,' said Mara.

'That he will,' said the boy. 'He's a very kind man to animals. My father was telling us that he never liked to see anything suffer. A very nice man.'

'So we'll shake hands on the deal, then, will we? You'll take care of my old friend, Brehon MacClancy and I'll pay you with a nanny goat.' Turlough proffered his hand, omitting, Mara was relieved to notice, the traditional spit on the palm, and the boy shook it gravely. By now his mother had come from the house and was standing smiling in the background. She did not come forward and seemed happy for her crippled son to make his own bargain with the king. Mara went across and greeted her but kept the discussion to the weather and how dry it was for the time of year. Conn, she thought, would be about fifteen, old enough to make his own decisions. His mother was smiling and slightly tearful, watching her crippled elder son shaking hands with the king.

'Don't you bother with that digging, Conn,' she called out. 'I'll finish it off, myself. You're a man with a job now. You get up there to Gobnait's place and find out when she wants you to call to take the Brehon for his walks.'

'I'll get Cumhal to find a nice well-mannered nanny goat,' said Mara as they walked away. 'That was a great idea of yours. Well, that's one of my problems solved for the moment.'

Turlough turned a surprised face towards her. 'What other problems have you?'

'I have to find who it was that committed the secret and unlawful killing of Brehon Gaibrial O'Doran,' said Mara feeling mildly exasperated.

'Oh, I shouldn't worry too much about that,' said Turlough. 'Let's face it. He wasn't much of a loss, was he?'

Fourteen

Bóslechta
(Cow Sections)

The owner of a bull or a dangerous cow should ensure the safety of passers-by. Every roadside field should have a stout fence or hedge and the best and most secure are those that have a fringe of blackthorn as their top layer.

'Niall's missing,' said Cael as soon as they came into the house late in the evening. 'We have searched the house and the garden and all around. Cian went right up to the top of the mound, but he couldn't see him anywhere.'

'Niall!' Mara was startled. Her mind had been on Peadar O'Connor. The lame boy's words had brought him back to her mind. There were two men who had a strong and very positive motive for murdering Gaibrial O'Doran. One was Boetius. It would, she thought, have been almost irresistible to a man of no conscience, to learn, from the drunken conversation of the five young men, that the man who stood between him and a well-paid, lifelong post was trussed up in a lobster pot and at his mercy. Murder, she well knew would not be beyond Boetius and his masters in London; Stephen Gardiner, in particular, would be very appreciative of his success and would hope that he would subtly change Brehon law into an accordance with English law.

The other, of course, was Peadar. Conn Bacach's words had recalled him to her mind and she had to acknowledge that Peadar's motive was the strongest of all. He had been condemned to banishment and for a young man without family or resources such as money or a trade, well, that was a death sentence.

But Niall! She had almost discounted his motive, his desire to get away from his master and to get back to Ossory. Why not just write to his father and say he was ill-treated?

'What happened?' she asked and her eyes went to Cian and then to Art who was standing in the background looking uneasy.

'Nothing happened,' said Cian. 'I swear to you, Brehon. None of us said a word to him. We were all busy. Art was pumping water and I was making a bonfire in that sheltered place behind the house.'

'And I was helping Brigid to clean the pewter dishes,' said Cael, holding up a brush and bar of soap in evidence.

'So how long has he been missing?'

'An hour or so, I suppose,' said Art hesitantly. 'When Cian came back, he said, "Where's Niall?" and I said I didn't know and so he went to ask Brigid what she wanted him to do.'

'And I noticed that his pony, or at least the pony we lent him, well that's gone,' said Cael. 'And then we had a really good search. We have searched the house and the garden, went everywhere, even up on the mound to see whether we could spot him on the cliffs.'

'Perhaps he's gone back to Ossory,' said Cian with a slightly hopeful note in his voice.

'Nonsense,' said Mara. 'Nobody but a fool would think that pony could do a journey like that. Even with a good animal, that would be a three-day journey.' She began to regret that she had said goodbye to Turlough at the stable when he had taken his horse out. If the boy was really missing, then it would be handy to have some of his men to search for him. 'Perhaps he has just gone for a walk to the cliffs, though I suppose we would have seen him if he did that, because we came from there and we've been around that area for almost an hour, I'd say.' She looked around. 'Where's Ríanne?' she asked.

'Beating the wall hangings down on that wall. But she doesn't know anything about him. I went down to her,' said Cael, 'and she said, "I haven't the faintest idea." That's what she said and how she said it.'

Mara suppressed a smile. Cael had put on a slightly English accent and had delivered the words in a bored, contemptuous tone of voice.

'Go and get her, Cael, will you? Tell her that I want to speak to her.' Really, thought Mara, I could do without this.

Where was the wretched boy? The obvious place to go for a walk was towards the sea, but surely she and Turlough would have seen him. On the other hand, he might not have wanted to be seen. She suddenly thought of the small, sheltered laneway where someone had built stonewalls and had planted slips of blackthorn in their shelter. No trees grew in this windswept place but every farmer and many fishermen needed a good strong stick so the blackthorn had been planted behind the walls and had flourished. The thickly growing blackthorn bushes would provide a screen. If Niall had heard their voices and had not wanted them to see him, he could have sheltered behind these and they would not have noticed him.

Ríanne's face was blank and innocent when she arrived.

'Cael said that you wanted me.'

'I wondered whether you know where Niall is.'

'Oh, isn't he here?' Ríanne looked innocently around the room as though expecting to see Niall concealed by a chair or stool.

'No, he's not. My scholars have searched the house and the garden. I think that Cael has already told you that he is missing.' Mara watched the girl narrowly. A natural liar, she thought.

Ríanne did not argue. Her face seemed suddenly to shut down, the mouth expressionless, the eyes blank and innocent. She made no further comment and Mara waited. There was something, some secret concealed and Ríanne knew about it. She could swear to it. She guessed that behind the façade, thoughts and explanations were rushing through Ríanne's head. After a long pause, Ríanne lifted her eyelids and looked at Mara with an innocent expression.

'You mustn't worry about Niall,' she said sweetly. 'You know what boys are like. He's probably gone for a walk on this lovely windy autumn day. He's like that, you know. Prefers his own company.'

'Well, I think that we'll look for him,' said Mara. This was no June day, this was October. The light would fade early in these days, so it would, she thought, be urgent to find Niall before that happened. She had a slightly uneasy feeling about him.

'I'd say that he has probably gone back to Craggy,' said
Ríanne helpfully. 'He likes walking around there.'

'Why?' asked Mara bluntly. There was nothing for anyone
to see in 'Craggy', or its adjacent townland, named 'Island'.

'Goodness knows. Well, you know boys!' said Ríanne.

There was, thought Mara, a very false note in the girl's
voice. 'I think that we should search for him,' she said, getting
to her feet. 'I'll tell you what, Ríanne, you search Craggy, if
you wish, and we'll go down towards the cliffs.'

'There was, undoubtedly, a flash of alarm on Ríanne's face,
but she tried to conceal it with one of her shrugs. 'I might as
well go with you to the cliffs,' she said. 'I still think that is not
where he went; he hates the sea, but I don't want to be stumbling around up there by myself. Or would you come with
me to Craggy, Brehon? I'm sure that is where he went. Shall
we go there first and then if we don't find him we can easily
cross over towards the cliffs.' Again the false note was very
apparent. Mara gave her a long look and then turned to Cael.

'Ask Brigid would she keep the supper warm, Cael? Tell
her that we will be as quick as we possibly can. And call Cian
and Art. If they come with us we can spread out. Now, Ríanne,
you can come with us or not, just as you please.'

I dread the sea, she thought, as they all set out, Ríanne trailing
reluctantly behind. There was something remorseless about the
sheer power of the waves. The night had been windy and as
they went across the headland of Doon MacFelim they could
hear the crashing of the waves against the rocks. It was still low
tide, though, and there was no sign of the waterspout.

'Brigid said to tell you that there are four panniers missing,'
said Cian in a low voice. 'And that there are four cakes of
bread, some apples, and two jars of buttermilk and half a cheese
gone from the supplies that she put into the larder.'

Mara's eyes met his. She was conscious of a feeling of relief.
There was no doubt that Niall was an odd, morose boy.
She had experienced a momentary panic in case the boy had
been driven to take his life, but now it looked as though he,
and probably Ríanne, had planned to leave and to return to
their own home. But why? After all, the king had promised
to provide them with an escort back to Ossory. It was a two

to three days' ride and times were troubled. Ossory marked a border zone between Gaelic Ireland and the English-occupied area around Dublin. And, of course, the O'Briens of Thomond and the Fitzgeralds of Kildare, not to mention the Desmonds of the south, were always at loggerheads. What on earth would be the point of the two young people riding unaccompanied through this territory. What could be driving them to make this hasty and unannounced flight? She thought about tackling Rianne, but then decided against it.

'Just slip back and check on Rianne's pony,' she murmured to Cian. 'And you might look around to see whether those panniers are hidden anywhere.' She would keep an eye on Rianne. She was fairly sure that the girl knew where Niall had gone. There was an uneasiness about her, but no panic, no worries about a boy with whom she had grown up. No, Niall had some enterprise, some mission and she was beginning to guess what it might have been. It was, she thought, unlikely that they would slip away tonight. Already the sun was setting and soon it would be twilight. No, she thought, they planned to disappear early in the morning, but if so, where had Niall gone now? And, of course, he had taken his pony with him. That, she thought, was significant.

'No sign of him,' announced Rianne in loud tones.

'No sign of the pony, either,' said Art and Rianne shot him a glance, a worried one, thought Mara and she was now even more sure that an escape was planned. But what was Niall doing down here at the cliffs just as dusk was falling and he could have been indoors, playing the part of an innocent, with his friend Rianne. If they were going to depart at first light, it would have been sensible for the two to seek their beds at an early hour.

There was no sign of the pony when they reached the cliffs. The tide was coming in fast, flooding over the sands of Bones' Bay and sending up clouds of spray from the spit of rocks that stretched out into the sea. Even the large slabs of terraced rock were shining wet and it would not be long before they were submerged by the saltwater.

'He must have gone up to Craggy,' announced Rianne. 'I was right, after all.' There was, noted Mara, not a trace of anxiety in her voice. Whatever Niall was doing, then Ríanne knew all about it and found no reason to worry.

'Look in the little laneway,' murmured Mara in Art's ear and he left them instantly, striding across the grass with long strides. Art was a finely built boy, Mara thought, already as tall as his father. She wondered whether he ever had a wish to join his foster brother Cormac in his training to be a warrior. Or perhaps his mother's dearest wish that her only child would be a lawyer one day was of too much importance to him. It had been a bargain between Cliona and Mara. Cliona would be wet nurse and then foster mother to the delicate baby that Cormac was, back in the far-off days of 1510 and, in return, Mara would accept Cliona's son into her law school and endeavour to make him a lawyer. It had worked out well, thought Mara as she watched him. Art was a good scholar, a great friend, and a good influence over the mercurial Cormac.

And then she forgot about the past. Art had just taken one glance into the laneway and was on his way back.

'The pony is tied to one of the blackthorn bushes,' he reported quietly and then: 'here comes Cian.'

Cian was running at top speed. For a moment Mara worried, but as he came nearer she could see that there was no bad news. Cian's face was triumphant and smiling.

'You three go on,' ordered Mara. Cael and Ríanne had stopped and were looking back as the pounding feet sounded behind them. Just as well, she thought, not to betray to Ríanne that plans had been discovered. Ríanne, she thought, as she saw her gaze flirtatiously into Art's face, was not in the least worried about her lifelong friend, Niall. And surely, even if they had differences, she should be. It looked as though the girl knew quite well what Niall was doing.

'Well,' she said, as Cian drew up beside her.

'Her pony is there, just eating some oats, nothing different about him, but two of the four panniers were hidden in the rafters of the stable and all of the food is in two of them.' He spoke in a low voice, but the note of triumph was apparent.

'So it was all well planned,' mused Mara, 'but why did Niall take his pony down here. Why bother? Just to save himself a walk of a few minutes? That's nonsense, isn't it? Especially if they planned to leave tomorrow, and the theft of the four panniers and of the food seems to point to that, doesn't it?' She was now fairly sure that she knew what Niall was up to – it fitted well with thoughts that she had earlier in the day – but now she waited to see whether Cian would think of it.

'Well, he probably has two of the panniers with him since they are not in the stables. Let me think. Why would I take a pony on a very short walk,' he said aloud. And then, with a quick flash of excitement on his face, he said, 'I know. I'd take a pony if I had something pretty heavy to carry. And it must be something that would fit in the panniers. You know the size of them, Brehon, don't you? They are the ones that Brigid fills with food for us if we are out for the day. I think he has gone to fetch something, something hidden.'

'Well done,' said Mara. 'That's very likely. But what? And it must be something heavy, mustn't it?'

'But not too heavy,' said Cian lowering his voice. Ríanne had stopped and looked back, almost as though she hoped to hear what they were talking about. 'Wouldn't be a piece of furniture, or anything. You couldn't get that onto a pony. It has to be pieces of silver, doesn't it? But where did he get it? Did he steal it from his master? That's not so likely, is it? Brehon O'Doran had not had time to get the fines that he imposed, so I don't suppose that he had too much, certainly not enough for Niall to need a pony to carry it.'

Mara did not answer. Ríanne, Cael and Art were standing on the edge of the cliff peering down and she moved forward to join them. There was an ominous rumbling sound from the fissure in the rocks. Soon a few big waves would erupt through the opening. She looked down over the cliffs, thankful that the wind had dropped somewhat. There were several large, pale-green shapes in the water and she guessed that they marked the entrances to caves. These would flood at high tide, though, and so were of no interest to her at the moment.

'If we go down the path here, at the side, we'll get onto the limestone flats,' said Art. 'It's not dangerous, Brehon. Cormac and I and my mother often went down there when we were waiting for my father to come back. We used to gather mussels from the rock pools.'

'You lead the way,' said Mara. She did not look at Ríanne, but hoped that she would not make any signal to Niall, if he was within earshot. I'm tired and hungry and I want this business wrapped up as quickly as possible, she thought impatiently and then turned a puzzled face towards Art. He, too, was listening intently. It was difficult to hear anything above the tumultuous thunder of the waves crashing against the rocks, but then, when she thought she must have been mistaken, she heard it again.

And it was the voice of a woman.

And then Mara remembered her earlier thoughts when she had sniffed at the dregs in the mug from which Fergus drank before lapsing into a doze. She put her finger to her lips and started to move rapidly down the half-concealed path that wound through the rocks and down towards the beach.

'Let me go first, Brehon. I know the way.' Art was just behind her and she stood back to allow him to pass and then followed closely on his heels. She was impatient to solve this part of the mystery and perhaps it might also solve the secret and unlawful killing which she was investigating. She sensed that the others followed her, but they did so in dead silence, the sandy path that Art had chosen masked any sound of footsteps and the roaring of the sea would be in the ears of those further down.

They had gone about three quarters of the way to the spread of deeply fissured limestone flags when there was an angry shout from below. Not a woman's tones this time, but a harsh, half-broken voice filled with fury. Mara stopped abruptly. The voice seemed to come almost from beneath her feet. And then she saw why Art had demanded to go first. Beside the path which he had taken, there was a hole, not large, though wide enough to receive a man's body. These cliffs, made from the limestone that fractured easily under the power of rain and seawater, were probably riddled with holes, none of them quite as spectacular as the blowhole on the cliff, but forming a vertical tunnel to the beach below. Or to a cave. The next words that came: the woman's lighter tones and the bellowing of the boy, seemed to have a curious echo in them. A cave, of course. They were right above a cave. The voices came up from there.

That made sense and it fitted with her earlier thoughts. She was worried, but stayed obediently behind Art he as threaded his way through the protruding rocks.

A cry rang out once more and then a woman's figure, low in stature, but squarely built, came out onto the limestone. 'Gobnait,' whispered Cael in Mara's ear and she nodded. The woman was moving rapidly and did not look up. Let her go, thought Mara. I can deal with this later on. The woman, she was not surprised to notice, had two long leather pouches, one in each hand. But then she stopped, took two steps to one side and waited. Her head turned back towards the cave entrance from which she had emerged.

And then Niall erupted from the cave. He was bleeding heavily from a cut on the right side of his forehead and he lurched like a drunken man, almost catching his boot in one of the long fissures engraved into the flat slabs.

'Gobnait,' called Mara.

But it was too late. Before the word reached the woman, she had swung the leather pouch in and hit the boy once again on the head. Niall staggered under the blow. For a moment it looked as though he would regain his balance, but then he staggered in a zig-zag pathway. Gobnait gave him one glance, but then hurried on towards the rapidly flooding beach, a pouch swinging from each hand.

'Niall,' screamed Ríanne. 'Niall, take care!'

The voice startled him. He looked up. Mara could see blood streaming from his forehead, dripping down over his ear. Art still kept threading a careful way through the rocks and she did not urge him to go more quickly. He was the only one who knew that path. But Niall had strayed dangerously near to the edge of the limestone pavement. Gobnait stopped, looked up at the five figures coming down the path and then quickly and neatly dropped the two pouches into a rock pool. Hesitantly, and still sending glances up towards Mara and her companions, she turned and went back towards Niall.

Whether she meant to help him or not, her movement was disastrous. Niall shrank away from her. He took one step backwards and staggered, his arms flying out in an effort to keep his balance. But it was no good. One foot had caught

in the deep-set rut. He wrenched at it, but his movement had
been too impetuous, too uncoordinated and he overbalanced
and tumbled over the edge of the limestone pavement and hit
the sea with a crash that momentarily rose above the noise of
the waves.

'It's all right, Brehon,' yelled Art. 'It's not deep. Cormac and
I learned to swim there when . . .' The rest of his words were
drowned in a terrible scream that came up from Gobnait.

She had gone straight to the edge of the water and was
looking down, her mouth wide open and scream after scream
forcing its way out, dulling the sound of the wind and waves.
Mara pushed past Art and went swiftly across the deeply lined
stone pavement, an inner caution, though registering the information that it was not slippery, warning her to be careful of
the deeper ruts, here and there. She had barely reached Gobnait's
side by the time that the woman had hastily pulled off her
woollen mantle and her boots.

'Wait,' shouted Mara, putting all the authority she could into
her voice. 'Wait, Gobnait!'

But it was no good. Dressed only in a long *léine,* Gobnait
had leaped into the water. There was a swirl of foam and then
the creamy froth turned a dark red. There was blood, but for
a moment Mara could not see where it came from.

'No, Art, no,' she shouted with all the command that she
could force into her voice. 'No, no one is to go. Make a rope.
Use your mantles.'

They obeyed her instantly and she leaned over, holding one
spur of rock firmly with her right hand and peering down
into the turbulent water.

And then she saw it.

It was an immense fish – no, not a fish, an eel, she thought,
seeing the long sleekly shining body and the gaping mouth
– a giant eel, longer than the tallest man, as thick as a man's
body. Its teeth were bared and it turned and twisted.

'It's a conger,' shouted Art. 'Stay very still, Niall. Don't
provoke it.'

But it wasn't Niall who was bleeding. It was Gobnait. Her
mouth gaped wide and scream after scream came from it. She
hit the water frantically with her two arms, but her legs remained

very still. All around her there was a pool of blood, darkening the white of her *léine* and turning the water around her into a dark shade of purple. She was immensely courageous, this Gobnait. She twisted in the water, splashing noisily, trying to keep afloat, but still one leg was held in the grip of the creature's mouth. Niall had managed to pull himself up onto a rock, but Gobnait was in terrible danger.

'Grab this, Gobnait,' shouted Art. And Cian gathered up the makeshift rope, scrunching it into a bundle and slung it into the centre of the pool. It unravelled quickly as soon as it hit the sea and straggled out in a long line. Gobnait reached desperately for it, but a wave swept it from her. She had stopped screaming now and Mara hoped that her body was not shutting down with pain and loss of blood.

'I have to go in, Brehon,' said Art. Already he had shed his boots. His knife was in his mouth and without a glance at Mara, he dived into the water, his hands stretched out over his head, a sharp clean dive that took him into the centre of the pool. His arrival, amid the crashing of the waves was hardly noticeable. With two powerful strokes, he was at the tail of the enormous beast. Mara stood very still. And neither Cael nor Cian said a word. Ríanne was sobbing helplessly, but that sound seemed to have gone on for a very long time, seemed to form a monotonous sound in the background, just like the incessant roar of the ocean.

Art seemed to be treading water, his chest and shoulders rising above the sea level, using two hands to stir small circles. The knife was still in his mouth and a ray from the setting sun caught a spark from the blade and illuminated his face. Mara caught her breath. She dare not shout to him to move away. Any retreat now would attract the attention of the beast. Its mouth still gripped Gobnait's leg. The woman no longer screamed. Was she dropping into a state of unconsciousness? And yet her hands still beat the water and she still floated.

And then Art struck. There was a quick flash of light and then the knife suddenly slashed across the centre of the beast, right through the spine. There was a spurt of blood. Art seized Gobnait by the hair. For a moment all was confusion, the long black body of the eel convulsed, jerked up and then fell back.

Art was swimming strongly now, using his legs and one hand to claw his way towards the rocks. Cian was already there, waiting for him. In a flash he had shed his *léine*, ripped the linen down with his knife and then handed it to Cael. In a moment, he, too, was in the water and Cael, intuitive to her brother's unspoken command, was tying knots in the piece of cloth at the same time as moving rapidly down the limestone pavement towards the beach. Mara followed instantly. Cian had now reached Gobnait and had grabbed a fistful of her clothing. He had instantly seen his sister's move and he also turned to go back out to sea. The twins, both of them working from that almost miraculous communication of minds, had realized that it would be almost impossible to pull the unconscious and badly bleeding woman up the steep slabs of rocks onto the limestone pavement.

'Cael, that boat!' screamed Mara. And without an instant's delay, Cael turned, ran up the sandy beach and began dragging a light, upturned coracle from the place where it had been left, jammed between two rocks. She had already freed the boat by the time that Mara reached the small sandy beach. Ríanne had passed her, running fast, her sobs ceased. In a moment she was beside Cael and then the two girls were hauling the boat down the sand, each holding the rope attached to its stern. Mara turned her eyes back to her own two scholars who were dragging Gobnait through the sea. Soon they would leave the shelter of the almost enclosed rock pool and then it would be a much harder task. Niall hesitantly stepped into a rock pool and then stood still as the water ebbed around his knees.

But now Cael had launched the boat. The girls must have planned something because neither girl was in the boat, but both were wading through the water, pushing it along, its prow turned towards the entrance to the rock pool. Of course, no one would leave oars in a boat, so this was the only thing that they could do. But would the boat be of any use? Gobnait was a heavy woman, and might bleed to death if they tried to lift her into the boat.

But she had underestimated Cael's intelligence, had forgotten how much time the twins and Cormac and Art had spent by the sea with Art's father, Setanta. Cumhal, her farm manager, taught all of her scholars to swim, but Setanta had taught them a lifetime of lore of how to keep safe, of how to use balance and buoyance, how to rescue a man without jeopardizing everyone else, and above all, how to keep a cool head and how to survive on this dangerous and rocky Atlantic west coast. Wishing desperately that she had learned to swim, but recognizing that a woman of her age wading through the Atlantic waves could only be a hindrance, Mara watched and prayed.

The girls were now near enough to see the woman and her injuries and Cael had shouted something to Ríanne. The girl had heaved something overboard and Mara breathed a sigh of relief. Of course, most boats held a tarpaulin, a piece of rough canvas smeared with tar, used sometimes to shelter the crew from a downpour, other times to carry a load of fish from boat to pier. They had taken the decision that Gobnait's injuries were too severe to allow them to manhandle her into the boat. But now the tarpaulin floated on the water and this could be slipped below her. Cael relinquished the boat to Ríanne and walked towards Cian and Art who were just emerging from the rock pool, dragging the tarpaulin behind her.

'Niall,' yelled Mara, putting all the power that she possessed into her voice so that it would carry across wind and waves and reach the boy who still sat, hunched up, on the rocks, seeming imperious to the heroic efforts of Art and Cian. 'Niall!' This time she roared his name. The tide was coming in fast. Already Cael was up to her waist in it. They needed another person to hold the fourth corner of the tarpaulin and to get the injured woman back onto the beach as soon as possible. Niall was not hurt; she was fairly sure of that. He was frightened, perhaps, and, yes, he had had a shock, but she did not have time to waste on that while two boys of his own age were hazarding their lives to rescue a woman who had, perhaps, rescued him from the ferocious conger eel. He did not move, though, and she gave up. As soon as Ríanne had guided the boat to the edge of the surf, she seized its prow and began to haul it up the sands, beyond the reach of the sea. To her approbation, Ríanne instantly returned once the boat was safe and went resolutely into the sea, sending clouds of spray rising up as she moved with long strides into the waves.

And now there were four of them. Five would be better. Mara tried one more shout in Niall's direction, but then gave up. They were managing cleverly. Art still kept a grip on Gobnait's hair, but Cian had let go and had managed to get two corners of the tarpaulin into his hands. The two girls each held a corner. The sea crashed against them and once a wave went over their heads, but they still held on, standing as still as blocks of stone as Cian edged backwards, head turned over his shoulder, judging his footsteps and keeping a steady pace, ignoring the surge of the sea. When he reached Gobnait's body, he shouted something which Mara could not hear and then bent down low, crawling or swimming, perhaps, his head submerged and the two corners of the tarpaulin in his hand. He was only invisible for a couple of seconds and then he rose up again, dripping, his hair plastered to his skull. Now the tarpaulin was under Gobnait, but there was one more task. Cian moved up close to Art. Mara narrowed her eyes, but she could not quite see what was happening until Cian moved back again. Now she breathed a cautious sigh of relief. Art still had one protective hand clutching Gobnait but the other hand clutched one corner of the tarpaulin. Now the four corners were held and a square of the foam-capped sea was covered with the tarred piece of canvas. Cian shouted something and Art nodded. He let go of Gobnait's hair. For a moment the heavy body floated free and then began to sink. The four youngsters spread out, each holding the corner of the tarpaulin. Mara held her breath, and she could feel with an ache of sympathy, how they must be feeling, afraid to breathe, afraid that after all their trouble, Gobnait might float off or the tarpaulin might sink with the weight of her inert body.

But it didn't happen. Cian shouted again and this time Cael and Ríanne cautiously moved to one side. Now their backs were to the sun, setting in the south-west and Art and Cian slowly moved until they were facing them again. Gobnait lay inert in the centre of the tarpaulin and the four took cautious, sideway steps through the churning sea and towards the beach.

And then Mara took a hard decision. There was nothing that she could do here in Bones' Bay, nothing except watch and pray. She could not swim, something that she regretted bitterly. She could not swim, she was fifty years old and she would be of little use in any rescue attempt.

Not allowing herself another moment to think or even to cast one more glance at the intrepid four and their burden, she began to run up the beach, trying to make as good progress as she could despite the wet sand hampering her footsteps and clogging the hem of her gown and cloak.

It seemed an endless time until she reached the limestone slabs, carved by the waves into slabs that almost looked like a set of steps. They were wet and slippery and full of small rock pools so she slowed down. A broken ankle would be a disaster, two extra minutes inconsequential. She could see the row of cottages above her, lining the small roadway that led to the harbour. She breathed a silent prayer that there would be assistance to find there. Surely, by sunset, some would have returned from fields or seashore. Resolutely she did not turn her head back towards the sea. There was nothing else she could do and she could not risk delay.

As soon as she reached the roadway she began to call, '*Cabhrú, Cabhrú, Cabhrú,*' she screamed, using the native word and hearing the rocks send an echo back of the *oo* sound at the end of the word. First one door opened and then another. There was no delay. These people who lived by the sea were used to emergencies. A couple of men appeared, carrying ropes, one woman held a blanket bunched up under one arm.

'We need something to bind a wound, linen, anything. Gobnait was mauled by a conger eel!' The wind coming up from the sea was strong but Mara used every ounce of her long-learned skills in the outdoor law court and projected her voice against its strength. Two of the women turned and re-entered their homes. Figures rushed past her, leaping down the rocks with an almost inborn skill and by the time she had turned back to the beach again, the first of these was already splashing through the surf. By the time that Mara was on the sands, the tarpaulin was being held by eight figures. By now the water was only knee high, but still the tarpaulin's weight floated on it. They would leave it to the last possible moment before lifting, thought Mara as, with the other villagers, she

watched and waited. By now the new rescuers would have
seen the blood soaked garments and perhaps the gaping hole
on the woman's leg. For as long as possible they slid her
body along on the water, but then they stopped. There were
a few words spoken, lost in the wind, but their purport was
obvious when, first the two girls, and then the two boys,
had their corner places taken by the men from the village.
There would be no rushing this last step. Gobnait's life would
depend on it. Already other men had arrived and stood
waiting. For a moment Mara's eyes went to Niall's figure,
still hunched on the rocks, but then they went back to the
rescuers and their burden.

A wave came crashing onto the beach. A big one. One in
every seven, Setanta used to tell the scholars. The figures in
the sea again braced visibly against its power as it retreated,
and then a familiar voice roared, 'And after the next wave.
Wait till I give the word. On the count of three!'

It was Pat, Gobnait's husband, Mara realized with a shock
of commiseration. She wondered for a moment where Fergus
was and then remembered the boy, Conn Bacach. He must
have taken up his duties immediately. Mara prayed that he
would have the sense to keep Fergus out of the way if he heard
about what was going on down by the waterfront.

The next wave was a small one. It rolled in and then
slipped out again without much disturbance of the water. The
figures in the water stood very still as it slid past and Pat's
voice rose up, '*A haon, a do, a tre.*' His voice was loud and
steady and even the noise from the ocean seemed to fade to
a background accompaniment.

'And now!' he roared and the tarpaulin rose up in the water,
its weight taken mainly at the four corners. Mara waited, as
the others waited. Nothing must be allowed to distract the
rescuers now.

Another wave hit them before they emerged from the surf,
a bigger one this time, but it did not shake them. And then
the first three set foot on the sand. And step by painful step
they began to move up the beach. Other hands came forward
to grip the tarred edge of the makeshift stretcher. Ríanne
dropped out first, shivering, her shoulders bent. Mara went

down and put her cloak around the girl and then Cael came up and the two girls huddled together. Cael was white and Rianne shook with sobs. Cian and Art still bore their share of the weight and Mara did not call them. Gobnait owed her life to Art and she could not take him away at this stage.

Step by painful step they staggered up the beach. Mara wondered for a moment why they did not lay the woman down, but the next wave washed up by her boots and she realized that the tide was coming in rapidly. One glance at the damp sand around her showed that this beach would be submerged at high tide. The rescuers knew that and they made for the rocks. For a moment it looked as though they would climb the limestone slabs, get the injured woman indoors, but a harsh cry from Pat stopped them.

And as Mara drew near to the body, she saw the blood pump from a bared leg.

'Get the priest,' shouted a woman.

'Get cloth, bandages, anything!' said Mara exerting herself to use her most effective tones of command and instantly some woman came forward.

'Get carrageen moss.' The voice was high and quavering and Fergus appeared, moving down the limestone slabs with a surprising agility.

'That's a great idea, Brehon.' Conn Bacach limped down after him, his voice calm and matter-of-fact.

Mara tried desperately to remember what Nuala had said about bleeding. 'Pressure', that was the word that she had used. She snatched a swathe of old linen from a woman's hand and pressed it onto the gaping wound. In a second it was warm and sticky to her hand. It was tempting to remove it and to get a clean piece, but she remembered Nuala's words. 'Pressure,' she said to herself and pressed down hard.

'More!' she said imperatively and another cloth was handed to her.

'Let me do it.' Pat took the cloth from her, muttering, 'I knew no good would come of that business.' Before Mara slid her hand out, she felt the weight of his: hard, heavy and calloused, above her own, pressing down almost too weightily, though the cloth beneath his hand did not stain instantly – a good sign, she thought. After a few moments she slid her hand from beneath his, straightened up and glanced around. One of the women was bringing the two soaking wet girls up towards the roadway and another was trying to urge Cian and Art to follow them. The physician had arrived to cries of welcome and to garbled explanations about what had happened. And Fergus was at her side, bearing a large clump of carrageen moss, torn from one of the rocks.

'Excellent,' she said, rapidly taking a cloth from a woman and wrapping the seaweed in it. It might help, she didn't know, but she handed it over to the surprised physician.

'Come along, boys, go instantly and get out of those wet clothes!' And then, with a flash of inspiration, she said in the old man's ear, 'Would you go with them, Fergus, and make sure that they do what they are told. They're both soaking wet, but they don't want say that they are cold. You know what those young scholars are like!'

It worked instantly. He nodded knowingly, smiled at her and then said in his cracked, old voice, 'Come with me, boys.' And with Conn Bacach limping behind, the four of them climbed the limestone pavements and went down the road. Mara waited until she heard a door slam and then she walked across the lowest of the pavements until she reached the edge of the small deep pool where the bloody remains of the conger eel floated on the surface and beckoned to the boy still sitting hunched on the rocks.

'Come, Niall,' she said imperatively. 'I need to speak with you.'

Fifteen

Berrad Airechta

(Shearings of the Court – Court Procedures)

Heptad 49

There are some people who are excluded from giving evidence in all circumstances:
1. A castaway.
2. A landless man.
3. An alien.
4. An insane or senile person.
5. A prostitute.
6. A robber.
7. A man who ingratiates himself with everybody.

There was no movement from the boy Niall. He sat immoveable, the tension in his slight figure was visible even from a distance. He did not turn his head when Mara called, just sat gazing out to sea, sat as though waiting for something or for someone. She called again, but still he did not respond. Her voice would have carried to him. Several people on the beach turned their heads and then looked curiously across at the solitary figure, sitting hunched up on the rocks at the far side of the conger eel's pool. For a second Mara wondered whether to go to him, but a moment's thought convinced her that it would be a mistake. He was a young, agile boy, wearing knee-length *léine* and mantle and she was, she had to face it, a woman approaching old age and hampered by ankle-length clothing. He could easily duck around the rocks, and then manage to flee to where his pony was tied up in the little blackthorn-fringed laneway.

And so she ignored him for the moment while she pondered what to do.

The beach was a hive of activity, only the figure of Gobnait, still lying on the tarpaulin was ominously still. The physician had arrived. His name was passed from one to the other of the workers and a deputation escorted him to the body. Soon a string of commands triggered another wave of movement as people hastened back up towards their cottages to fetch required articles. Mara wondered whether she should go down, but she wanted to keep a close eye on Niall. By now she was fairly satisfied that he would not be able to scale the cliff behind him and that his only way from the beach would be to pass close to where she was sitting. She beckoned to a small boy and he came to her instantly.

'Would you do an errand for me? Would you go up to the alehouse and tell the king's soldiers to come down here to the beach. Say that the Brehon wants them. Would you be able to do that?' she asked, wishing that she had something with which to reward him.

He grinned at her, showing a pair of large new teeth in the front of his upper jaw.

'I'll say the king's wife and then they'll know who I mean,' he said.

'You're right,' said Mara humbly. He had a point. There were too many Brehons hanging around in this case. To most of the people of Doolin, Fergus was still the Brehon and then there was Gaibrial O'Doran, the so-called new Brehon and even Boetius used the name of Brehon when he wanted to impress the village people.

By the time the boy had reached the grassy cliff, more people were coming down. A woman carrying an armful of blankets, another with still more strips of linen fluttering in the sea wind, a pair of men carrying a door taken off its hinges. In this treeless coastal area there was always a shortage of wood and she had seen a door used as a stretcher before now. Mara took heart from these signs. Gobnait must still be alive, she thought. A body could be easily carried back on the tarpaulin, but the door pointed to an anxiety not to jolt the leg and start the blood pumping out again. She waited patiently. It would, she thought, be impossible to question Gobnait for several days, but in the meantime she could find out what she needed to know from Niall. Everything was beginning to fall into place. The events of that night that followed on from that day on the eleventh of October when Brehon O' Doran had judged the cases of arson, theft of copyright, rape, assault and neglect and issued his harsh judgements. Those five foolish young men, smarting under unjust sentences, had created an opportunity for the murderer to act beneath the cloak of their deed. It had been, she thought, not a planned crime, but an impulsive one.

The small boy must have run full speed because very soon the king's men were marching down the road. They took in the situation on the beach in a glance. By now Gobnait's inert form had been carefully transferred onto the door. The leader of the men issued a crisp command and they took their places in between the four men who already held the corners. Now the makeshift litter could be moved with the utmost care and with the minimum of jolting. Mara waited, watching its progress, but not moving from her position on the rock. She cast another glance over at Niall, but he hadn't moved either. She saw his head turn once, but then he looked out to sea again. What was going on in his head? Surely he didn't think that he could make his escape? From time to time, she looked thoughtfully towards the rock where Gobnait had dropped the two canvas pouches, but Niall made no effort to go near to them and she was content to wait until the return of Turlough's men. This affair should now be conducted with dignity and according to the law.

As soon as the soldiers returned to the beach she beckoned to them and they came over quickly.

'I want that boy brought up to the Brehon's house at Knockfinn,' she said, pointing across to Niall. She had little sympathy for him. Ríanne, at least, had redeemed herself by her efforts to save Gobnait, but Niall had done nothing, had not come to Art's assistance, had even not helped Cian, nor had he come across to see whether Gobnait lived or died. She turned back to the soldiers.

'But first of all, I want you to search those cracks and puddles in the rocks. The woman dropped two canvas pouches some-where there. I saw her and I saw the splash of water. And search the cave behind. I have a feeling that there might be more of these pouches in there.'

There had been a flash of colour on the side of one of the canvas pouches and she thought that it had looked familiar. A search of the cave would verify her guess so she waited patiently, noting that Niall had twisted his head sharply as though alarmed when he saw the soldiers tramping across the rocks. He did not move, however, but sat there. She wondered what was going through his head and then began, despite her feelings of anger, to be rather sorry for him. He was, after all, only a child. His happy life at the MacEgan law school had been disrupted by his father's ambition for a cleverer younger brother. He had lost his friends, lost his position in the family, lost, perhaps, his view of himself and his hopes for the future when he had been bundled off with this man, a Brehon, yes, but a stranger to him and not, thought Mara, seeing before her the pompous, merciless figure of Gaibrial O'Doran, a man to take charge of a vulnerable boy of that age. She kept a careful eye on Niall, ready to alert one of the soldiers if he made a move, but he sat as though frozen. She wondered what was going through his head. Fear, perhaps, regrets, almost certainly, and, perhaps, given his age, a certain wild and unfounded spring of optimism that somehow things might work out eventually in his favour.

Hope must have died, however, when one soldier found the two pouches, lifting them out of their watery hiding place, holding them aloft and allowing them to drip. It was hardly a minute later when another two emerged from the cave. This time the men were holding quite a burden in each hand. Mara could see that by noting how the hands hung down as each clutched its find. They crossed the stones and slabs very quickly and were by her side in an instant. She rose to meet them.

'This is what we found, Brehon,' said the leader of the little troop. He held up his own find and nodded towards the hands of his comrades.

All in all, there were nine pouches and now that they were under her eye, Mara verified their origin immediately. Each one of the pouches bore the shield of the O'Brien clan embroidered onto it, the white arm holding up the silver sword against the background of blue and saffron. The O'Brien crest. And, of course, she recognized it instantly. She herself, as Brehon of the Burren, received a pouch like this on every quarter day: *Imbolc, Bealtaine, Lammas* and *Samhain*, as her stipend for keeping law and order in the king's kingdom. She gazed at the pouches with a lump in her throat. Her own practice was always to empty the silver into her locked chest and then to return, immediately, the empty pouch to the messenger. Fergus, however, had not done that. Probably far earlier than she had suspected, his brain had begun to soften. He had hoarded his money, had felt it to be insecure in his house and then had taken the decision to hide it in the cave beside the sea. He had always been a walker, of course. Even back in her youth, she remembered the tall figure striding the cliffs, blackthorn stick in hand. He made his own sticks, had quite a collection of them, instructing her on how year after year he watched a branch, growing up straight in the shelter of the wall and then slanting away from the Atlantic gales, and telling her how he kept an eye on a branch until the handle was the right size and then he cut it off just near to the root and had stick and handle all in one piece. The people of Doolin and its surrounding townlands were used to him walking across cliffs and rocks. No one would have thought to follow him, to wonder what he was doing.

Until recently.

Mara opened her satchel. 'Put these in there,' she said and waited until the nine small pouches were stored within it. They would be quite a weight to carry, but she did not want to expose anyone else to temptation. There was more than two years of a Brehon's stipend in there and there would, she surmised, have been more. Her mind went to Gobnait's snug and shining little house and to the display of plate. She, who had once been among the poorest of the poor, had not been able to resist the temptation of showing off to her neighbours.

But Gobnait had not been the only person who penetrated the secret hoard of Fergus.

'They'll be heavy for you, Brehon,' said one of the men tentatively, but he did not offer to carry the satchel. Glances had been exchanged between them and they probably, from the weight of the pouches, had a good estimate of the value of their find.

Mara smiled at them. 'I'll manage,' she said. 'I'm used to carrying law books.' She looked across at the figure on the rocks and her glance hardened. She had called to him repeatedly, had given him the opportunity of coming to her and of making full confession of all that he knew. He had not responded and now she would have to compel him.

'Two of you fetch that boy and bring him to me at the Brehon's house; you three please come with me,' she said. She wondered for a moment about Ríanne, but then decided to leave her. She, Cael, Art and Cian would all have been frozen to the bone. Let them sit by a fire, sip hot drinks and relive the successful rescue of Gobnait from the jaws of the ferocious conger eel.

Niall, she thought, needed to do some talking now.

She allowed them to go ahead of her. Each one of the men had a grip on Niall's arms and they marched him along. He had protested when they came to arrest him. Childish of him. He should have known that a half-grown boy like himself would be no match for this pair of sinewy and experienced men-at-arms. He had tried to cling to the rock, but they had jerked him to his feet and hauled across the limestone slabs and pulled him until he was on the road. He appeared stiff; cold and frightened, probably, she told herself, and a little sympathy softened her.

The house smelled of good soup and of roasting meat when she pulled open the door and she had a moment's compunction for Brigid still keeping the supper warm. She ignored the boy and hastened to make her apologies.

'Oh, Brigid, I'm sorry, but something terrible happened. Gobnait, the woman who is looking after Brehon MacClancy, has had an accident; she fell into a deep pool by the sea and was attacked by a giant-sized conger eel,' she explained as she opened the kitchen door. 'Art and the MacMahon twins rescued her, well, Brigid, you would have been so proud of them,' she added knowing that while these young people were scholars to her, to Brigid they were almost like her own children. 'But they got soaking wet, of course,' she went on, 'so, I wonder,

Brigid, could you put together some dry clothes for them. Three of you,' she addressed the soldiers, 'could take the bundles and three ponies so that they can get back quickly into the warmth. And one of you, please go to find out news of Gobnait from the physician. You other two bring the boy into the parlour and then wait in the kitchen in case I have need of you,' she said clearly, with her eye on Niall. He appeared subdued, but he was a boy who did not show all that was going on in his mind and she remembered that his pony was still tied up in the small blackthorn-lined lane.

She allowed Niall to wait for a while as she approved the clothing for the four young people, rejecting Brigid's sugges-tion of blankets, but applauding the choice of a fur-lined mantle that one of Brigid's girls found in Ríanne's room. A wedding present, she thought. It would keep the girl warm on her return journey. She would not have had as adventurous a childhood as Cael and Cian. The twins had been quite neglected and allowed to live out-of-doors when they were young. Cael had led the life of a boy until fairly recently. Ríanne would be the one of the four most likely to suffer ill-effects from her exposure to the Atlantic chill in the month of October.

'It was Ríanne,' said Niall as soon as she had closed the parlour door behind her.

Mara took her time. She selected a comfortable seat beside the fire, put her satchel on her knee and then looked up at the boy. He was standing just where the soldiers had left him at her command, standing stiffly erect, his young face was very white, the adolescent blemishes standing out vividly against the pallor.

'What was Ríanne?' she queried after she had allowed a minute to elapse. And then when he said nothing, just looked sullen, she added, 'Do you mean that Ríanne authorized the death of her husband or that she actually cut his throat herself?'

'I know nothing about the death of Brehon O'Doran,' he said stiffly. 'I didn't do it.'

'Take down that cup from the shelf,' she said. A row of well-cleaned pewter cups and ewers now decorated the shelf above the fireplace. The boy came across hesitantly, reached up, took the cup in his left hand, and then, when she made no move to take it, he placed it on the table.

'I see you are left-handed,' she said. She had previously noted this, but she was anxious to see now how he might react to her words. It was difficult to tell. The light from the candle fell upon his face but then he turned it slightly aside, bending down and studying the floor.

'You don't ask me why I remark on your left-handedness,' she said. He was very tense, she thought.

He did an odd thing then. He picked up the cup in his right hand, this time, and he ran his left forefinger across the rim, tracing a line from the right-hand side to the left-hand side of the vessel. And then he did it again, more quickly then, making the movement into almost a slashing gesture. He replaced the cup onto the table and then he looked back at her. His face was even whiter.

She nodded. 'I see that you can guess the way the investigation is going. Yes, the physician from the Burren thinks that the cut in Brehon O'Doran's neck was made by a left-handed person.'

This time he used his right hand, rather awkwardly, she noticed. The movement now went from the left-hand side of the cup to the right-hand side. He turned back and looked at her with a spark of interest in his eyes.

'I think I get it,' he said speaking with more animation than his usual reluctant and surly response. 'I suppose that if a left-handed person slashed the Brehon's throat, then the wound would probably be deeper on the right-hand side of the man's throat.'

Mara half-smiled, despite her worries. She did love to watch clever young minds working out a puzzle. Nevertheless, she told herself to be cautious and careful. This was a bright boy and bright boys often lie easily, often guess what is in the interrogator's mind, and forestall a question. She frowned a little. That gesture miming the stroke of the knife had looked familiar. Niall, she thought, must be made to tell all that he knew.

'What were you doing in that cave?' she asked.

His eyes went to the satchel on her knee, but he said nothing.

'You went to steal Brehon MacClancy's silver,' she said bluntly. 'You knew that it was there, didn't you?'

'I followed Brehon O'Doran, there,' he said stiffly. 'I was wondering what he was doing. I saw him. It was on the morning of the day before judgement day and he was on the cliff and he was staring down. I wondered what he was doing and why he was not moving, so I went into that little laneway and I kept an eye on him. He was not looking out to sea. He was looking down. After a minute, he even lay down on the grass, so that he wouldn't be seen. He had crawled forward and he was staring down onto the rocks beneath. And then, I saw him sit up. He wasn't looking down any more. His head was turned towards the village. And then I saw her. I saw Gobnait. She was climbing up those limestone flags. She had something in her left hand. I could see how it was clenched up. I was wondering what it was, but I didn't move. I guessed that my master was wondering, too. He was a man who always wanted to know what was going on. I had watched him with people. He wormed secrets out of them.'

'And so you waited there, in hiding.'

'I'd have been a fool to do anything else, wouldn't I? And he wasn't a man to excuse you for spying on him. A word out of place and the stick appeared.'

'And what did Brehon O'Doran do next?' It crossed Mara's mind that Niall was making a long story out of this. Was he giving himself time to think? Time to put forward other suspects. Nevertheless, let him tell his story in his own way.

'As soon as the woman had gone out of sight, he crept down the pathway. I couldn't see him for a while, but I guessed where he was going. I heard his boots on the rocks when he got down, but I didn't risk going anywhere near. I just went back, went back into the house so that I was busy studying when he arrived.'

'But you went to the cave, afterwards.'

'I told Ríanne about it. I wanted her to see it. I thought that we might get a chance in the afternoon. He was so pleased with himself when we were eating our dinner at noon that I knew that he had found something. He couldn't stop smiling to himself. But he had a lot of preparation to do during the afternoon for the judgement day. He knew that the king was going to be there and he had all his law books out. I thought that he might want me to copy out sections, but he didn't. He was making sure that he had memorized them, wanted to show off how learned he was, how he could speak without any notes, and so he sent me off. He told Ríanne to get out, too, because she was singing upstairs and stopping him concentrating. He said that he didn't want to see us before suppertime.'

'I'm surprised that you told Ríanne about the discovery. I thought you two were not very friendly.'

Niall hesitated for a moment. He looked slightly awkward. 'We were great friends back in Ossory,' he said after a minute.

Mara allowed this to pass. There were more important issues than whether or why the boy and girl had, for some reason, pretended to be at loggerheads. It was fairly obvious that Niall had decided Ríanne would be a more credible witness to his presence in the house through the night hours if she appeared to be hostile to him.

'So you and Ríanne went off together.'

Niall nodded. 'We pretended to go towards Craggy, just in case he was peering out of the window after us, but then we cut across and went down the little laneway with the blackthorn bushes and when we were sure that no one was around we climbed down the cliff and went onto the beach. The tide was out,' he added.

'And then?'

Niall frowned. 'And then the old man, the Brehon MacClancy, came along. He didn't see us because we hid behind one of those big boulders. But he was looking all around him, looking to see whether anyone was there. And then he climbed up the rocks and he went into a cave. We heard his boots echo, just as I heard Brehon O'Doran's boots that morning. We were whispering to each other and wondering what he was doing. And then he came out again. And Ríanne said that her grandfather went soft in the head when he was old and he used to hide things in the cellar. Any little bit of silver that he could lay his hands on, he used to take it down and put it in a chest. And then he started to take the plate from the buffet and bring that down too and his steward had to go down every night when the old man was in bed and bring it back up again.'

'So when Brehon MacClancy came out again and went back to his house, you and Ríanne went in and discovered his secret?'

Niall nodded a little shamefacedly. 'We had a bit of trouble finding it. And then we remembered how tall he was and we started looking high above our heads. There was a streak of silver quartz on the left-hand side of the cave, a couple of fathoms high and under it was a broken section of rock, almost like one of those little cubby holes beside fireplaces. I made a step for Ríanne with my hands and she climbed up and found the little pouches, all lined up there. We opened one of them and we could not believe it when we saw the silver. I wanted us to take one of them. I thought that the old man wouldn't miss one bag. Everyone knew that he had lost his wits. Silver was no good to him. He wouldn't know what to do with it. I was saying that to Ríanne. But she didn't want it touched. She was sorry for him. Anyway, she said that it was no good to us, either. We were both stuck with Brehon O'Doran. She was married to him and I was apprenticed to him. Anything we got, he would take away from us. So we just left the bags there, just where the old man had put them and we sat on the beach, just talking.'

'Talking about what?' asked Mara.

Niall gave a half shrug and then stopped himself. He was, thought Mara, anxious not to offend her in any way now.

'We were just fooling, deciding what we would do if the money were ours, just fooling,' he repeated, looking at her with a tentative, uncertain expression on his face.

Mara sat back on her chair. 'But there was only one thing stopping you from putting those dreams into practice,' she said. 'And that one thing was the life of a man who is now dead. What do you say to that?'

'It wasn't us?' said Niall. 'It was nothing to do with us.'

'I think,' said Mara, 'that you should start telling me the truth, the whole truth and nothing but the truth. Don't make up anything, don't try to make things sound good for you.

Just tell me the whole truth and allow me to be the judge. Of course, if you are guilty, you might think that you should lie, but sooner or later I will find out the truth and you will have lost any grace that you might have gained now by owning up to the crime. What did you mean by saying that it was Ríanne?'

He looked uncomfortable. 'Well, it was both of us, really, I suppose,' he muttered. 'But when he didn't come back that night we started to make plans. We were just fooling, really. We hoped that he might have had a heart attack, or that the fellows with the bows and arrows might have shot him, or that pirates had snatched him. And if that happened, if he really did disappear, well Ríanne agreed to take one of the pouches. I persuaded her that the old man wouldn't miss one of them. And then we would go back to Ossory and say that Brehon O'Doran had disappeared. So then,' concluded Niall, 'I went out and found him dead. And we were very frightened.'

'Found him dead, or decided to finish him off, which was it?'

'I found him dead,' said Niall steadily.

'Show me your knife, again,' said Mara. It had been, she thought with compunction, remiss of her not to have double-checked it after her preliminary glance. Somehow, though, she had never truly, even after Fergus's accusation, believed Niall to be guilty, or even to be capable of this deliberate and decisive murder. The motive seemed weak. After all, if he were unhappy, he could write to his father and complain. He had the look of a well-cared for boy; his mantle was made from thick wool of the finest quality and dyed a deep soft black. The discovery of the nine pouches filled with silver, had, however, changed matters. No, he did have a strong motive.

He produced his knife readily and instantly. And that impressed her. During his time as a law scholar in the MacEgan Law School, he would have known of the importance of knives as evidence to a crime. She took it and examined it carefully. It was a very old knife, she thought, the hilt of it had been worn very smooth. It was ingrained with the dirt of many years and as she turned it over in her hands, holding it carefully by the tip of the handle, she could see no traces of blood, and what was even more heartening, there were no traces of recent cleaning. The knife, she thought, was really quite filthy.

'It was my grandfather's knife,' said Niall. There was a note of slight anxiety in his voice, but it was, she thought, brought on more by a worry that she might retain it, rather than a fear about what she might discover from an examination of it. Not just the hilt was uncared for; the blade itself was dull, and the point had been broken at some stage, though not recently, she thought. She ran a finger tentatively down the blade and then pressed a little more heavily. The knife, she thought, could not be used to sever tissue and sinew. It was far too blunt.

There was a clamour of voices outside. And then the door was pushed open. Ríanne appeared at the doorway, swathed warmly in her fur-lined mantle.

'Oh, Brehon, what are you doing with Niall's knife?' she cried. 'He didn't kill Brehon O'Doran; I'd swear to that.'

'No,' said Mara. 'I don't suppose that he did.' The knife, she thought, would not have killed a mouse, not to mind a grown man. She thought of the little house by the sea and sighed unhappily.

'You all go and have your meal in the kitchen,' she said as Cael, Art and Cian appeared behind Ríanne's shoulder. 'You go too, Niall. Here's your knife. Cael, tell Brigid that I will have just a bowl of soup and some bread. In here, please. I want to sit and think quietly.'

Sixteen

Brecha im Gaca
(Judgements of Theft)

The penalty for theft is greater if an object is stolen from a house or yard, than if it is stolen from a deserted place or a seashore.

It was three days before Mara went to see Gobnait. The reports of the injured woman had been good. The physician had stitched the wound on her leg and the bleeding had not reoccurred. She had regained consciousness on her journey back to her house and was said to have asked for food when she arrived. There had been some fear of an infection setting in on the leg, but that had not yet happened.

'It's the carrageen moss,' said Fergus earnestly when she met him on the hillside. 'Conn and I go out every day and gather some. They don't allow me to go too near to the fire, but Conn is a good lad and he boils it up for me and we make a poultice with it mixed in with some old stale bread. It's saved her life,' he said proudly.

Conn Bacach, thought Mara, was proving to be a great success. She did not know what Pat would have done with a senile man while he was nursing his sick wife, but Conn had taken to spending the whole day with Fergus and not going home until his charge was safely tucked into his bed. Ríanne and Cael went to the village every day to enquire after the invalid and to help Conn to entertain the fidgety old man. Cian and Art, somewhat disgruntled at Mara's refusal to discuss the case with them, had developed an obsession with fishing, going down every morning to the little beach, keeping a sharp look-out for the chance to kill another conger eel. Niall, still tight-lipped and unhappy-looking, took it upon himself to build a proper stack from the sods of turf that had been tumbled on the ground behind the house just before Turlough had moved Fergus into the care of Gobnait and her husband Pat, and he laboured on it from dawn to dusk, refusing any help or advice from Cumhal or from any of the boys.

Boetius arrived unexpectedly one afternoon.

'I'm thinking of going back to England, back to London,' he said abruptly as soon as Brigid had ushered him into the parlour where Mara sat thinking. 'Have you any objection?' he added.

Mara thought about the matter and then shook her head. 'No,' she said. 'No objection. You are free to go.'

'And yet you have not solved the case,' he said with a look of malicious enquiry in his light green eyes. 'I'm surprised at you, Brehon. I would have thought that you had your pick of suspects. Perhaps you could have done with some help after all.'

She ignored that. 'And your claim to the Tuath Clae lands?' she queried.

He shrugged. 'I've decided to leave it until the old man dies,' he said. 'He can't last too much longer. To be honest, caring for him is something that I don't wish to take on. I've looked into the matter. The seven acres, without the post of Brehon, are not worth the trouble. And I don't suppose that I will be allowed to have that. You are too prejudiced against me. So I am returning to London and will claim the acres and the house when the old man dies.'

'As you will,' she said indifferently. She was relieved to be rid of him. He, in his turn, she thought, was looking forward to going back to London. This wild and desolate Atlantic coast, living among simple fishing and farming people, was not to his taste. He probably missed the sharp wits and the gaiety of King Henry's court in London.

And when he had gone, she went into the kitchen to get directions to where Orlaith lived. It had been on her conscience that the woman might be owed some wage. She had been summarily sent home by Brigid, appalled by the state of the house, but that had not been altogether fair. In all probability, Fergus neither cared nor even noticed what sort of state the house was in. Gobnait had, apparently, found her willing and obliging and eager to tell her everything about the likes and dislikes of Brehon MacClancy. Orlaith had worked for Fergus for about ten years, had arrived soon after the death of Siobhan and, after the departure of the housekeeper soon after that event, she had never had anyone, except a single man, to cater for. Fergus would not have cared or noticed any such details as unwashed floors and cobweb festooned ceilings. And, of course, once he was removed into Gobnait's care, she would have fallen into even more idle ways. The new Brehon, Gaibrial O'Doran, would probably have soon got rid of her.

Mara set off, not bothering to take her horse from his stable, but tucking the knife into her satchel. Orlaith, she thought, should have been questioned before now. No doubt the piece of silver that she intended to present to the woman in return for her services would erase the memory of a casual question.

And then, she thought, once she had an answer to that question, she would go down towards the harbour and pay a visit to Gobnait. Brigid had donated for the invalid one of her delicious calf's foot jellies, her sovereign remedy for all ills and Mara consented to carry a small woven basket to keep this safe from harm. The knife, that good knife, with its handle carved from alder wood, the blood-tinged knife that she had taken from Ciaran, the knife which he had declared he found on the beach; that knife reposed in the bottom of her satchel. And her satchel, still weighed down with the nine canvas pouches, was in her right hand.

'So, how are you, Gobnait?' she asked again once they were alone. Fergus was missing, out walking with Conn Bacach when she arrived at the little square house by the sea. Pat had been easily persuaded to take a half an hour rest from the nursing and go down to the beach to see to his lobster pots while the Brehon talked with his wife.

And so she and Gobnait were alone. There was a slight unease about the woman as she eyed Mara and Mara waited to see what would be said. Gobnait was looking well, still pale from the loss of blood, but her eyes were bright and keen.

'Never seen such a beautiful jelly in my life,' said Gobnait, eyeing the wobbling shape. 'Look at the colour of it! Look at the way the light shines through it. I've never seen such a beautiful red.'

Her voice was nervous and Mara knew from the sound of it that Gobnait guessed why she had come and that she had guessed why Pat had been sent off to the beach. There was no time to be wasted. The jelly had already been admired. Mara reached down into the depths of her leather satchel and fished out one of the canvas pouches. It had been carefully dried by her bedroom fire, but the seawater stains still showed streaks of white salt.

'One of the ones that you dropped into the puddle of seawater,' she explained and watched the woman's face.

Guilt crimsoned the white cheeks, but that was understandable.

'I found it,' said Gobnait after a minute. She sat up very straight and there was energy in her voice. 'I found it, I found the two of them in one of caves down there by the shore. I was going to try to find out who they belonged to.'

It was a brave try, but Mara greeted it with silence and Gobnait sank back onto her pillow and looked at her.

'I think,' said Mara, 'that you knew very well who it belonged to. I think that you followed Brehon MacClancy and you saw him going into that cave. Perhaps two or three times,' she added. Fergus would, of course, have a dim notion in his head that he had to check on the safety of his treasure and it was probably a daily routine for him.

'I don't suppose that you meant any harm to him,' she said aloud. 'You were probably worried about his safety when you had him first, before you realized how sure-footed and agile he still is, even when climbing rocks, even those big boulders up on the Pooka Road. You probably followed him, in the first place, to make sure that he did not fall, or get trapped by the tide.'

She waited for a moment, but Gobnait said nothing and so Mara continued.

'So you followed him and peeped in and then you saw him reach up and take down one of the pouches. You may have even seen a glint of silver. The sunlight in the evening at this time of the year would shine right into that cave. And when he had replaced the pouch, you probably withdrew behind one of the rocks.'

Fergus, thought Mara, was never a very observant man, even

at his best. He tended to be lost in his thoughts and the people around him were never as much of interest to him as were the texts that he read.

'And then,' continued Mara, 'you went in and you saw all of the pouches. You reached up and took one down and counted the silver.'

The woman stared at her in a horrified way. Mara began to feel sorry. After all, this was a woman who had been at death's door only a few days ago. The confession had to be made, but she should get the business over and done with as quickly as possible.

'Just tell me the truth, Gobnait,' she said making her voice as gentle as she could. 'You were tempted and you fell. It happens to all of us.'

Gobnait gave her a startled glance of disbelief.

'Let's get this over and done with before Pat returns,' said Mara a little more sternly and Gobnait instantly responded.

'He knows nothing about this,' she said hastily. 'God help him, he has no *mas* on anything except those old fish that he catches. He did ask about that silver cup, but I told him that the king sent it down for the Brehon to feel at home and he never looked at the things that I bought at the fair again.'

'You took one of the pouches,' suggested Mara.

'No, I wouldn't do that,' said Gobnait indignantly. 'I just took a piece of silver from one of them, and then a piece from another, just so as himself wouldn't miss anything. They were a consolation to him, poor misfortunate man. I'd say he went into that cave every single one of the days that he was with me. I used to be wondering what he was doing scrambling around the rocks. First I just put it down to him being in his second childhood, so as to speak, but then I got myself a bit bothered about him. And that was how I found the silver,' she ended.

'But Brehon O'Doran saw you one day. The day before he was murdered.'

She was startled, visibly startled. 'I never saw him!' Her tone was slightly alarmed, but the alarm subsided after a moment.

'Well, I never!' She thought for a moment and looked at Mara with a tinge of curiosity. 'He never said a word to me.'

Her face darkened. 'I suppose that he was going to bring me up before the next court. He wouldn't be a man that would hesitate to disgrace a poor woman. Thank God that he is dead.'

'Did you have any hand in that death?' Mara asked the question for form's sake. She was by now fairly sure of the murderer's identity and Gobnait, she thought, was guilty of no more than theft. The answer came back readily.

'No, I didn't, Brehon. I didn't even know that he saw me. And I wouldn't have killed him for that. I'd have sworn blind that I never saw no bags, no silver. He'd have found it hard to prove anything against me. I've always been a respectable woman. Ask the priest.'

Mara concealed a smile. The woman, she felt, was probably telling the truth. Long experience had made her very aware of lies, and of unease. Gobnait was almost cheerful now. She bore the look of a woman who had got something off her mind.

'Just one more question, Gobnait,' she said gently. 'Why did you take two pouches this time? You told me that on other occasions you just took a little silver from each of the bags?'

'I thought you might be going to take Brehon MacClancy away from me; I thought we might lose the house and all,' said Gobnait frankly. 'You'd been asking questions about him being out at night and I thought someone had been telling tales. It's true, of course. He had taken to going out in the evening and there was no stopping him. He'd fidget and get in a bad mood. Pat thought that I should stop him. We had an argument about it that evening, the evening when that Brehon O'Doran was killed, not that we knew anything about it at the time. Pat wanted me to stop him going out, but I said that there was a good moon, and that he would come to no harm. But then when I heard about the killing, when I heard about that next day, well I swore I wouldn't let him out again after sunset. I'd lock the door and hide the key and let him fuss all he wanted. But, you know, Brehon, with all those walks that he takes these days, he's ready for his bed as soon as he has finished his supper. And that's a fact,' finished Gobnait, eyeing Mara's stern face a little uncertainly. Her face had whitened again. And then, after a minute, she asked in a low voice, 'What's going to happen to me? Pat will die of shame.'

It was a bleak little cry for mercy and Mara melted. After all, the woman was doing good service in caring for Fergus. No one had been hurt by her small pilfering. It might very slightly lessen the inheritance which would inevitably soon come to Boetius, but on the other hand, the king was now maintaining Fergus and would have a right to take a fee for that service. In any case, her bravery when she jumped into the water to rescue Niall from the conger eel went a long way towards atoning for her crime.

'I'll speak to the king about it, but I'm sure that he would want you to keep what you have. But if you want anything more,' she said, hastily thinking that she should not be seen to endorse theft, 'if you want anything else, please ask for it. The king is very grateful for your care of his valued friend and would want to give you anything which you felt was necessary for the comfort of the home he has provided.'

Fergus, she thought, would not have the slightest interest in a buffet piled high with silver plates, nevertheless, it was important to keep Gobnait happy. She had no easy task and it would get worse.

'There's just one more thing that I need to say to you, Gobnait, and I will say it to Pat, also. Brehon MacClancy must not be left alone. You must always know where he is and there must always be someone with him. Will you promise me that? If it gets too much for you, or for Conn Bacach, then the king will hire someone else, but he must not be allowed to wander around alone. It could be dangerous.'

'Yes, of course, Brehon. I was thinking that myself. I'd never forgive myself if anything happened to him. Poor misfortunate man. And him such a good kind creature. And nowhere is safe nowadays, is it? To think of a secret killing happening in a place like this, well, I never thought that I would see the day.'

Seventeen

Gúbrecha Caracniað
(The False Judgements of Caratniad)

A just king will have frequent conference with his Brehon and must be prepared to inforce a fair judgement by means of force, if necessary. If there is disagreement about a verdict, the matter is referred to the king and the Brehon must be prepared to defend the ruling.

Turlough arrived on the following afternoon. Mara had thought of sending for him, but then had hesitated. She knew that he had urgent business in his chief and largest kingdom, that of Thomond which during his reign had extended east, almost as far as Ossory. There was, she thought, no great urgency about this affair. Brehon Gaibrial O'Doran had no sorrowing relatives thirsting for vengeance or demanding solutions. His widow seemed very happy, her laugh rang out through the house as she and Cael teased the boys and mocked at their fishing exploits.

But the matter would have to be settled. Murder could not remain unsolved, or else the fabric of justice in the kingdom would suffer. The people of north-west Corcomroe would have to be told the truth about what happened on that Friday night after judgement day. Mara's face, when she went out to greet her husband, was very grave.

'What is it?' As always he was very sensitive to her mood.

'Come and eat first, and then we'll go for a walk and I'll tell you.'

'Not another murder?' he queried as he threw his reins to his steward.

'No, nothing like that!' For a moment, though, her heart skipped a beat. What if there were to be another murder? It was not, she thought, outside the bounds of a probability. Not all murders were done with a knife. There were other ways of killing. A man or a woman can be choked until the breath leaves the body, can be poisoned with a mixture of herbs, can be pushed into the sea and drowned, can be bludgeoned to death with a blackthorn cudgel. She felt a wave of relief come over her to know that she could share her burden of responsibility. She watched Turlough eat, listened absentmindedly as he teased Brigid with accusations that she was in the pay of his enemy, the Earl of Kildare, and was trying to make him fat so that he could not fight, threw ridiculous questions at Art and the twins about fictional and absurd law cases, talked with Niall and Ríanne about the arrangements for their journey back to Ossory and then got to his feet, declaring that he needed to walk off all that food.

'I think I know who killed Brehon Gaibrial O'Doran,' she said when they were alone together and walking towards the cliffs.

Turlough turned an interested face towards her. 'You're a great woman,' he said. 'I was thinking about it last night and I could not for the life of me make up my mind about who was the murderer. I suppose it was Boetius MacClancy, was it? And yet, you know, he's not the sort of man that would get his own hands dirty. I'd have said that if he wanted to kill a man he would get someone else to do it, perhaps one of those silly lads.'

'You're probably right,' she said humbly. Turlough laughed at his own lack of brains, deprecated his scholastic achievements, but he had a great shrewdness and judged his fellow men with an accuracy which often surprised her. She had wasted a lot of time investigating men who were unlikely to murder and had overlooked one possibility.

'Priests talk about the soul, and poets talk about the heart, but, of course, when it comes down to it, I suppose man is ruled by the brain,' she said aloud and saw him look at her with a puzzled air.

'The brain,' he echoed. His brow was creased with a slight frown. She wondered whether he was beginning to guess. 'What has the brain to do with murder?'

She could not avoid the issue any longer. 'Turlough,' she

said quietly, 'I believe that Fergus killed Brehon O'Doran. I don't want to use the word *murder*,' she added. 'He killed because, perhaps, he thought that he should, perhaps he felt that the man deserved death, perhaps he didn't really know what he was doing, perhaps even to put what he imagined was a dying creature out of his misery.' Her mind went back to the words of the boy Conn about how Fergus wanted fish and lobsters killed quickly. 'I don't know, Turlough,' she continued. 'I think none of us can have much insight into what is going on in Fergus's brain now.'

He stopped. And she stopped, too, looking up at him. Turlough's weather-beaten face was dark red in colour. The wind from the Atlantic was blowing strongly in their faces. She could taste the salt on her lips and feel the sting on her cheeks, but Turlough, she knew, had flushed with rage and his pale green eyes were angry. This was not going to be easy; she had known that and had rehearsed her arguments again and again. Turlough had a great affection for Fergus and, as a young king, had looked up to him because of his knowledge, learning and his kindness.

'I'll never believe that.' The words burst out from him and he began to walk again, walking swiftly. She allowed him to go ahead of her. He needed a few moments alone. When he reached the blackthorn lane he turned and came slowly back towards her.

'I'll never believe it,' he said again, but this time his voice lacked its positive assurance.

She said nothing. He had to find his own way through his thoughts.

'I know he's old and forgetful and that he imagines things sometimes,' he said after a moment, 'and I suppose he does do strange things sometimes. But Fergus. He was so gentle, so controlled. You'd never hear him shout at the scholars. He was so patient with the stupid ones. I've only once seen him strike one of them and that was when he was driven out of his mind by the lad's defiance.'

It was a good phrase, thought Mara. Cumhal and Brigid used it often. *You'll drive me out of my mind!* Brigid would yell at a girl who had not remembered to scald the milk pans, or had allowed the hens to walk upon the spotless kitchen floor. But, of course, neither Cumhal nor Brigid were ever really driven out of their minds. Control, she thought, remembering the babyhood of her own strong-willed son, was learned gradually, starting at about the age of three and strengthening all of the time with most people until adulthood was reached. But it was the brain that controlled actions.

And when the brain went; when all of the learned norms of behaviour gradually seeped from the mind . . .

'I just can't believe it,' said Turlough and there was a break in his voice. Mara slipped her arm through his, but still said nothing.

'What made you think of Fergus,' he said when they reached the edge of the cliff. 'Why on earth should Fergus kill a man who had done him no harm? I know that I told you that he was upset, but he probably forgot about these judgements an hour later,' he added.

'Nuala thought that whoever slit the man's throat was left-handed,' said Mara. 'She wasn't quite sure, but thought the wound looked like that. Of course, this wasn't that helpful because it turned out that there were a lot of left-handed people involved in this case: two of the five young men who were sentenced so unjustly are left-handed. Niall, the apprentice is left-handed and so, of course, is Fergus. Fergus, himself, told me, oh, long ago, that there were an unusual number of left-handed people in this part of Corcomroe. He had a theory that some powerful chieftain had sired a lot of left-handers and it got handed down through the generations. And, of course, because he was left-handed he was very good at teaching left-handed scholars to write a neat script and I used to ask for his help from time to time.'

'There you are,' said Turlough more cheerfully. 'Could have been anyone, then, couldn't it?'

'And then there was this knife found on the beach, left there by Fergus, or perhaps thrown over the cliff; I don't know; though it does look as though the blood was cleaned from the hilt with wet sand.' Mara reached into her pouch and took out the knife, pointing with her finger to the dark line between handle and blade. 'His housekeeper, Orlaith, and Gobnait, both identified it as belonging to Fergus. You recognize it, too,' she said quickly as she saw his expression.

'I gave it to Fergus,' he said reluctantly. 'He had a terrible old knife. I gave him a new one, a silver one and he thanked me politely and left it on the shelf above his fireplace. He said it was too grand for him, so then I gave him this one.' Turlough stared at the knife for a moment, at the shaft of alder wood and the well-honed blade. The wind from the ocean stirred his grey hair and he smoothed it down impatiently. 'Proves nothing though,' he said. 'He could have lost it. He's just absent-minded, doddery, I suppose you could say, but I can't believe that he would hurt anyone.'

'He was out that night, Turlough. Gobnait's husband, Pat, found him down on the beach, but he had already told me himself that he was out that night, a night of the full moon. He said that he was up on the Pooka Road over there.' Mara cast a quick look at the expanse of white limestone on the other side of the bay. The year was dying and the days were shorter. The sun had sunk down below a swathe of black cloud in the south west and the golden light had warmed the silvery sheen of the stone and the enormous boulders that littered the surface had each a black shadow etched beneath its rounded base. There was something eerie about the place even in daylight and Turlough grimaced.

'They shouldn't let him out by himself at night,' he muttered.

'I've had a word with them about that,' said Mara and then she waited. Turlough's lips were compressed and his eyes had an angry, baffled look about them. For a moment she half-wished that she could have left this murder unsolved and not given him such pain, but she knew that her office required her to solve the crime and communicate her results to the people of the kingdom. Turlough was a just man and when he had recovered from the shock he would be the first to say that justice must be seen to be done.

'What did Fergus say?' he asked after a moment where she could see that he struggled to control his fury.

'He told me that he had seen someone cut the new Brehon's throat; he even mimed the gesture; he was quite confused, thought it might have been Donal, the young musician, then thought it might have been Boetius and then Niall, who does look quite like Donal, but afterwards he denied having seen anyone. The image that seemed strongest in his mind was that of a hand holding a knife. It was, I think, his own hand.'

'That's nonsense,' he said angrily. 'He would have heard talk, picked up snatches of conversations, and it all became muddled in his poor old brain.'

'Do you remember saying that Fergus had been gathering sloes, on the day of the murder, you said that Gobnait was making sloe wine with them?'

Turlough nodded. His large hands, she noticed, were clenched tightly closed and he had a baffled look on his face.

'I think, but, of course, I cannot prove this, nevertheless, I think that Fergus went wandering along that lane that evening in order to pick more sloes – he had probably enjoyed the wine-making and wanted to relive the experience. I noticed that there were a number of sloes lying around on the laneway, not as if they had just dropped one by one from a branch, but as though handfuls were spilled out of a bag or a basket. I noticed them when I walked along it with Niall on the following morning. Fergus may even have seen the five lads tie up Gaibrial O'Doran and leave him under the waterspout. And who knows what came into his head at that moment, Turlough? It could have been an impulse of pity, a desire to put a creature out of pain, or it could have been something else, some confused notion about justice, but I think that Fergus killed O'Doran quite soon after he was tied up, perhaps within minutes. The five young men said that the body was stone cold when they returned.'

'The water would have cooled it,' said Turlough shortly. 'I've no knowledge of medicine, but I know that much. A corpse left out in the rain becomes stone cold very quickly, they stiffen in the sun.'

'You're right,' said Mara. 'But fishermen and farmers too know these things. They, all of them, when they came back later on to release him, thought he had been dead for hours.'

And then she waited while he gnawed the edge of his moustache, his eyes staring out at the foam-ridged waves of the turbulent sea. She would give him time. His was the ultimate decision.

'Have you asked him about it?' When Turlough broke the silence he spoke in a low voice.

Mara shook her head. 'It would serve no purpose, merely distress him.'

'No point, I suppose,' admitted Turlough. 'Can't we just leave it at that? There are no witnesses, are there? Nothing to prove it beyond doubt. I think we should say no more. Don't worry about the girl, Ríanne. I'll see that she is compensated.'

Mara's mind went to one of the triads that her young scholars chanted on a daily basis and she recited it to herself.

There are three doors through which truth is recognized: a patient answer, a firm pleading, appealing to witnesses.

She could not appeal to witnesses. None had seen this killing of the unjust judge. She had tried the patient answers. Now was the moment for firmness.

'No, Turlough,' she said decisively. 'The people of the kingdom must know the truth. I can't allow this matter to fester beneath the surface, allow surmises, false accusations. I want to put the facts before them, tell them of my conclusions.' She looked at his sorrowful face – there was, she thought, a hint of a tear glistening in one eye, but he said no more and did not try to move her from her decision.

Mara delayed judgement day until the festival of *Samhain*, the last day of the Celtic year. Fergus, she thought, was sinking more and more into an oblivion of all cares and he enjoyed himself like a child, fishing in rock pools, gathering the last blackberries, watching the birds and gently brushing the silky hair of young Conn's goat. There was little danger that he would understand what was going on, but she suggested to Turlough that he take the old man and his companion on a three-day visit to the Aran Islands. They would stay at the castle there; eat good meals; walk by the sea; do the things which the once-learned Brehon of Corcomroe now enjoyed above all other.

And then Mara prepared for judgement day.

The morning dawned with a violently red sky, a sign of a

storm to come and by four o'clock the heavens were filled with smoke-grey clouds. The *Samhain* fire had been lit on the highest point of Knockfinn and there was an odd atmosphere of apprehension and excitement among those who congregated around it. *Samhain* was a time of year when the sun had descended into the realms of the underworld and the dark forces were in the ascendency. Several people on the outskirts of the crowd wore masks as it was believed that creatures from the abode of the dead, unfettered from the control of the sun, walked the earth on that evening and that the living had to hide their identity from the undead. There was an eerie undercurrent of sound among the people, voices hushed by the howl of the wind and by the moan from the nearby ocean. They surged towards her, huddling together, almost as though banding against the evil spirits. Mara moved forward and stood in front of them.

'This is a sad moment for me,' she said and noted the sudden shock and surprise on faces near to her when the traditional solemn greeting and announcements were omitted. Mara took a long breath and raised her voice to be heard over the wail of wind and water. 'It feels to me like the ending of much that I have cherished and believed in. Thirty years ago Brehon Fergus MacClancy stood beside me as I faced the king and swore to be faithful and unswerving in the administration of the ancient laws of Ireland and in my pursuit of justice and truth. And now I have to stand here before you all who have been served so well and so faithfully by that man for over fifty years and I have to tell you that I believe that it was he who committed the murder which has torn your community and cast suspicion on many. Under our law no blame can be attached to Fergus MacClancy, who has lost his wits due to old age and is under the protection of the court, but the truth has to be known by the people of the kingdom.' There was, she thought, compassion and understanding on the faces nearest to her as she endeavoured to explain the old man's state of mind and described what had happened at this place two weeks previously. And then she was silent, waiting, but no one spoke. No questions, no comments. She had not expected either.

The howling wind had now strengthened in ferocity and the flames from the *Samhain* fire rose higher. There was a clap of thunder from out on the Atlantic and then a flash of lightning zigzagged over the silver-white boulders on the cliff above. A few large and heavy drops of rain splashed on the rock before her. She remembered the priest's words at last Sunday's Mass: '*Ita, missa est.*'

'Go,' said Mara. 'It is ended.'